LISETTE AUTON

The
SECRET
of
HAVEN POINT

Illustrated by
Valentina Toro

PUFFIN

PUFFIN BOOKS

UK | USA | Canada | Ireland | Australia
India | New Zealand | South Africa

Puffin Books is part of the Penguin Random House group of companies
whose addresses can be found at global.penguinrandomhouse.com.

www.penguin.co.uk
www.puffin.co.uk
www.ladybird.co.uk

First published 2022

001

With thanks to Inclusive Minds for connecting us with their Inclusion Ambassador
network, in particular Rebecca Thorne for their input.

Typeset in 12.5/18.5pt Bembo Book MT Std by Jouve (UK), Milton Keynes
Printed and bound in Great Britain by Clays Ltd, Elcograf S.p.A.

The authorized representative in the EEA is Penguin Random House Ireland,
Morrison Chambers, 32 Nassau Street, Dublin D02 YH68

A CIP catalogue record for this book is available from the British Library

ISBN: 978-0-241-52203-5

All correspondence to:
Puffin Books
Penguin Random House Children's
One Embassy Gardens, 8 Viaduct Gardens, London SW11 7BW

This book is dedicated to Alex David Gray★

★ 'Aunty, what are you doing?'

    'Editing my book.'

    'Who are you going to dedicate it to?'

    'I don't know yet.'

    'You could do it to me, Marky or Mum.'

    'OK, I'll have a think about it.'

    'Me. Dedicate it to me. They can have books two and three.'

On Language

A Note from the Author

In *The Secret of Haven Point*, Cap'n teaches Alpha and all the Wrecklings that language is really important and powerful. He is able to teach them that because *I've* been taught it too, by incredible disabled people who I've had the good fortune to meet and work alongside and then call my friends. I made conscious choices in this book about the way the characters choose to describe themselves. These choices are based on the way I describe myself as a disabled person. I also asked my disabled friends about the language they use to describe their impairments and conditions, and then I used those words too.

Person-first language: Some people choose to use the phrase 'people with a disability'.

Identity-first language: I choose identity-first language when I say 'I'm a disabled person' and it's the way my characters describe themselves too. It means that I focus on the fact that I think my body and brain are brilliant exactly the way they are. It says that society needs to change – not me. *Disabled* is a strong, empowering word. There is no shame in using it!

Individual choice is very important, and we must always respect each other's decisions and be kind to each other when it comes to the words we choose for ourselves, and the ways in which we describe our own impairments.

I loved writing this book and getting to know all the characters, but I'm a bit nervous about my words going out into the world, not least because of the pressure I felt to get everything 'right'. There are millions of books with non-disabled characters, and no one expects an author of one of those to get everything 'right'. Those books feature lots of different characters doing all sorts of things, and if, as a reader, you don't like it, you can easily put that book down and pick another up instead. There are still too few books with disabled people getting up to things. That means there is a lot of pressure on a disabled author like me to represent everybody by using all the 'right' words. So I have done my very best to write the story I wished *I* could have read, and write the characters that were missing from *my* bookshelf.

I really, really hope that if you enjoy this book you might ask your librarian, your bookseller, your teacher for more books with disabled characters written by disabled people. And if they can't find many, perhaps you could ask them to find out why. And then, just maybe, we can make a big enough noise that tells the IMPORTANT PEOPLE that these books are very necessary and wanted. And maybe then, if you'd like to be an author too when you grow up, *your* book describing characters in the important words that are right for you will find a home. Then there will be lots of books full of all sorts of disabled characters, having lots of different sorts of incredible adventures, written in different sorts of the 'right' words that fill the shelves, so that everybody can have a choice about which powerful and important words they read.

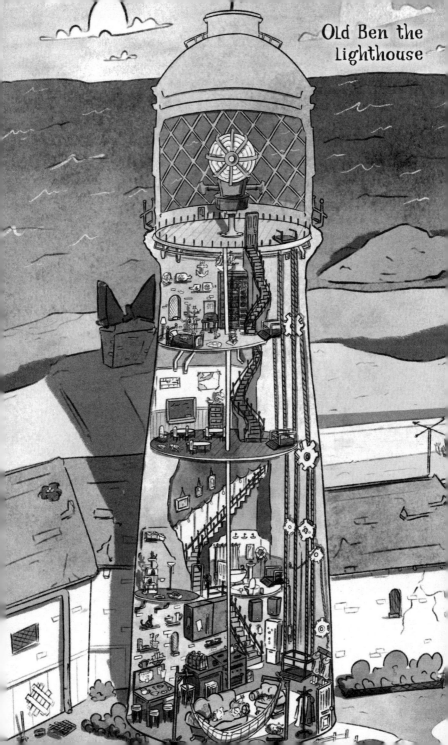

Old Ben the
Lighthouse

Haven Point

Chapter One

Here are the facts:

1. My name is Alpha Lux. *Alpha* because it's the first letter of the Greek alphabet and I was Wreckling number one. *Lux* because the box I was found in had LUX SOAP FLAKES written all over it.

2. My face looks like a flame-grilled jellyfish.

3. I was raised by a mermaid.

4. I always tell the truth.

I'll give you a bit of time to let that sink in.

Ready?

Then let's begin . . .

Chapter Two

I was Haven Point's first Wreckling, but I certainly wasn't the last. There are forty-two of us now, not including the mermaids. When you're a Wreckling, you mainly spend your days squabbling, eating and planning adventures. Well, at least that's what my gang does. Oh, and Wrecklings also carry out *wreckings*, which is how we got our name.

These days we leave blankets in the Lux Soap Flakes box, and it's under the porch so no new Wrecklings have to get damp and cold like I did.

★

There was a full moon the night Cap'n found me. He thought I was a dead 'un, nowt but blisters and scrawn.

Back then he lived in Old Ben, the lighthouse, all by himself. (The mermaids only started coming ashore after I arrived.)

Cap'n was outside because he's terrified to sleep on a full moon. He says it's the height of sea-magic and he worries that the waves in his dreams will steal him away. So imagine this: he's leaning on the rat-a-tat tree where the woodpecker lives, watching storm clouds roll across the horizon with the big sea-magic moon in the sky, Old Ben with his red and white stripes standing to attention behind Cap'n just like his shadow.

The full moon sets Cap'n's nerves on edge. It's like he can feel the blood pulsing through him in time with the waves. All his senses are heightened and shadows are making ordinary things look sinister and unreal. And then . . .

(This is where you get to meet me.)

. . . he hears the cats fighting. They sound like babies squalling, and Cap'n is fed up of them unsettling the kitten that lives in his beard. He sighs and gets the broom from the porch.

The whole world is made of shadows on a night like

this. His boots crunch along the gravel and then *shloop* into the damp grass as he follows his ears, chuntering to himself as he goes.

There's a box by the wall and he thinks the bloomin' cats must have got themselves stuck in there. It's a really old box; it probably came from one of Cap'n's wreckings. (I'll tell you about them later.) And printed all over the top it says:

Lux Soap Flakes - cares for special things

I guess it did just that.

I love it when Cap'n tells me this next bit, cos he acts it out and does all the faces. He's really good at them.

Cap'n sees that the lid of the box has been closed in that way where the four flaps fold over each other. He doesn't wonder how the box got folded back up after the cats got in. Instead, he's on guard with his broom drawn like a sword because he knows furious cats are about to come hurtling out at him, and the kitten in his beard is mewing and scrabbling.

He holds his breath.

He pauses.

Then whips open the box, closes his eyes and prepares to be attacked.

Nothing happens.

He opens one eye.

He opens the other eye to see if it tells him what the first one did.

He sees me.

'Holy Neptune!' he whispers.

Then he drops the broom and goes helter-skelter skidding on the shloopy grass and rings the huge brass bell, which has a handwritten label above it that says:

EMERGENCY USE ONLY

I mean, I was there and I don't remember any of it. But it's a damn good story the way he tells it.

Chapter Three

At Haven Point, we're all bound by the laws of the water. Did you know that waves make different noises, depending on how the day is feeling? When it's angry, the sea is just this low-down, rolling roar that sets your tummy a bit iffy.

Today is Sunday and it's indifferent. I knew it the moment I woke up. I could hear the sea gliding in and out, like it can't even be bothered to make waves. A sound like can't-be-botheredness.

If it stays like this, it'll be perfect for tonight's wrecking.

None of the other Wrecklings are up yet. Not Jericho or Willis, or Badger – my best friend who goes everywhere with me, except for this morning when I've left her snuffle-snoring in her hammock. She's not an actual badger – that'd be silly. She has a pitch-black Afro with one white streak, which is where her name comes from.

She can't get to In Deep with the mermaids anyway; none of the other Wrecklings can. And that's where I'm headed today – In Deep – to see Ephyra and the other mermaids for the first time in ages.

I'm leaning over the thick whitewashed wall at the end of the lighthouse garden. From here, I can see all the way out to the foghorn that squats on the cliff edge, and the lift beside it that leads down to the beach – and, beyond it all, the sea. This is the exact place where I was found in the box nearly twelve years ago. I love it when I have this spot all to myself. You don't get hardly any time alone here. Moments like this, with no one yelling? Brilliant.

I head through the gate, knocking twice on the wall as I go. That way I know I'll return. We're a superstitious lot here – I reckon it comes from Cap'n and his seafaring days. The sea is wild and we'll do anything we can to calm it. Knock on the wall, cross our fingers and think of knots: we're all for it.

I walk towards the foghorn. It's a white bell shape, like a short windmill, but instead of blades it's got two black horns sticking out of the top. I strike out to the left of the foghorn and reach the lift that will take me from the clifftop down to the beach. I press the button and wait, taking in a deep lungful of salty air.

Beyond the rickety steps that start beside the lift and zigzag down to the beach, I can just see the edge of Camel's Island, the humpback lump of rock that separates our bay from the salt beds.

I turn and look back at Old Ben, the lighthouse. His posh name is Old Benevolent – he's a burst of bright red and white stripes on the clifftop, surrounded by a little clump of ramshackle houses and outbuildings, all kept in place by the thick whitewashed wall. The wall needs to be solid because when the wind howls – which it often does – the sky and sea churn, trying to outdo each other, and it feels like the wind could whip us all up and drop us over the cliff edge into the sea. When the lightning flashes, the whole bay lights up and makes your eyes burn. Not literally. You wouldn't like that. My left eye must've got burned when I was a baby, Cap'n says. It melted, fusing my eyelid with my cheek. My left ear too, so it works, kind of, but it's just a hole with no fancy bit to protect it, or to wear shells in like Ephyra does. When the wind howls, it just goes straight on in there and stays.

Haven Point, Wrecklings' territory, is like our very own island, even though we're attached to the mainland. I sometimes lie on my back, stare up at the sky and imagine that I'm soaring like a seagull and I can look down and see Old Ben in the centre of Haven Point – he's like our castle with all our higgledy-piggledy buildings surrounding him. I flap my wings and catch an uplift to glide round the edges of our territory. I fly from the point where the salt beds touch the sea, all the way up the cliff face to the green, grassy Leas where Old Ben stands guard behind the whitewashed wall. I drift south and skirt the edge of our allotment at Spuggie's Lawe, then west to the quarry with the white horse we painted on the hillside, and north right up to the old pillbox. I finish the loop to land back at Old Ben.

Every good castle needs a moat because they keep people out. The way we do that here is with the Boundaries. They're the reason why you don't find us on any map and why you've never heard of us before. They are our invisible moat that keeps us safe and hidden from the Outside. At the start of every year, we sing the Boundaries. Everyone, even the toddlers. We fuel their power.

Cap'n made the Boundaries when he first moved here and set up his home in the abandoned lighthouse where he could watch and wait for his sister who was lost at sea. He'd pace round and round, hoping for her return. I know what it feels like to wait for someone.

The big word for the thing that started to creep inside Cap'n when he lost his sister is 'agoraphobia', which you say like *ag-or-a-foe-bee-ya*. It means he doesn't go outside. He can force himself when it's an emergency, and he has to, but Cap'n feels better when he's indoors.

When he first arrived at Haven Point, the only way he could keep going outside was to sing made-up songs to help him feel safe. He hoped the songs would guide his sister home, but they never did.

And that's all we know about his sister. Cap'n clams up if we ask about her. I don't even know her name.

After some time Cap'n realized there must be sea-magic in his songs because they'd built an invisible wall round his lighthouse, the moat protecting our castle. Eventually, Old Ben and the whole of Haven Point disappeared from memories and maps. Vanished.

That's a good thing, by the way. Because there was

more than just the Boundaries in the sea-magic of Cap'n's songs: they became an invitation and a map too. You see, everyone who finds this place and becomes a Wreckling is disabled. If you're not, you're an Outsider, and no Outsider has ever made it past the Boundaries. Cap'n, without even realizing it, made us a home here to live as we want, exactly as we are. No need to change, or hide, or have to try to do things the 'proper' way.

I don't remember life beyond the Boundaries. I was a tiny baby when I arrived. Haven Point is my home, my life, all I've ever known. From what I can gather from the other Wrecklings, well, the world outside Haven Point is cruel. I'm not scared of much, but I am terrified of the Outside, of Outsiders.

★

The lift pops me out at the bottom of the cliff, just along from the sea caves, and I trudge down the beach. The soft sand knackers my legs, and the seagulls slumped on their nests caw in sympathy.

I'm nearly In Deep, nearly with Ephyra.

Ephyra is my not-mam, my not-big sister – she's my everything.

She's a mermaid, the one who came when Cap'n

rang the **EMERGENCY USE ONLY** bell, way back when he found me.

She's the one who always comes.

We share the sea with the mermaids. Marsden Rock, which looms offshore, just in front of me, is really mermaid territory, but we have their permission to climb it. It's massive. At high tide, the rock rises out of the sea and you have to swim out to it, but it's low tide now and it looks like it's been plonked on the wet sand.

Marsden Rock is flat, as if a sea god had reached up and beheaded it with a trident. On the side, there's a metal ladder and a pulley system to raise us up to the top. It's a tall rock. Like, really-don't-go-near-the-edge sort of tall, and it's always covered in seagulls. Badger has to watch out if she gets close to Marsden Rock because she always gets bird-luck poop spattered on her head. I reckon it's because the birds appreciate that she can imitate all their calls, and they want to mark her as one of their own. But she hates that it gets her hauled in for a bath by Norma.

Marsden Rock is as big as a football pitch on top, though I wouldn't recommend playing it up there. We tried once, but ended up just sitting around, waiting the whole time for someone to go all the way down the ladder, swim to get the ball, and then come back up again.

Beyond Marsden Rock is In Deep. That's where the mermaids live and no Wreckling goes there. Ever. Not even Cap'n.

Except, of course, for me.

I'm the only one who was given the special saltwater charm that allows me to enter the mermaids' home. Well, it's more like a lair. The word 'home' makes you think of crumpets and curtains and cats, and it's really nothing like that at all.

★

The bored waves still keep me in trudge-mode even though the sand is easier to walk on here – hard, licked by the sea.

Then I feel it.

I've suddenly got goosebumps. The bad kind.

Something's wrong.

I glance back over my shoulder. Is Badger sneaking up on me?

No. Was that something on the clifftop? Something catching the light?

I shake my head to knock the silly out of me. A small glint on the clifftop doesn't mean it's *her* coming for me. She couldn't get through the Boundaries anyway – she's an Outsider. Sometimes the sound of the sea eats my sensible head and makes my mind race.

It's not the first time I've got goosebumps like that, and this last fortnight it's happened more than ever, to the point where I haven't been able to hide it like I usually can. Badger caught me looking over my shoulder the other day when we were eating pilfered stotties and pease pudding on the cliff edge. 'Do you think it's *her*?' she asked.

I pretended I didn't know who she was talking about, hoping she'd get the hint and shut up. She didn't. 'You know, your *mam*?'

'Don't be daft,' I said.

I pinched a bit of her stottie, knowing she'd duff me up and would miss me catching my breath.

★

I'm *really* excited to see Ephyra. I've heart-missed her. Recently, Ephyra and her mermaid clan have had Important Meetings and Things and I haven't been invited.

Ephyra took my charm away to make sure I couldn't go In Deep by myself any more.

I humphed. She patted me on the head. I growled. She kissed me and swam away.

But this morning there was a shark tooth on my pillow, with its gummy edges still bloody. A proper mermaid invitation if ever I saw one.

★

At last, I'm standing in front of a mass of scrubby bushes at the edge of the shore, in line with Marsden Rock. This is No Entry, the only entrance to In Deep. It's covered with plants that smell of cat wee, brambles with dagger thorns, and the kind of nettles that sting so deep they reach your bones and then knack for weeks.

You can only get to In Deep if you go *through* No Entry. That's sea-magic for you.

In Deep is the part of the undersea where Ephyra and her Northern Clan live. She's the head, which makes her the boss.

The fairy tales got it half right about mermaids, as most fairy tales do. They say that mermaids use their song as a trap to attract the attention of sailors and lead them to their death. Which is a bit overdramatic and completely misses the point of the really useful bit.

And that's exactly the way the mermaids want it.

The mermaids' song stops memories from forming. There are some gossamer strands of the fantastical left inside sailors' heads and these grow into legend as all good sea stories do.

There's only one sailor who has ever outwitted the mermaids, and he runs our lighthouse.

★

I take a step into No Entry – and a bramble snags on my leg.

That never happens. I usually glide straight through. When I bend to remove the bramble, the dagger thorn lurking just beside it doesn't shimmer and disappear like it should. Instead, it slices my right arm from my jutty wrist bone all the way to my elbow.

At first, there's no pain, just shock.

Then I see the blood and all the 'ow' comes in one heat spike of every swear word only Badger knows I know. I sit down fast, not cos I want to, but because that's what my legs do. The edges of the cut are white and the blood is red and it's dripping into the damp sand, making patterns in its ridges.

I tried to enter without my saltwater charm.

That's what excitement does: turns you into a newbie and makes you go all helter-skelter into half-baked unthinkings.

Suddenly the burrs and dagger thorns shimmer, showing the hidden path I couldn't find, and there's Ephyra.

'Hey, my sweet,' she says, making a grand entrance with her arms raised. She's dangling my silver urchin-spine charm from her fingertips. Then she realizes I'm all bloody.

'Alpha! What have you done?'

Ephyra plops down beside me and kisses my forehead, takes my hand. She's the only one who's ever kissed my scarred face. Cap'n says it's the first thing she did when we met and that's how he knew I'd be hers and she'd be mine, even though Ephyra herself didn't know it yet.

'You forgot you didn't have your charm?'

My charm. The first time Ephyra put it round my neck and we walked through No Entry together. I toddled then, barely came up to her knees. She said I needed to find my water legs. Back then I thought everyone went In Deep. When I found out I was the only Wreckling who'd ever been there, this special bit of me filled up with honey as sweet as when the bees have been feasting on lavender. I felt gooey and warm. When I asked Cap'n what it meant, he said it was love.

I nod in response to Ephyra's question. Then remember I'm cross she took it from me, and I don't want her to know that my excitement at seeing her made me forget.

So I shake my head. 'It's your fault. If you hadn't *unlawfully* taken and exercised *unlawful control* over my charm with intent to deprive me *thereof*, I would've been fine.'

'Kelvin been teaching criminal-law classes again?' asks Ephyra.

'Yup. That's the first time I've ever been able to use any of it, mind.'

'Feeling a bit smug, are we?'

'Nope, not smug. Vindicated, correct, injured – and mainly just really angry.'

'Why angry? At me?'

'Yes, of course at you! You took my charm! I've got a gouge out of my arm because of you!'

'Fair enough.'

Ephyra looks at me. She's not one of those adults who try to make it better when you don't want them to. I hold on to my rage for seven more seconds, then I let it go. It's impossible to stay angry at Ephyra.

Mermaids aren't magic – they get really huffy if you call them that – but bits of them really behave as if they are. Like their legs. Mermaids have tails, not legs. But if they're wearing their saltwater charm, then what they need appears, which are legs, *land legs*. That's how Ephyra reached me on the sand. Not that she uses them very often. Ephyra just about tolerates being on the beach or the salt beds, but now I'm bigger and more self-sufficient she won't come any further Up Top.

From the net bag at her waist, she pulls out a large clamshell and opens it.

Pine sap. It's like superglue. She trades it with Cap'n for squid ink.

She puts a blob of sap on her right index finger and takes my arm. 'Ready?' she asks. 'Think nice things.'

I say, 'Yes,' but inside my head I say *no*, so I clamp my teeth tight instead, hard enough to make the bit below my earholes jut out where my gills will appear. I close my right eye. My left one permanently does the job for me.

Think nice things. Override the pain.

OK.

Ephyra presses the sap on my arm and I completely lose my stuff, my happy things, and yell all those swear words only Badger knows I know.

Now Ephyra knows too.

'Potty mouth,' she says.

When I open my eye and look down, there's an amber track along my arm, like a slug trail. It's bloody, but that's just dried stuff that had already come out; the rest of me is now staying in. Mermaid healing works fast.

I snort. 'Potty mouth? Is that the best you can do?'

'Well, I certainly can't beat you, can I? Ready?' She takes my hand and hauls me up with her.

'I'm ready.'

I take a deep breath as she places the silver spine round my neck. The strand is long and narrow, almost invisible. It comes from an urchin that never stops growing, so many fathoms deep that it barely exists in memory.

Ephyra drops it over my head and, as soon as it lands on my skin, it scuffles round and round and digs, digs, digs. It's not painful, it's woozy – like landsickness, like the sea is claiming me as one of its own. Then it's over and I touch my neck. The spine is in my skin and on my skin, like the echo of a silver necklace.

Ephyra's charm is a vial of saltwater made of abalone, a shell with a shiny rainbow inside. The stopper is a pear-shaped pearl. My charm doesn't look anything like hers, but it's like they're two halves of a whole and, when they're together, it's electricity and balance. Same as us. When I asked why mine is just an urchin-spine strand, not anywhere near as pretty as hers, she said not everything beautiful *is* beautiful. Sometimes she speaks proper weird.

I *covet* her charm, which means I really, really want it. It's silly because I have no need for it. It's what allows Ephyra and her clan to be on land, gives them their land legs, just like my charm is the thing that allows me to get through No Entry and then gives me my tail and gills when I'm In Deep. Without her charm, Ephyra couldn't leave the sea. If she lost it on land, she would drown in the air. That's another reason for her sharpened teeth, as it is with all animals: to protect the things she needs.

I'm one of those things.

★

This time the brambles and branches shimmer, like Ephyra's land legs, and hand in hand we make our way through No Entry together.

The air becomes damp and cool as we walk inside the base of Marsden Rock, which seems impossible to reach from No Entry and yet we always arrive here. We come to a stop inside a cave that the sea has gouged out of rock. Sometimes the sea is a sculptor: it gave us the Stacks on the beach, like tall, skinny Cleopatra's Needle, which Badger perches on when we do wreckings, and Lot's Wife that stands to attention out beyond the foghorn.

Layers of yellow and gold sandstone lie above us, sparkle motes drifting in the air.

We face a gap in the rock the size of a lighthouse windowpane, in a perfect right-angled triangle. The edges are sea-smoothed and old. It's the only thing between us and the sea. The Triangle is what I call it. Mermaids don't go in for names, so I've had to do loads of labelling around here.

We wait.

You can't hurry this bit.

It took me a long time to be able to go In Deep without Ephyra. I'm not sure I was ever meant to learn, which was why she had to take my charm away.

You can't see when it's the right time to go In Deep. You have to *feel* it.

The waves dance at an angle behind the Triangle.

We're waiting and, when the waves form a web, we dive through.

Chapter Four

Waves thrash. Ear pressure builds. Bubbles. Kick, kick, kick.

Pop.

Ephyra has my hand.

She always does.

★

I can never remember how I get from the Triangle to here. One minute we're jumping and I have legs, the next I've got a tail and gills and I'm In Deep with the mermaids of the Northern Clan.

It's been a while, Alpha. We missed you. Henrietta is

sharpening a spear. Her voice is in my head without her having to move her lips, the mermaid way.

Cobalt hisses and the petrol-coloured, poison-tipped wings on her cheeks stand out proud.

Well, some of us did, says Henrietta. She swishes her knife so it licks the point of the spear.

Out of the corner of my eye, I see Cobalt slink back. Her ink-coloured tail blends into the reef as she watches from the shadows. I've learned never to take my eye off Cobalt. I've got a scar on my ankle to remind me.

I stick my tongue out at her, knowing that Henrietta is beside me to back me up, then I swim slow figures of eight. It feels like flying. I don't think I'll ever properly get used to being alive and breathing underwater like this. It's too wonderful to ever become boring.

A striped purple seahorse bobs beside me and nudges my arm with its nose.

Looks like you've got a friend, says Henrietta.

I can't play now. I try to shoo the little creature away. *Next time*.

It throws its little shoulders back in a strop, flicks its tail and shoots off. Ephyra and I once beat the seahorse herd in a race and I keep postponing the rematch.

I look from Henrietta to Ephyra. None of the

mermaids are alike: it's as though each of them has been coloured in differently. Ephyra is striking and fierce, all emerald peacock colours with knotty pale blue hair tangled with barnacles and fish scales.

Henrietta is wild. Her tail is orange and gold, and there are chunks of it missing. She dances with the white horses that leap on the crests of waves at midnight. It's highly unusual for a mermaid to change clans, but she told me that the Southern Clan were too tame and scholarly for the adventure seeker in her. They buried their heads in the Seaweed Scrolls for hours without a break. Henrietta was always in trouble, not for doing bad really, just for doing bored and unthinking. That's probably why we get on.

Why did you leave the Southern Clan? I asked.

My heart wasn't there, she said.

I don't like her saying that. It reminds me that, even though Ephyra and Cap'n have made Haven Point my heart-home, there's still something missing, no matter how much they try to fill it.

I know the missing is where my mam's face should be.

Mermaids aren't designed to be without a clan. Henrietta said she'd heard about the wreckings we carry out, and we sounded like her kind of home. Ephyra says that Henrietta's wanderings are handy to keep us linked to the rest of the world.

★

Give me a hand with this. Henrietta holds out a spear to me.

I look to Ephyra and she nods. *Back soon.* She gives one kick and shoots off. She's gone before I can complain. Why did she invite me back if she's just going to disappear on me? Something is definitely up. There's a reason I was held Up Top and not allowed In Deep, and I want to find out what it is.

You can't see waves underwater, but you can feel them wash over you in warm patches and cold bites. I touch below my ears, feeling the delicate fronds protecting my gills.

Henrietta slaps my hand away. *Stop touching – you'll clog 'em.*

I stroke once more just because I can't be wrong, and poke my tongue out.

She threatens me with her spear and then goes back to sharpening it. I try to kind of float-sit. There's a lot of thinking involved to make my body do what it needs down here. Ephyra says it's like that when she's Up Top. The natural isn't there – it's all process.

I watch Henrietta and wonder if she'll be easier to break than Ephyra.

So . . . I say.

Henrietta looks up. She doesn't have gills like me; none of the mermaids do. They don't need help to breathe down here. Her eyes are full of mischief-twinkle. The not-waves swoosh her hair around her. She's a big splodge of every colour that exists.

Mermaids are a *big secret*: no one but us knows they really exist beyond fairy tales and sea shanties. Imagine what would happen if the world found out about Ephyra and her clan? Doesn't bear thinking about. They'd be experimented on, tortured . . . maybe even kept in a cage and put on show so kids could prod them. Wrecklings escape to Haven Point to *stop* being prodded and poked and gawped at – and worse. I've read books. I know how valuable the mermaids and their song would be to baddies.

A shoal of silvery green fish cuts between us, moving like the starlings do over our Spuggie's Lawe allotment. They brush against my hair and I know they'll leave behind their scales like sequins. The fish at the front slow down and the shoal billows, moving as one. I'm mesmerized and forget I was asking Henrietta a question. The bulk of the shoal passes and she becomes visible through the stragglers.

So, what? she says, and I'm about to reply when she grabs three fish, slaps them together like a sandwich and rips them in two before popping the heads in her mouth.

Mermaids aren't quite how you'd imagine.

Henrietta shoves the rest of the fish in her mouth and sucks in their tails like spaghetti. She stares at me, cocks her head and smiles. Her teeth fit together like someone has drawn a zigzag across them and then cut it out with a penknife. *You want something?*

No, I say.

With a flick of her tail, she's beside me. *Yes you do.*

And then her fingers are prodding my sides and she's wriggling them, and I can't stop laughing, or get away, or breathe.

Suddenly Cobalt is there. I'd taken my eye off her. I kick out to try to get away from Henrietta's tickle fingers, but my tail connects with Cobalt's arm –

Her growl is a jackdaw meeting a storm. In a heartbeat, she's in my face.

Why is this fried landmass In Deep? Did you see her kick me? No sandin' respect, this one. She points in my face. *No sandin' respect.*

No one ever gets away with calling me something like that. I'm furious and ready to fight, but my body remains frozen.

Cobalt sneers. *Mussel got your tongue?*

Henrietta moves to put herself between us, but, before she can, Ephyra shoots through the water and thumps into Cobalt's side, knocking her away from me. The two of them twist over and over, a double mermaid somersault that would look like an underwater ballet dance if it weren't for the barbs in Ephyra's hands.

Henrietta grabs me by the shoulders and pulls me back from Cobalt's poisonous wingtips as they hurtle by.

Within seconds, Ephyra has Cobalt pinned to a jagged rock edge. Scarlet drops float away from Cobalt's thigh. When I see Ephyra's mouth, it is bloody, like the shark tooth she left on my pillow.

Ephyra unpins Cobalt, who slinks away into the shadows. Ephyra waits, her chest rising and falling. When she's sure the danger has passed, she swims back over to us.

You're supposed to keep her safe, she snarls at Henrietta, who bows her head and squeezes my shoulders, before she turns tail and is gone.

It's not Henrietta's fault, I say to Ephyra. *You're the one who slunk off and left me*. Even though I didn't know they were waiting there, tears explode out of me.

Ephyra immediately softens and curls herself round me.

You're right, she says. *You're right. I'm sorry. There, my sweet, my beautiful one.*

She strokes my hair back from my face where I've pulled it to hide my tears. She takes one of them from my face. It's a bubble that doesn't mix with the rest of the sea. She holds the tiny orb on the tip of her finger.

I'm not though, am I? I say.

What?

Beautiful. I say it so quietly in my head that I don't think she's heard. There's a pause.

She stares right into me. *Your face shows your might, your survival. You are battle-scarred and you wear it with beauty.*

She holds out the tear that's still on the tip of her finger; it splits in half, forms two perfect spheres in which tiny oceans roar. She places one on the inside of her wrist and one on mine. They stick fast like limpets. She smiles and curls her body tighter round mine.

Cobalt is jealous, Ephyra says.

Of me? I ask.

Of course of you. Ephyra laughs and strokes my cheek along its scars.

I let Ephyra touch my face just for that moment, then shake off her fingers.

I ask her a question to change the subject. *What's going on? Like,* really *going on?*

Ephyra sighs. *We don't know. Something's not right. I'd tell you, but we don't know. I should never have left you alone for a moment, especially with Cobalt on edge more than usual, but I thought there might have been news. Never mind for a moment, I should never have allowed you back down full stop! I missed you and that got in the way of sense.*

Henrietta could find out what's up, I say. *Ask her old clan.*

She taps my forehead. *See, we need you for those brains of yours.*

Gerroff. I bat her hand away.

Ephyra unfurls herself from me and does a slow somersault as she stretches. I join her.

She whirls a little faster. I go faster still and soon we are whooping and looping and laughing, and everything feels nearly OK again – but Ephyra's right: there's something heavier than usual lying in the water.

★

When Ephyra leaves me at the No Entry bushes, I hand over my charm before she even asks. The tiny orb stays on my wrist. Ephyra smiles. Then she puts my charm inside her net bag.

'Just for now,' she says. 'To keep you safe.'

'Forever' and 'now' are interchangeable for mermaids though, because their time is so much longer than ours. Now *could* be my forever.

She holds my cheeks in her hands. 'Tell Laura I've gathered more tellins and grey tops for her.'

My face must look as blank as my brain is.

'Shiny shells,' she says, and laughs.

I'm still puzzled.

'For their wedding!'

'Oh,' I say, giggling.

Laura is engaged to Maura. They're two of the grown-up Wrecklings. Laura and Maura are going to get married in nineteen sleeps. I know this because there's a countdown chalkboard in the entrance hall. It's Flea's job to update it and he takes it *very* seriously. He's one of the kids like me. There are fifteen of us yelling and screaming and getting in everyone's business. We're having a party after they get married, which is brilliant because Wrecklings love a good party, Maura and Laura are super-lush people, and also cos of the epic name-rhyming thing.

Ephyra looks at me. 'Everything OK?'

'Course,' I reply, and stick my tongue out. She does the same back, but hers always looks more impressive cos it's forked.

'See you tonight at the wrecking,' she says.

Then she turns and the dagger thorns start to shimmer.

Just before she disappears, I yell after her. 'Ephyra!'

She turns round.

'Don't tell anyone I cried.'

She nods and walks away.

Ephyra will never tell.

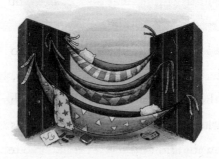

Chapter Five

By the time I get back to Old Ben, it's naptime. I'll duff you up if you laugh. We all have a long one, late in the afternoon, before a wrecking – we can't afford to have people nodding off halfway through.

As I walk along Old Ben's hallway, lined with our sou'westers and shoes, and above them bits of old ships on wonky shelves, I try to get my head round what just happened. Not the fight with Cobalt – that's par for the course with her. With Ephyra. I've never seen her so uneasy before. And, before that, the prickly feeling I got on the beach – is that part of it?

'Hey!' yells Badger, as she prods me in my side. 'Gotcha!'

'Oi!' I go to clip her round the head, but she laughs and ducks.

Badger is funny and clever, and can do all the bird calls, and also is blind. Badger uses a cane, but she also does this thing called *ekko-low-kay-shun*, which is spelled in the dictionary as 'echolocation'. It means she bounces clicks off walls and objects and it helps to tell her where she is. It does *not* mean she can see everything all fancy in her head like some comic-book superpower. It's just a tool that helps her out, same as her cane. Rahul, one of the older Wrecklings, helped her to work on this skill and make it stronger once she got here. Not all visually impaired people do it, can do it, or want to do it. It's just if they're 'that way inclined' according to Rahul. Turns out Badger was.

I've known her for the four years since she arrived at Haven Point, and I've been her best friend since ten minutes after I met her, when she told me that I was, whether I liked it or not. She said she'd never had a best friend before; all the other Outsider kids ignored or babied her, and she was interviewing for the position.

I told her to stuff off. She said the job was mine.

Now I admit defeat. 'You got me. Nice one.'

Badger bows and we walk into the base of Old Ben.

Every time I go in here, the first thing I do is look up, my eye following the metal railing by the steps, round and round, up and up round the inside of the lighthouse tower with its white walls. The paint is peeling in patches and some of it is yellowy with damp. Despite all of us constantly working on it, Old Ben still manages to look shabby.

Even though it's naptime, it's noisy. What with the sea, the wind and us – well, it's bloomin' chaos. It's never quiet here, but the noise is always ramped up by the thrill of a wrecking to come.

The toddlers are at Maura and Laura's cottage. They don't do the wreckings yet, too small and sticky. All of them were born here. A brand-new generation of Haven Pointers who've only ever known this as their home. Flea was the last one we found in the soap-flakes box, so he gets the same surname as me, which is cool. It's like having a proper little brother.

Cap'n has retreated to his quarters upstairs. Sometimes you can see when it's a bit much and he needs closer-together walls to support him. Sometimes he conducts lessons from inside a cupboard. That's fine by us. Do whatcha have to do.

Minus the toddlers, Cap'n, snotty Willis and those

who live in the cottages, that leaves thirteen of us who sleep in the dorm in the lighthouse base, the youngest being Flea and the oldest being Jericho. Flea *thinks* he's in our gang, but he's too young. Large *is* in our gang, with me and Badger and Jericho. He leads the wreckings, but he doesn't stay here with us. He sleeps at Maura's, even during naptime, because sometimes his breathing goes funny. Large is really tall – you might have guessed that – and he has the kindest eyes I've ever seen.

I'm last in line to brush my teeth. You may think this is because I'm rubbish at queuing, but it's actually a very clever move. Cap'n says we're falling apart enough without putting our teeth on the line too, so he's obsessed with making sure we brush them. He checks to see if the toothbrush heads are wet, all thirteen of them standing in a row, wedged upright on a roll of astroturf which is splattered with toothpaste speckles. Unless you're first, or last, and you've made sure everyone's done when you go to grab your toothbrush, you can bet someone will use your hand as target practice with their minty gob spit.

Flea does it now (I rest my case).

I go to help Jericho and Badger with the lockers. These are Old Ben inventiveness at its best. They are on wheels and stay up against the wall usually, but at night or naptime we all roll them into the centre in rows. Then we use them to hang our hammocks on. Two lockers, facing each other, equals room for three hammocks, one each for me, Jericho and Badger. The whole of the lighthouse sounds like it's clicking its fingers as we all lock them into position and get ready to kip.

Tip one: sleep diagonally on a hammock; it stops the comedy roll.

Tip two: don't tell people this immediately as you'd hate to miss out on watching the comedy roll.

'You owe me a postcard for the extra jam I sneaked past Willis for your porridge, Alph,' says Jericho as he puts his brakes on.

Willis. Ugh. He's very definitely *not* in our gang.

Jericho has freckles on his nose and cheeks and a mop of orange hair that matches the flames on his wheelchair.

'Where do you fancy?' I ask.

'Surprise me,' he says. 'No, actually, somewhere cold.'

Badger and I hang the ends of our hammocks over the hooks on the lockers and tie them tight with a bowline. Most useful knot in the world, first one we're taught when we arrive. You learn it quick if you're in the dorm because hammocks aren't comfy if they're not suspended. Then they're just net on a cold floor.

Jericho transfers from his wheelchair to the bottom hammock, and I fold up his wheelchair and lean it against a locker.

'Remember to chain it,' says Jericho.

There's been a recent spate of wheelchair theft. Well, not theft exactly, more . . . wheelchair modification. Jericho rigged Kai's chair so that a reinflating whoopee cushion was hidden underneath to make it sound like Kai was trumping every time he moved. Kai got him back and Jericho still hasn't quite got rid of the squid ink that stained his hands. Hence Jericho insisting on me chaining up his wheelchair.

'You started it,' says Badger, who is now snuggly in her hammock.

'Yes,' says Jericho. 'The key part also being to finish it.'

After I've secured his wheelchair, I grab the old index-card box from my locker. It's got all my postcards in it.

I flick to the blue section where the cold places live. There's a Norwegian fjord with 'Greetings' printed across the front. The faded writing belongs to Mrs Edwina Shrub and the stamp is dated over fifty years ago. She had a pleasant time apparently, but didn't much care for pickled fish. I'm on Edwina's side. It's rubbish here when it gets to midwinter and pickle time.

'How's about this one?' I say as I hand it to Jericho.

He gives it a good look. 'Perfect.'

'Want me to put it in your locker?'

'Nah,' he says, like he doesn't care. 'No need for the hassle. I'll just keep it here.'

I nod and return my postcards to my locker. Then I place both hands on my hips with my back to the edge of my hammock and spring. You've got to have a good bounce to get in – can't wuss out or you'll go splat. Once you're used to them, hammocks are the comfiest things in the whole world. Now this is the clever bit. Instead of us all having to be crammed in like sardines, I wind the handle, which is linked to a cog on the side of the locker, and my hammock slowly rises above Jericho, then above Badger who is in position already, until we're no longer side by side but stacked up like bunks in a submarine.

We don't own much stuff, so what we do have all fits in one locker. Like my box of postcards and the baby clothes I was found in.

We share everything we have. It's fair that way: no

one has loads of possessions while someone else has nowt, cos often when people arrive here they do so with absolutely nothing. We don't need to buy stuff, so we don't have money. We're good at bartering though, giving value to things other people might think are rubbish or useless.

I get the postcards from Kelvin, who found them in a trunk that came ashore during a wrecking. Kelvin covets the bird quills I collect. I covet his postcards.

Jericho says he wants to see the world and he does that via my postcard stash. But I know he pretends that they were written to him by family members who love and care for him. How do I know he does that? Because I do it too.

Cap'n has done an amazing job here, but you can't smooth all the hurt edges. And they always feel sharper before we go to sleep.

Twenty minutes later, I'm still awake. Badger is snuffling in her sleep, airy sighs that usually comfort me, but now they just make me angry because she's asleep and I'm not. Someone trumps on the other side of the lighthouse, followed by a little giggle.

There's too much going on in my head: the tension with the mermaids; Ephyra not being able to hide her worry; but, most of all, it's that feeling of being watched. I know there was nothing on the clifftop – it's just my imagination running away with me.

Should I tell Ephyra about it though? What about Badger? Should I tell them what I thought I saw? *Who* I thought I saw?

Is it her coming back for me?

That's a thought too far.

Her face is always in darkness, but every time there's that flash of light, that spark, like I saw on the clifftop today. I think you can only dream what you know, and I don't know my mam. That's why I can never see her face.

Don't keep secrets. Don't tell lies. They eat you up inside.

I'll tell Ephyra about it. She'll hug me and tell me I'm being silly, then it'll be OK. And I'll tell Badger.

Ephyra, then Badger.

My eye is heavy now.

Badger snuffles again. Teetering on the edge of sleep, I don't mind at all.

Chapter Six

Our routine is ruled by the moon and water, and wreckings – where we lure and rob unsuspecting ships – are a part of that routine, just like eating and cleaning our teeth. They're part of the deal Cap'n made with Ephyra when they both first came here. The mermaids use their song to stop sailors' memories from forming so we can 'repurpose' their goods; in return, we keep the mermaid clan safe and hidden.

That's where our name comes from: the wreckings. When I arrived, Cap'n called me his little Wreckling, and it stuck. When *we* get to choose a name and make it ours? There's power in that. We're proud of us, what we do, who we are, our bodies and brains.

We're proud to be Wrecklings.

The mermaids' forgetting song has only one antidote – razor clams. Every Sunday, without fail, we gather together and drink our razor-clam soup to protect our own memories, and then, after our Sunday-afternoon nap, it's time for the wrecking. Our allotment provides us with food, and our know-how keeps us ticking over, but you can't be self-sufficient and isolated from the world with just those. That's where the wreckings come in. Otherwise, how would we survive?

I asked Cap'n why what we take from the unsuspecting ships isn't stealing and bad. He said we're seafaring Robin Hoods, that he only lets us take stuff from companies with a 'dodgy reputation'. I asked how he knows which ones those are. He tapped the side of his nose and walked away – always does when I come out with those sorts of questions. Like when I ask about his sister. Even if I plait his beard to make a hammock for his kitten, he still doesn't give stuff up about her.

★

We're in position, down on our bay, in front of the sea caves. Marsden Rock looms out of the water, threatening in the dark. We're all silent. You can feel the tension in the air. I'm waiting for Large to give the signal: claps and torch flashes.

Cap'n always makes sure that it's a black night for a wrecking. There's a tiny sliver of moon giving the sky the texture of velvet.

'You ready there, Large?' I whisper.

Two quick claps. Two flashes. He's ready.

I stretch and bounce on my haunches. It's not nerves, not these days. It's excitement and something small running up the back of my neck that was once fear, but is now just a memory of it. I feel a familiar pressure on my thigh as Badger leans against me.

'What's on this one, Alph?' she asks.

'Cap'n says it's gold doubloons.'

'Really? Pirates!' Badger's unseeing eyes grow wider.

'Nah, yer sea lettuce. Gold doubloons? When has anything exciting like that ever happened? It'll be the usual dull stuff like bits of pipe and tins of soup.'

Badger sighs. 'One day, Alph. One day it'll be pirates.'

I put my arm round her. 'Aye, lass, one day.'

I hear Large clap three times, see the three torch flashes. It begins.

Badger and I scurry along the beach towards the Needle, hunkering down to try to hide from the wind. I wish I'd worn my hat over my balaclava.

Two claps.

My stomach flutters.

One clap.

Large is in position with his crew at the water's edge, grappling hooks and nets ready for the haul.

Fourteen paces at a sprint, and the last is a splash. Wet left foot in the sea and I know we're on target at the base and Badger begins her climb to sentry duty at the top of tall, skinny Cleopatra's Needle, the highest of the Stacks. You can always rely on Badger. Her ears are the best in all Haven Point; anything untoward and Badger will let us know immediately.

I look for the ship. It'll be out there. I'll see it soon.

Three claps.

Two claps.

I crouch down.

One clap.

'Ears, silly,' whispers Ephyra as she rises out of the waves beside me. I clap my hands to the sides of my head.

Our foghorn sounds on the clifftop. It rumbles your gut, like the noise wants to eat your insides. Ephyra dives back into the sea, ready to give her mermaid crew the signal.

She is sinewy and powerful, like a cheetah. Cobalt would usually be with her, but I'm guessing she's been relegated to anchorage duty, holding our target ship in position while we wreck. She'll hate that. *One—nil to me.*

I can just about see the ship now. It's small, only one mast and no pirate flag. Badger will be disappointed. Again. It's just beyond the sandbar out to sea past Marsden Rock. Old Ben was designed to warn ships about that. But, of course, tonight it doesn't, and that's the whole point of a wrecking.

The singing begins. Soft at first, it could be mistaken for the bubbles caught in rock pools. Mingling with the kittiwakes and the cormorants and the booming of the waves, the singing rises and falls as the mermaids dive under the sea, heading towards the stranded ship. They leap but don't splash; they're too strong and skilful for that.

It's a race against the sunrise, and the mermaids' song won't keep the memories of the crew unformed for long.

A red tinge dances on the sand. Daybreak is beginning.

I can just see the mermaids hauling themselves up the side of the ship. That's my cue.

I wrench away the curtain of seaweed at the base of the Needle and pull out my cart. Jericho and Willis will be doing the same right now, from their own hiding places.

But then I get it again – goosebumps and a funny tummy. The *thinking-someone-is-watching-me* feeling. I look behind me.

Something bright catches my eye up on the clifftop further over to the west from Old Ben – and I stumble.

I know every tuft of grass, every rock and molehill. There's nothing up there except the pillbox, and definitely nothing to catch the light like that.

Years ago, we used to use the pillbox as our den. It's a square concrete building on the cliff edge, looking out over Camel's Island and the Needle. It once had a door to the rear, though that crumbled away long before Cap'n and the Wrecklings arrived. We tried using wood to build a new one, but the wind always tore it off and it would be gone by the time we returned. The wind always wins around here.

There's a slit in the wall where a Second World War Home Guard soldier would have sat and pointed his gun out, protecting the rugged north-east coast from a deadly seaborne attack. The pillbox made one heckuva hiding place until the roof started to crumble and Cap'n made it a no-go zone. Which we, of course, completely ignored – until Jericho nearly got flattened.

Cap'n didn't need to tell us off; our shocked faces were enough for him. And now no one is supposed to go up there at all.

I haven't taken my eye off the clifftop, but now, when I squint harder, I can't see anything. I take a step back, just in case the strange glint appears again – but still nothing. Maybe I imagined it, like I did this morning, or perhaps it was moonlight on something dropped by a magpie. But that's telling myself lies because I know that there *was* a something. A something that ought not to be there.

I hear the other carts racing ahead of me, so I give my head a shake and get a shift on. That glint's made me fall behind and I *never* lose!

I drag my cart to the tideline, my shoulders straining in their sockets on the dry sand. It's easy once the wheels hit the wet.

'I beat you, Alpha! That's another postcard you owe me.'

I shrug and pretend like I don't care. The only good

thing about being whooped by Jericho is that it means I wasn't beaten by Willis. If he'd won, I would have been proper narked, but here he comes, last as always, spitting out sand. At least when I stumbled I didn't face-plant.

'Enjoy your trip?' I ask Willis. He glares at me.

'Shh,' says Large. 'I can't concentrate with you muttering.' He looks out to sea, scanning the incoming tide.

We fall quiet behind him.

'Here we go!'

The bay explodes into action. Large yells at the crew to *haul faster, harder* as they throw their nets into the sea. I splash into the water to help, gasping as the cold bites into my thighs. You never get used to that.

Working two per rod, the Hauling Crew hook the larger crates that the mermaids have brought into the shallows from the ship and drag them to shore. The Shore Crew form a human chain to transfer them on to the handcarts. Heaving, yelling, the smell of sweat building the harder we work.

I call to the group: 'Keep the noise down. Don't distract Badger.'

She's on top of the Needle, perched like a meerkat, her ears standing to attention for any sound that isn't

ours. Badger would have caught it if anything was amiss. Though she's focused out to sea, not on the pillbox . . .

But we've got the Boundaries! We're safe. The mermaids are safe. No one can find us. No one can get through.

Jericho's cart is filled first and he starts off at a cracking pace, grunting as it barrels over the bumpy, lumpy surface towards the base of the cliff. He passes it to the Knot Crew, whose job it is to securely attach the loot to the ropes, and transport it Up Top. They put the goods in crates and attach them to the pulleys to be yanked up into the air and then hauled up the side of the cliff. The crates are always covered in white chalk dust that sprinkles down the cliffs as they bash into the sides. You can tell who's a member of the Knot Crew by their grey hair.

I'm straining to pull a metal box on to the beach, half in the water, half out, when I see the glint again.

This time, no question, it's a definite *something*.

My chest feels tight suddenly, like I have to remember how breathing works. Has Badger heard anything unusual? I look over, but the box blocks my view of her.

I wave to catch Large's attention, but he's not looking either. Wrecklings are notoriously nosy and rubbish at keeping out of other people's business, so why now, when I need someone to neb, is no one bloomin' looking?

A thought thwacks into my head. What if the glint is only for me? Like in my dream? *What if it is my mam?*

That puts a cold feeling in my chest that has nothing to do with night or water.

I stand to look again and I mistime a wave.

The box lunges at me, forcing me on to my back, crushing the air out of my chest. It bends my right foot back at the ankle and I gasp and swallow lungfuls of salty water.

I try to yell, but the wave is joined by another that is bigger and stronger. The box pushes further into me, pinning me down.

Pressure pounds in my lungs.

In my mind, the glint flashes. Again and again, teasing me.

This time I nearly see my mam's face in its shadow.

Then black.

Chapter Seven

I'm caught in the shallows with waves that pound and I can't even gasp for air. My head floats away from my body. I leave my lungs behind, then desperately kick to get them back.

I don't know which way is up. Follow the bubbles?

It's black. Can't see bubbles.

I don't have air left to *make* bubbles.

The sea has never been this heavy.

This cold.

There's an amber slug moving towards a glint. My mam is somewhere in its shadow. I reach for her –

Cobalt's winged face leers out of the black and snatches the amber slug in her mouth. Spatters of honey

fire out of the slug, fire over me, over my shadow-
mam –

I'm trapped down here with the fire. I touch my face.

I can't see my mam's face.

I can never see her face.

★

I cough and splutter. I'm lying on my side as burning
water foams out of my mouth. Someone strokes my
face. When I open my eye, Ephyra is haloed by the red
of the growing dawn. Her pale blue hair is peacock
iridescent. 'You worried us there for a moment.'

'It's a skill I have.' I roll on to my back and look up at
all the concerned faces staring down at me. 'I'm reet.
Show's over. Come on, chop-chop!'

Large bends down and thwacks my shoulder. 'Twit.'
And, with that show of affection done, he straightens
up. 'You heard her, back to it!'

Ephyra gives my forehead a quick kiss, looks at me
long and hard, and then she's gone.

The others go back to hauling and heaving.

The ship is gently rising, the sandbar giving up its
prisoner. Thanks to the mermaids' song, it will sail out
of the bay, the crew none the wiser for their little

detour. Well, until they reach their destination and realize their cargo's missing.

I leap up and wince. My ankle knacks where the box bent it backwards. A shooting pain zooms right up my leg. Clumps of sand fall from my hair and tumble out of the creases in my trousers. Before I limp over to help the Knot Crew haul the last of the crates up the cliff, I take one last look at the spot on the clifftop where I saw the glint.

Nothing.

But a nothing could always be a something.

'Howay, lass!' shouts Large. 'These aren't gonna haul the'selves.'

One more glance, then I set off up the beach, half running, half hobbling.

Chapter Eight

I don't tell Badger about the glint when we walk back to Old Ben after the wrecking. I don't tell her when we go to breakfast the next morning, or when we're playing football, or at lunch. I tell Badger everything. But *not* telling's not a lie. So that's OK.

Each time I walk, my ankle yells the not-lie at me. Things aren't straight in my head yet. I'll tell her when they are.

★

We're all crammed in together for the weekly post-wrecking debrief, with the hammocks unstrung and the lockers pushed back against the walls. 'I call this session to order!' shouts Cap'n.

The chaos does not subside. It never does first yell.

Flea has brought in a football that's getting kicked around; it's being bounced off the circular white walls, causing scuffles to break out. The noise soars up the tower, floating in a cloud at the top and dropping back down at random intervals as echoes.

'You miserable Wrecklings!' yells Cap'n. 'I warned you!'

Normally, I'd be right in the middle with the football, but my ankle's still sore, so I lean against the wall and watch. It means I can get my hands over my ears at the same time as Cap'n squishes down the ears of the kitten in his beard and takes up the beater.

It's not magic or owt, the kitten in Cap'n's beard. It's not even the same one from when I arrived (that *would* be magic). We get a bit overrun by cats here. No one has the heart to get rid. They're 'very friendly' creatures as Rupert said with a wink. When I asked him what he meant, he said cats are very good at multiplication.

Whenever there's a runt in a litter, someone brings it to Cap'n for him to look after. He puts it in his beard until it's strong enough to fend for itself. Sometimes I think the kittens look after Cap'n more than he looks after them.

Cap'n gives the brass gong by the door an almighty *thwack* and the lights flash on and off. The air is filled with the usual 'Wey, yer beggar!' and 'Nee call for that, mind!'

It has the desired effect.

Us Wrecklings settle down, some squishing on the floor, some on the steps that run loop-de-loop, dangling their legs through the railings.

Cap'n begins to dissect the wrecking from the day before, making notes on his inventory as the Unpacking Crew yell out what they found: engine oil, assorted garden tools, a crate of stationery including three boxes of highlighter pens . . . Maura stands by his side, translating his words into sign language.

I stop listening. I've perfected the listening face though, along with the occasional nod and a non-committal *hmm*. That bit is important, the non-committal *hmm*. I once accidentally signed up for a month of potato-peeling duty by being eager at the wrong moment and then I had to pretend for an entire month that I *had* wanted to peel a ton of potatoes. Cap'n knew. He made a point of walking past every day and chuckling.

The thing is, I know the glint is a possible Boundaries issue and I should tell Cap'n what I think I saw. But that's the thing – it is only a think. And seeing Cobalt's head underwater, which I know *wasn't* there, has made me doubt what *was*.

I don't have any proof, and without proof . . . well, we call that 'doing a Willis'. He's forever trying to bring in even more rules and regulations with nothing to back them up. He's such a pain. I *really* don't want to do a Willis.

I have the perfect position by the door to the yard. Once we've OK'd our crews, I'll be free to sidle out and no one will notice I've gone. Investigation time.

If it's nothing, nowt's lost. If it's a something and I solve it? Maximum bragging rights.

And if it's my mam back to get me . . .?

Can't think about that. Makes my knees jelly.

'Shore Crew, anything to report?'

They all look at each other and at the floor. Wendy, one of the Shore Crew, stares at me. I shake my head slowly. 'No, Cap'n,' she says.

I'm just about to head for the door when Willis stands

up, looking ridiculous in his suit. The whole room groans.

'I don't want to tell tales, but –'

'Don't then!' yells Flea, who ducks for cover behind a pillar when Willis spins round to see who's spoken.

I grin.

'I feel it my place, as Health and Safety Officer, to log an incident on the beach.'

The crowd boos. Willis holds his head up high so he can look more down his pointy nose than usual, his eyes resting on me.

I stop grinning.

'Alpha Lux stepped away from her risk-assessed duties as Third Handcart Operator, and –'

'Third! I'll give you third . . .' I take two steps towards Willis, my fist raised. I would have stepped further, but there's something heavy attached to my leg. I look down and it's Badger, her arms tightly wrapped round my calf. I try to throw her off, but Badger shakes her head.

'Not worth it, not here,' she whispers.

I sigh and deflate myself.

Willis's grin grows larger and his voice warbles. 'And in doing so there was an incident on the beach that could have led to her *death* by drowning.'

'Wish it had been yours!' Flea doesn't quite have time to hide behind his pillar.

Willis huffs. 'Has that threat against me by that urchin been noted, Cap'n? Has it?'

'Yes,' answers Cap'n with a sigh.

'Well, I don't see you noting it.'

Cap'n stares until Willis drops his eyes. 'It has been noted. Flippin' fishsticks, can we move on?'

'I don't see there being a resolution to this situation as of yet!'

'Oh, for goodness' sake,' says Cap'n. Maura grins at Cap'n as she translates. 'Right. Alpha, are you OK?'

'Yes,' I say.

'Do you promise not to do whatever you did again?'

'Yes.' I nod convincingly.

'Right, problem solved. Moving on to Any Other Business.' Cap'n takes a deep breath and is just about to speak again when he's interrupted.

'Cap'n, I do not believe this has been adequately dealt with.' Willis glares hard and this time refuses to drop his eyes.

The silence Cap'n had been seeking at the beginning of the meeting descends. He untangles the kitten from his beard and places it on his shoulder where it washes its paws and then starts licking Cap'n's right ear.

Cap'n giggles. 'Sorry. Tickly. Where was I?' He sighs and then smiles at us all. When he does that, you can feel the room relax. 'Beloved Wrecklings, it's a perilous job we ask of you and, no matter how we try to manage the risks, there will always be danger. Alpha, why did you enter the water?'

'Well, to help, Cap'n. It's all about the team,' I say as I give Willis a proper stare. He doesn't have a ruddy clue what being part of a team means.

'Noble. And the incident occurred because?'

I pause for a moment.

I could tell Cap'n about the glint now. It's the perfect time to arrange a search party. In fact, the search party will probably be mine to choose and lead . . . but what if there isn't anything there? Well then, I'll look like a right –

'Because?' Cap'n asks again.

'No reason, Cap'n. It won't happen again, mind.'

'Damn right – best not. Who'd peel all our potatoes?' Cap'n winks, and the lighthouse erupts into cheers and laughter.

I hear Cap'n calling again for Any Other Business as I slowly edge my way over to the door.

Chapter Nine

I sneak out and the icy sea wind grabs me. It often hides in alcoves, waiting to ambush you and topple you over.

I take a deep breath. The air tastes particularly salty, as it always does when the waves are white horses. It's like the sea rolls up into the clouds and the saltiness is sprinkled on us.

I let the breath out just before I have to cough.

Willis, ugh.

He's perfectly designed to make you want to kick him in the head. I know that's not the way to win a battle *yada yada yada*, words are more ferocious than fists *wiffle wiffle wiff*. But really, are they? They certainly don't feel as good as connecting with his nose.

I haven't met a word yet that can cause an actual nosebleed.

'Whatcha *doooin'*?' Badger is sitting cross-legged on the wall that stops the wind uprooting Maura and Laura's roses.

'You were inside!'

'I was, now I'm not.' Badger is almost magic.

She plops off the wall and falls into step beside me, her tongue clicking as she goes, the sounds bouncing off stuff to help her find her way. She says that, back in the children's home, they made her be quiet, told her that her clicks were *attention-seeking* and that she'd *never fit in*. That was the final straw that made her run off to Haven Point and become a Wreckling. Unlike me, she wasn't one of the first, but she is the best. After me, of course.

By the time Badger arrived there were loads of us; she's never known it quiet here. I love it now, but I loved it then too. Two weeks after I was found in the soap-flakes box, Peter arrived. He's a *lot* older than me, but not as old as Cap'n. Age doesn't matter here; you're friends or you're not – and we are. Anyway, Peter was sitting on the front doorstep and nearly gave Cap'n a heart attack. Peter says that, even though he can't hear, he almost heard the swears Cap'n shouted out – they were *that* loud.

Peter won't tell me the swears.

Peter also won't tell me exactly how he got here and that's not him being mean: he says he doesn't know. But he does know that he was lonely. Peter is Deaf so he uses BSL – British Sign Language – to communicate. BSL is speaking with your face, your hands, your whole body. Outsiders made a bit of an effort to communicate with him at first, then gradually ignored him. And, because he could get by OK through lip-reading, it was easy for Peter to become invisible. Like Haven Point.

He doesn't know how he knew about us, just that one morning he woke up, packed his things and started walking. He had no idea what he would find, but somehow he was certain it would be where he belonged. Peter and I worked out the dates on our fingers once. The day he set out was the day Cap'n found me in the soap box.

After me, after Peter, others started arriving too. Badger said she ran away, as she often did, but that last time she somehow knew she wasn't ever going back. It was like a map had been drawn in her head that she had to follow and, at the end of it, there was Old Ben on the horizon and she knew she'd found home. It's like that for all us Wrecklings.

★

Badger doesn't speak, just waits, because she knows I can't keep a secret in her presence.

We walk out of the gate at the bottom of the garden and turn back to hug the thick whitewashed wall. It's the thickness of three people and smoothed with age. It provides a perfect cover from nosy glances. We both knock twice on the wall as we leave it behind.

We take the quarry route up to the white horse. I'm pretty sure the glint came from the pillbox, which is in the opposite direction, but, if the glint isn't a something but a some*one*, they could be watching us. I don't know how that makes me feel, but I do know how to be practical. If we get higher, I can watch *them*.

It's easy going over the Leas. The grass looks and smells bright and rich. When we reach the end of the Leas and begin to climb, Badger slots her arm through mine.

I know this *make-me-talk* trick well.

The tufty terrain is trickier for her, but her clicks and cane mean it's manageable. We've been up and down almost daily for the entire time we've lived here. She doesn't need any assistance whatsoever. In fact, it's harder walking two abreast and we keep sliding, then having to hold our hands out into the bright yellow dust to stop ourselves slipping back down.

The hill climbs steeply along the quarry edge and, no matter how many times you do it, your lungs don't get used to it.

Step. Slip back. Hold. Step. Slip back. Hold.

Ledges in the quarry are stacked with bright yellow goldenrod and little white flowers, bigger than daisies.

I tip my imaginary hat to the white horse we painted on the hillside. I nudge Badger. She does it too. Being blind is no excuse to be rude.

Badger doesn't let go, even when we nearly fall. She knows something's up. And she knows that closeness breeds intimacy, which breeds . . .

'I think I saw a glint on the clifftop,' I say.

She stops and unlinks her arm. 'During the wrecking?'

'Yeah, just before that box got me.'

'I knew summat was up. Even you're not foolish enough to get tangled up like that. Is it something to worry about, Alph?'

'Doubt it.'

'Not sure about that though, are you?'

'Nope.'

She links her arm back into mine. Not because she needs me, just because we're best friends. But it weirds me out because I'm not telling her everything and I don't know why.

★

We stand together on the edge of the quarry, where grass gives way to sunset-coloured mud and dust. Perfect for sliding down on Maura's second-best tea tray.

You can see to the edge of our world from here.

'Is there time to fly?' asks Badger.

'Aye,' I say. 'A quick one can't do any harm.'

I take hold of her left hand in my right, then we step away from each other, facing out towards the sea. We raise our other arms so our baggy jumpers make us look like flying squirrels and cross our fingers and think of knots.

She has no fear. Is that because her eyes can't tell her how far the drop is?

I close my good eye, but I can still see the image of the trees below burned on my retina, the size of the ones in Flea's plastic farmyard.

'On three,' Badger says.

We yell out the numbers together. 'One. Two. THREE!'

We take a deep breath and lean all our weight forward. I know suddenly that we've timed it wrong, balance off, past the point of no return –

I open my eye, and then *WHOOSH*, the updraught hits. Our tiptoes remain on grass tufts and the air holds up our bodies.

Badger cries out in relief and glee, and I cry out too.

A seagull caws and we join in, our hair streaming upwards, our baggy jumpers taut, two gliding squirrels completely free.

I feel the wind begin to drop and so does Badger.

We let go of each other's hands and chuck ourselves backwards, landing *whump* on our backs in the grass, feet dangling over the precipice.

'That's got to be the last time, Badge. I didn't think that was going to hold us.'

'You're such a wuss. Anyway, you knocked on the wall, didn't you?'

'Yes.'

'Well then, we were bound to be OK.'

I don't answer. Badger curls into me. 'Tell me what's

in the clouds,' she says quietly, and I begin to make up stories from the sky.

★

I wake because I'm damp and the breeze is making me shiver. Dusk is dancing along the edges of the sea, painting the grass tufts a shimmering silver. I twirl my ankle. It's stiff, but not sore any more. Each time I wiggle it, I think about how the sea didn't want to let go of me. I shudder. First time I've been scared of it.

I stretch gently so as not to disturb Badger and sit up.

It's there! A quick flash and then it's gone.

I nudge Badger awake.

She leaps up, immediately adventure-ready. As she's standing above me, she does this brief flicker, like something just slapped her. When she speaks, her tone of voice is totally different. 'Howay, Cap'n will be proper radge if we don't get back in time for tea.'

I'm baffled and about to tell her so when she grabs my hand and hauls me up from the grass. As she does, I realize she's telling me something. Peter is Deaf and uses BSL. Badger can't see. This is the way they communicate with each other: signs and squiggles by touch, finding a common language. Obviously we all nicked it cos it's great to be able to share secrets when no one else has a clue what you're saying. She fingerspells on to my palm, unleashing a torrent of words.

I pretend like I'm struggling to stand so she's got time to spell out everything she doesn't want to say aloud.

I manage not to glance over my shoulder at the bush behind as I stand up and brush myself down. 'Who made *you* boss?' I say, falsely telling Badger off.

She fake-thumps me, but although we're just pretending it's still really hard. So I thump her back.

We make small talk about Flea's football team all the way back to Old Ben.

My ears aren't as good as Badger's. No one has ears as good as hers, but even I can hear the snotty breath every now and then as Willis stalks us back home.

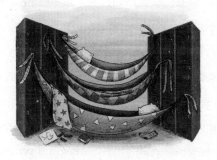

Chapter Ten

It's dark now so I can't go and find Ephyra. That's one of our Haven Point rules: we do not go out after dark, especially not alone. This rule is nothing to do with protecting the mermaids or us from scary Outsiders, but everything to do with having barely any outdoor lighting and a cliff to fall off, sea to drown us, machinery to trip over and teetering ramshackle buildings about to thunder down on our heads.

We duck down by one of the outhouses, and Willis stalks past and goes into the cottage at the end of the terrace where Kelvin lives. Probably about to grill him on some law to get me imprisoned forever.

'Do you really think it's a nothing?' asks Badger. I

don't want to lie, but I can't tell her the mam thing, not yet. 'Do you?' she repeats.

'Nope,' I say. 'I don't think it's a nothing.'

'Where do you think you saw it?'

'At the pillbox.'

'The *completely-banned-from-going-there, Cap'n-would-string-us-up-if-we-ever-went-there-again* pillbox?'

'Yup, that's the one.'

Badger doesn't even pause. 'Right, make a plan, one of your good ones, not a rubbishy one, then we'll sort it. Won't we? Hinvestigators R Us! And, if we're going to do that, we might as well make it a double whammy and go in the dark,' she says, grinning.

'What about Willis?'

'Are you gonna be beaten by Snot-nose? You'll work it out. It's choir tonight to practise for the wedding so I can't come. And don't you dare even *think* about going without me.'

We shake on it, with spit to make it official, then wander over to Old Ben in a casual *we're-not-even-thinking-about-breaking-the-rules* sort of manner. We're just entering the hall when a hand grabs my wrist. 'Gotcha!'

'Sorry, Alpha!' yells Badger before she runs away, giggling.

'Bath time,' says Norma as I groan, and she marches me along the corridor.

★

'It's completely pointless,' I tell Norma for the ninety-seventh time. 'I'll only get mucky again.'

'And, as I've said, *tough.*' Norma stands on a stool by the bath and pours a jug of water over my head. That shuts me up. Norma is married to Malcolm, and together they are the engineers whose greatest triumph is making the foghorn automatic. They both have dwarfism. That's why you find handles at my thigh height and hooks in the middle of doors.

'How's your ankle?'

I honk some water out of my nose and push my hair away from my eye. 'Fine.' I don't tell her that actually the hot water is really helping.

'What made you fall?'

'Nothing,' I say, and go bright red. *Why is everyone suddenly interested in the thing I don't want to tell them?* She stares at me, cocks her head to one side. I can't lie, so I slide back and dunk my head under the water.

When I pop back up, she's still looking at me. Not worried as such, but it's definitely more intense than usual. I get into scrapes all the time; her and Maura are constantly bandaging me. 'Sure it's nothing?'

I don't answer. Not speaking is not lying.

'You can talk to me, Alpha. You know that, don't you? I'm always here for you. We may not always agree . . .'

'Mainly on baths,' I say.

She looks a bit sad, and then says, 'Yes, mainly on baths, but everything I do is for your own good.'

I don't like her looking sad so I flick water at her. She flicks back, and soon there's more water outside the bath than in.

★

By the time I get back to the base of Old Ben, the table is stacked high with a towering battalion of unmatching crockery and three bowls full of forks, knives and spoons.

Large is guarding it, making sure that everyone lines up in a reasonable sort of queue, and that those who need a bit of help get it.

I always wonder how Badger's ears can cope with mealtimes. I don't really understand decibels, probably because neither does Cap'n and he was the one who tried to teach us about them, but the sound in here at mealtimes is definitely Nuclear Decibel Setting.

The toddlers all sit with Maura. You need to avoid that table because it's just a bit, well, messy. Some of the adults don't come to meals as they've got their own kitchens in the cottages, or they're working or resting, but everyone else is here.

I get to the front of the queue and grab two bowls and two spoons for me and Badger. She's already got bread and forks and has gone to bagsy a spot by one of the stoves round the edge of the room.

I think about earlier. I can't believe Willis followed us! I didn't know he had it in him. I shouldn't have fought back so much at the meeting. He already hates me, but now he's going to be watching me all the time to try to spot stuff he can use to grass me up.

The soup smells rich and meaty and, as our bowls get filled, I realize how hungry I am. I push my way back through the queue and spot Badger in the far corner. I say corner, even though there isn't one in the tower base. It's odd how we use some words even when they're not accurate.

We try our best to make words right here. They're important: they show you care and you understand.

Take, for example, walking across this room towards her. I'm walking it, while some other people here wheel, or crawl. So, if I was talking about all us Wrecklings, I'd just say *moving* instead. Cap'n says words are mighty. That they're sometimes used by powerful people to make other people appear weaker, even when they're the ones with lion hearts.

Cap'n can be a pain about many things, but I think he's right about that.

Badger has found a spot next to Jericho. She's also nuked the toast by the time I reach her. She tells when it's ready by smell, but, by the time she can smell it, it's burnt. I wish I'd remembered knives to scrape the black bits off, though to be honest there wouldn't be anything left if I had.

'Sorry, Alpha,' she says. 'I think I might have incinerated it.'

I sigh and hand her the bowl. She sticks her thumb over the edge to work out how far up and how hot the soup is.

'How long do you think he was there?' she says.

'Who was where?' asks Jericho.

'Nobody,' I reply at exactly the same time that Badger says, 'Willis.'

— 80 —

I glare at Badger. She can't see, but she can bloomin' well feel it.

'What did he catch you doing this time?'

'Nothing,' I say as Badger says, 'Looking for the glint.'

Before I can even glare at her this time, she rams a massive amount of soup in her gob, mumbles, 'Choir practice,' and runs off.

Jericho watches her until she's disappeared out of the door. 'What glint?'

I'm so fed up of Badger not knowing when to shut up that I don't reply.

'Like that, is it, eh? You're up to something, Alph,' says Jericho. He stares at me.

My eye doesn't blink. His do.

'I *like it* when you're up to something,' he says. 'You're not going to tell me what it is though, are you?'

I shake my head, but a little grin is tickling at the corner of my mouth. 'Not yet.'

Jericho lets out a massive 'Ugh!' and I turn to see what set him off. Willis has just pushed in the queue. Everyone groans and mutters, but they let him get away with it. It's easier than having him on your case.

'He *actually* does my head in,' says Jericho.

My soup has something crunchy in it that doesn't bear thinking about. I spit it on to the stove and it crackles in the flames. Jericho spits into the stove too, just because.

My mind whirs, like bits of thoughts I didn't know I'd been having are suddenly whisked up together.

I have a plan.

It's an exceptional plan. One of my best. One that serves the delicious dual purpose of finally exposing Willis as the complete and utter twerp that he is, *and* lets me and Badger sneak off to investigate the glint. Two for one.

'Jay, my man,' I say. 'Fancy getting one up on Willis?'

I already know the answer to that question. Just like me, it's what Jericho lives for. He smiles and nods. We huddle over the stove and I tell him my idea.

Chapter Eleven

The whole place is rocking. Everything is dark with red round the edges.

I can't breathe.

The heat. In my lungs, skin crackling, smell of hair burning. Her face in the shadows. The flash of gold.

And I'm rocking.

'Alpha. *Alpha!* Wake up, please, you're scaring me.'

I recognize the voice and hold on to it as a rope to guide me from sleep to wake.

There are two feet wedged in the small of my back. I buck in my hammock as she shoves me up and then drops me down again.

'It's OK, Badger. I'm awake now.'

It's the glint, the plan, the watching feeling, the wondering about my mam, the *hope* all muddled up together into night terrors.

'That was a bad one, Alph. Haven't heard you like that for ages,' says Badger.

I sigh. Hopefully, not many of the others did either. That's one problem about dorm living – *zero* privacy.

★

I'm on lift-pulley duty with Large. Cap'n has his quarters at the top of the tower, and his classroom, where we have our lessons, is on the platform halfway up.

One of the first questions newbies ask when they arrive is why Cap'n doesn't bring everything to ground level to make it easier. Then we all groan as Cap'n launches into his favourite 'Ease Does Not Inspire Innovation' speech for the nine hundred and fifty-four billionth time.

Jericho is the last one to roll himself on to the lift. Large locks the arm into place and I wind.

'Cheers,' says Jericho as he disappears up into the tower.

The handle I use is attached to a small cog, attached to a bigger cog, and then a bigger one still, so that this section of the wall looks like the inside of a grandfather clock. The bell dings and the light bulb flashes when Jericho reaches the top and Large and I lock the pulley in place. Simple.

'Race you!' Large yells and is already off, leaping on to the first of seventy-six steps.

'Oi, cheat!' I run after him.

Halfway up, both of us slow down and cling on. Large waits for me to catch up. I may accidentally sick up a lung. We peer out of the window and take in the green of the Leas. It's scattered with wild poppies. Beside the window are wall cabinets full of tiny handmade ships in bottles. Cap'n says they're replicas of every ship he's ever sailed in. My favourite is *Seahawk*. It has three masts and a crow's nest for a lookout. Cap'n makes them himself, down to the tiniest detail.

I love watching him build them. I sit in his study and eat his biscuits as he paints and glues. He wears these binocular things on a band round his head that he pulls down over his eyes. He goes all concentrate-y and hums.

Just me curled up, cats purring, and him making and humming.

★

'You look ill,' says Large.

I smile weakly back at him. I haven't got breath for words yet.

'I'll carry you.'

With that, he grabs me round my calves and chucks me over his shoulder like I'm the bag of spuds by the kitchen door.

We're the last ones to arrive, but it seems we're sooner than Cap'n was expecting, because he's not in the room and it's mayhem.

I plop into the seat next to Badger. 'Ready for tonight?' she asks. The three of us worked through the plan when Badger got back from choir practice. She brought Belgian buns to say sorry for her big gob. She didn't need to, but I still ate my bun.

'Yup,' I reply. 'Is Cap'n in the cupboard?'

'Nope. Flea checked.'

'Not like him to be late. Bonus.' I promptly make a spitball and blow it across the room so it donks off the back of Willis's neck.

He growls and flings himself round from the suck-up seat right at the front. I suddenly need to fasten my shoe.

'Did you just do what I think you did?' asks Badger.

I'm about to reply when Cap'n comes in. 'Please, everyone, say hello to Peter. He'll be translating today.'

We all sign hello to Peter.

You can spell out names, but then you can also have your own sign name that's based on an essential part of you. Like your hobby or a play on your name. The thing about your sign name is that you don't get to choose it yourself, or everyone would be Captain Awesome. It's bestowed upon you and can be an honour, or a curse. Willis will tell you about that: his is the sign for 'snot'. I'm Soapy, due to where I was found. Badger is Badger, because sometimes it's just that easy.

We make the sign for 'fishing' for Peter because he's the best Wreckling by far for providing us with tea that once swam.

Then lessons begin. According to Maura, they're not *standard curriculum-based*, but that's because we learn the stuff we need to thrive here. Also, Cap'n gets bored and goes off on tangents.

Today is geography. We pull out globes that have bumpy ridges to show the high bits.

Flea's group are working on their volcano. It's a project we've all done before and we laugh at the young ones for having to do it, but it's amazing how many people grumble about being asked to help them, and then completely take over and won't back off. Large is helping them today. He never takes over.

Badger, Jericho and I are working on a mapping project of the sea caves below Old Ben. Badger passes Jericho a compass, pencil, rubber and ruler, and he begins to draw Cave Four. Imaginative name, I know.

'How you getting on there, troops?' Cap'n pulls up a seat and pops the kitten from his beard on to Badger's lap. She picks it up and rubs it against her cheek.

'It's slow-going,' I say. We've been working on this for weeks.

'The important things usually are,' says Cap'n.

I can't be bothered with Cap'n's wisdom today. 'Why were you late?' I ask.

He ignores me. 'How's your ankle?'

'Fine,' I say because I haven't thought about it once. But, now he's said something, I realize it's just not quite right. *I'm* not quite right. *This is all not quite right.* 'Or it was until you reminded me about it.'

'So, it's not the ankle then . . .'

Badger and Jericho will not look at me, or say anything. Heads down, they work hard at working hard and leave me to deflect the grilling. Friends, who needs 'em?

'Are we going to play a guessing game?' asks Cap'n. 'Or are you just going to tell me?'

My fingers become really interesting. I pick a scab on the back of my right hand.

'I'm sure your friends would be happier if you simply came out with it, then I'd go away and they'd be able to stop pretending to work. Jericho, you've nearly made a hole in that map.'

Jericho puts down his rubber and goes bright red. Badger concentrates on a lumpy bit of desk.

I can't have Cap'n thinking it's something to do with me tripping in the sea, and I'm worried if I don't say anything he'll suss it eventually or drag it out of me. I don't want to have to outright lie to him.

But if something's going on in Haven Point – the something that Ephyra wouldn't tell me about – then *he's* the one lying to me. If he's not going to do sharesies, then there goes his shot at finding anything out from me.

Cap'n is too clever to baffle. The only way to not have to tell him about the glint, and who I think it might be, is to give him something else to get his teeth stuck into.

'I had a nightmare last night,' I mumble. It's the truth, so I tell it well.

I carry on picking my hand until Cap'n gently places his on top of mine. 'Stop,' he says. 'You'll make it bleed.'

I stop, but now I don't know what to do with my hands. I'm worried they'll give me away so I sit on them instead.

'Was it the old dream?'

I nod. He's being too nice. He sits there and he has this presence that's warm and safe and it makes me want to cry. I can feel my eye begin to fill and my bottom lip does that stupid twitch thing that says it's about to lose it.

I feel guilty too for thinking the glint could be anything to do with my mam, when she abandoned me, and Cap'n and Ephyra gave me the only home I've ever known.

Cap'n's quiet manner pulls words from you, ones that you really don't want to give up. So I surrender ones I have no wish to say out loud, not in front of Jericho – but at least they're not about the plan.

'I still can't see her face.'

'That's natural,' says Cap'n. 'You know that. When something horrific happens, your brain sometimes wipes out the bits that hurt to protect itself. Sometimes that wiping out takes other bits with it too. Maybe her face will come back one day, when you're ready.'

He squishes my shoulder. His fingers are gnarly but strong, and I can still feel the heat from them after he's removed his hand.

Cap'n stands up and retrieves his kitten that's trying to tunnel under Badger's arm. 'I suggest you keep on going, gang. Did you know that whoever finishes drawing the map gets the honour of choosing the place name? I'm sure you can come up with something more exciting than Cave Four.'

He walks over to Peter and signs something to him, but he's got his back to me and I can't see what, then he leaves.

Badger waits until she can hear he's gone and then flings her head up. 'Whoa, Alpha, you're good!'

Jericho nods. I can feel what's in his look. He doesn't have a mam neither. But at least he knows what happened to his. Doesn't make it better, but it does kind of make it closed.

'You need to bow in the presence of my awesome-ness,' I say.

Jericho and Badger both do so, twirling their arms and doffing imaginary hats.

'What are we gonna call it?' asks Jericho.

'Call what?' I reply.

'The cave, silly. Weren't you even listening?' says Badger.

'Nah,' says Jericho. 'She was too busy basking in her own glory.'

They both bow and giggle again, then start to bicker about the new name for Cave Four. I try to join in, but my heart's not in it.

Chapter Twelve

Lunch is a mountain of sandwiches piled on a table in the hall between the kitchen and the back door. Bread-buttering duty has the same punishment status as potato peeling.

I take a pile of cheese-and-pickle butties and go outside. I pull my hood up to avoid wind-tunnel ear and ram a butty in my mouth. The bread is squishy, with floury crusts that will give me a lunch moustache.

Everyone who's sensible is hiding inside and snuggling down with Maura and story time. Maura tells epics. There's one about a pirate that Badger loves.

I sit by the whitewashed wall and look out to sea. The waves are being whipped up, and foam swooshes and lands in piles on the beach. It looks like someone put too much bubble bath in.

My head is as whirry as the waves. The glint on the cliff, Willis, and the missing face of my mam.

The butties are good for my tummy, but not particularly good for defogging my mind.

After I've finished eating, the wind drops just enough. It's perfect weather for surfing, which is excellent as it means I can get the gang all set up and zooming around, then they won't notice me sneaking off to see Ephyra again.

She'll help me sort out my head.

★

We lay sections of woven seaweed on the dry sand so that Jericho's rig can roll its way to the hard, wet sand.

'You look cool as,' says Flea, buttering up Jericho. 'Can I go first?'

'Don't make it too obvious that you're flattering me for personal benefit,' says Jericho as he finishes fastening his helmet.

Flea takes a while to work out what Jericho means, then his face falls.

'Nah, man! You are *well* cool. Like the coolest . . .'

Flea's voice peters out as Jericho laughs and hands Flea his helmet.

Badger bunks Flea up into the rig next to Jericho. Flea's so excited he's not just doing his usual bouncing, but also singing a nonsensical stream of joy.

'You'd better not do that as we're hurtling along, or I may accidentally chuck you overboard,' says Jericho, smiling at Flea.

I clip Flea in and make sure his helmet is securely fastened, then tap on top, just hard enough to get an 'Oi!' out of him.

'That pays you back for the toothpaste,' I say, and I thwack him once more.

Flea bounces as much as his harness will allow and lets out a massive *WHOOP*. Jericho releases the brake and powers the hand bike until the wheels of the rig bite into the damp sand and he starts to roll.

The ropes between the rig and the parachute tighten as the slack is taken up, then . . . *whumpf!* The wind snatches the silk from the sand and it soars. Flea and Jericho hurtle down the beach and we all fill the air with yells and whoops.

The beach fills with post-lunch Wrecklings, and Jericho and Flea career through them all.

It is mayhem. Joyous, shrieking mayhem. Which

makes it the perfect time to slip away to Ephyra. The mermaids have their own routines, just like we do, so I know exactly where to find her.

★

I climb up the rocky spikes of Camel's Island, which was once attached to the shore but became detached in the last big storm when the cliff crumbled. It's the quickest way to reach the salt beds, but I'm careful not to slip cos the raggedy edges love eating skin. I try to work out what I'm going to say to Ephyra. How do I tell her I think my mam's come back for me? It sounds silly in my own head, never mind trying to say it out loud. I know I have to tell her because we need to check the Boundaries, especially with whatever's up with the mermaids *and* Cap'n that neither of them are bloomin' talking about.

I reach the top of Camel's Island. It's flat and pitted with holes where the sea has burrowed. There are rock pools with spiky plants and fronds that flow as the wind ripples the surface.

It'll be like bartering. I'll tell Ephyra what I think's going on, dead plain and unemotional. Then she'll tell me what she thinks is going on and then we'll sort it together, like we always do.

I look up, but there's no glint today.

I hug the dry sand by the cliffs to make my way over to the salt beds, avoiding the inlets. Everything is covered in old seaweed and bird poo. I try to snort the acid smell out of my nose.

Walking on the dry sand means each step is only a half because you sink backwards, even though you're going forward. It's hard going, but I know better than to walk on the wet and disturb the clams.

Geography lessons with Cap'n tell us that the cliffs here are made of magnesian limestone, few examples of which exist in the whole world, which makes Haven Point as unique as those of us who live here.

I walk past one of the Stacks, a skinny tower that was once a cliff, a warning about the power of the sea.

I wonder how many years it will be before Old Ben teeters on the edge of the cliff, and who will be living there when it does.

What will happen to future Wrecklings as the tide claims victory over the land? I can't imagine us ever not being here. Lighthouses are beacons of hope for ships in trouble. Old Ben is a beacon of hope for us.

★

Ephyra spots me before I spot her. She whistles and waves from the salt beds and I make my way over to her, slipping on some of the flat stones that are covered in a thin layer of green moss. It jars my ankle.

She's kneeling at the edge of the nearest bed and has a finely woven hessian sack laid out beside her, a small garden rake in one hand and a trowel in the other. Her land legs do the slight shimmer that always makes me pause, just for a second. It's easy to forget that Ephyra doesn't belong on land.

'I thought you'd be playing on the beach with the others,' she says. 'I could hear Flea from here. You shouldn't be coming over here by yourself. *Safety in numbers.*'

I say nothing and kneel down next to her. Not quite the excited welcome I was expecting, and why shouldn't I be alone now? Not like it's night-time.

'It's lovely to have your company, of course, especially if I can put you to work hunting razor clams. Much faster with two of us.' She hands me the fork. 'How's your ankle?'

I shrug. She rolls her eyes.

We work in silence. I rake the salt into fine grooves,

criss-crossing it in sections until it flakes and crumbles into tinier pieces, which she then gathers in her trowel and tips into her bag.

The salt beds we've made here aren't massive like those I've seen pictures of in the books Cap'n keeps in his study. They're just enough for what we need, which is pretty much our way full stop.

The beds are set far enough back that the tide can't reach them. They're built of the bits of edges that Camel's Island gave up and we slotted them into place like drystone walls. We pour buckets of seawater into them and then the sun does the rest, evaporating the water and leaving behind layers of grey opalescent salt crystals.

I watch Ephyra out of the corner of my eye as we work; she's muttering away to herself. She's not beautiful. It's too one-dimensional a word and doesn't take into account her cleverness, her determination, her teeth filed to points so she can tear fish and seals to shreds. Mermaids definitely don't just lie on rocks all day, plaiting their hair. I chuckle to myself at the thought of Ephyra doing that.

'That's enough now,' she says. I don't know if she

means my giggle or the work, so I stop raking and help her carry the bag of salt to the water's edge. We hold a handle each and it sways as we walk. In our other hand, we each carry a bucket.

The silence between us is usually easy, but this time it feels like it needs words wringing out of it. Now I'm here, I don't want to give mine up.

At the edge of the sea, the air is sharp and makes my eye water. Ephyra sees me wipe it and gives me a funny look. She knows I'm not telling her something and I don't know why I'm not, after I really wanted to. Everything is confusing.

She puts her arms round me and we stand, looking out to sea together. Her shoulder is the perfect height to rest my head on, so I do.

'Where's everyone else?' I ask.

'Henrietta is holding court. She asked the Western Fins to come to a summit. It was a good idea of yours.'

I only know summits on mountains or when summat's wrong. I'm not sure what Ephyra means, but, as it was apparently my idea, I feel like I should. I wait for her to tell me more, but she doesn't.

She has a lot on her mind too.

I twiddle with her hair. Beneath this murky sky, it

looks less peacock and more seaweed. I can see a starfish caught up in the knotty curls and bits of old net cling on like barnacles. It has an ecosystem of its own.

She kisses my forehead and pats my shoulder absent-mindedly. Then she shoves me away and giggles.

'Careful,' I say as my foot nearly goes in the water.

'Careful,' she mocks back.

We both fill our buckets with seawater and take a handful of salt from the bag, bend forward and scan the damp sand.

We're treading carefully so our tremors don't give us away. We're looking for circular dips in the sand, about the size of a Connect Four counter.

Ephyra sees one first and crouches by the dip. I walk past her and spot one of my own.

When I first went hunting, I waited to see whether the holes spouted as I couldn't properly tell the difference between a standard bit of lumpy sand and a burrow dip. Now I just *know* and don't need to wait. That's practice, I guess.

I gently kneel next to it, trying not to disturb the razor clam living inside. I don't want to scare it and make it burrow away. We need it for our not-forgetting soup.

I use my thumb and forefinger to trickle a big pinch of salt on top of the dip, then I lean back on my feet and wait. Always remember to lean back.

I count Mississippis and on the sixth an arc of water fires out and the dip becomes a hole.

First time I did this, no one told me about the leaning-back bit and it squirted right in my eye – my bloomin' good one.

I yelled at Ephyra, but she just laughed and said it was a rite of passage. I've taught many Wrecklings to gather razor clams since and I've let every one of them have their own rite of passage too.

I quickly pour more salt into the hole before it can fill back up with wet sand and water and I lean back again. Sometimes it spouts a second time. No one told me about that either.

No second arc of water, just the magic as the razor clam begins to rise out of the sand. It's narrow and brown, like the handle of a big tortoiseshell spoon. I grab it before it knows it's been fooled. Not too hard or you'll crush the shell. And don't pull straight away – that can smash it too. You need to sort of test its weight until you can feel that it's lost its grip and given up, then you slide it out. The shell comes all the way first and then, once you've released that from the sand, the freaky white squidge follows. When it hits the air, it darts back inside the shell. Pop it in the saltwater bucket and that's your first razor clam caught.

'Why does salt make them pop up?' I ask Ephyra. I realize I've always just done it without ever knowing.

'No one really knows,' she replies. 'It could be that we confuse them and they think the tide has washed over them and it's time to come out of their burrows and look for food.'

I pour more salt in a spouted open hole. 'Or maybe they just really hate salt,' I say.

'Could be.'

I gently grab a clam as it rises out of the sand. 'Ephyra?'

'Yes, my sweet.' Only Ephyra can get away with calling me something tacky like that. I'd thump anyone else.

'What's a summit?'

She settles down on the sand. I drag my bucket next to hers and sit next to her. She wiggles so she's sitting behind me and I lean back into her outstretched legs. She begins to comb through my hair with her fingers.

I don't want to break the spell so I try not to yell when she reaches a ratty bit.

'We haven't had one for years, and I was hoping it wouldn't be necessary, that it was all just gossip. But something is brewing.'

Ephyra hasn't answered my question, but I let her off because this sounds properly interesting. I rake through the sand at my fingertips, turning it into mini cities while I wait for her to gather her thoughts and speak again.

'Henrietta keeps in touch with the Southern Clan into which she was born. From anyone else, it would just be gossip, like the stories that sometimes filter in from the Atlantic tides, but if *they* say something – well, they're so serious, there has to be truth in it.'

I wait for Ephyra to speak again. She's gone far away and I'm scared if I say something she'll hush up for good.

'There had been rumours for a while about a renegade commander who was seeking out mermaids. But there are always rumours about *something* hunting us down. That's been the case since we were born, just after the waves were.'

It's no good. I have to ask. 'What's one of those, a rentagrade whatsit?'

She explains with a smile: 'Renegade commander. *Commander* – high up and in charge of people. *Renegade* – gone rogue. Got it?'

I wiggle round to face Ephyra. 'Basically, a leader who's a baddie?' I ask. Ephyra nods. 'And after you?' She nods again. 'And no one's trying to stop him?'

'Exactly.'

We sit in silence. It's like the renegade commander has sucked the words out of us. After a long while, Ephyra speaks again.

'The Central Fins went quiet. Vanished. Henrietta and Verdigris swam over last week. Their lair was smashed up and empty. Whatever happened, it happened fast. That's why she's invited the Western Fins for a summit.' She pauses and then explains. 'That's a meeting, to see whether we can decide what to do.'

'Do you think they're coming for the Northern Clan next?'

Ephyra sees the look on my face and holds me tight. 'I don't ever lie to you. We don't lie to each other, do we?'

I can just about nod, then I shake my head; I don't know which one's the answer. I'm too upset. This is not how the conversation was meant to go.

Ephyra releases me and smiles. 'It's all just guesswork at the moment anyway. We don't know anything for definite.'

'Does Cap'n know?'

'No. Not yet. And neither should you. So keep it schtum, young mackerel.' She prods me in the sides.

Cap'n was odd at lessons this morning. I bet he thinks something's up too. Why don't grown-ups talk to each other?

'When will you tell him?' I ask.

'When there's something to tell. Once we've spoken to the Western Fins, we'll know more and we'll go from there. No need to alarm Cap'n unnecessarily before we find out what we're dealing with.'

She gives me another hug and then squishes me from side to side. 'Now tell me your thing. You've definitely got a thing.'

'Nah,' I say. She's right. You shouldn't alarm someone unnecessarily. Not when they'd worry about you and definitely ban you from carrying out a plan that involves sneaking away at night.

'Just Willis stuff,' I say. Which isn't a lie.

'Is he giving you more hassle?'

'Nothing I can't handle.'

'You'd tell me if there was something big, wouldn't you, Alpha?'

'Of course,' I say, and cross my fingers behind my back. 'Why are you not at the summit?' I ask to change the subject.

'Because I thought you might come here this afternoon. And you're more important.'

I pass her a bucket. I take the other and we move off to find more razor-clam dips.

I yell out to her before I kneel down. 'Last one to catch thirty is a dirty old pirate!'

Chapter Thirteen

By the time I make my way back to Old Ben, I've talked myself out of going through with the plan for Willis's downfall and Operation Investigate, and then talked myself back into it. Dusk is beginning to tickle the cliff edges in pinks and oranges. I wish I'd worn a scarf. Summer hasn't arrived to even begin to think about warming up the evenings.

The beach is empty. Jericho's rig has been locked away and the seaweed walkways are stacked back in the hut at the base of the lift.

As I walk towards it, I see Norma on the clifftop. I sigh. It'll scupper my plan if she's waiting to haul me off for another soapy dunk. At least if she does the decision will be out of my hands. But she turns and walks away. Must have had a row with Malcolm – they've been having lots of those recently.

That's decided then. We're on.

I press the button and wait for the lift to clunk down towards me. Marsden Rock glows in the disappearing light. It's almost as if it's breathing.

The seagulls are rioting as they keep swooping in to land and bagsy a roosting spot for the night. Airborne fights break out and I duck when one nearly crashes into me. The lift arrives just in time. Those seagulls are huge and angry. They could eat fingers like chips. Well, they *look* like they could.

When I reach the top, Jericho and Badger are lurking there.

'Where've you been, Alph?' says Badger. 'You were on the beach with us, then you weren't. I thought you'd gone investigating without me.'

'Never,' I say, and punch her a bit. Lightly, mind.

I don't tell them what Ephyra said about the Central Fins and the summit. Badger is rubbish at secrets, but it's not that. The secret belongs to me and Ephyra together. It's ours.

From out of the shadow behind Jericho steps Large. I look at Jericho. He shrugs and points at Badger.

'Badge . . .' I say.

'Ah,' replies Badger. 'You've spotted him then.'

'Someone is pretty rubbish at keeping their mouth shut,' says Jericho.

I shake my head and realize Badger can't see that.

'You're shaking your head, aren't you?' she says.

'How do you do that?' I say. 'And stop trying to change the subject.'

She scurries off to hide behind Jericho, who does a wheelie, then rocks on his back wheels.

'Where's Willis?' I ask.

'Base of Old Ben,' says Jericho. 'He's been rampaging all afternoon, looking for you. At one point, he went purple and I thought his skull was going to crack open.'

'Excellent,' I say. Then I turn to Large. 'How much do you know?'

He grins. 'Everything.'

★

Time to put stage one of my glint-investigation plan into action.

If Badger and I want to investigate without Snot-nose following us, or grassing on us, or generally just Willis-ing, we need him out of the way.

When we arrive at the base of Old Ben, Willis has Flea and his mates in a row facing him and is giving them a lecture about cleanliness. He's not getting far. They keep picking their noses and wiping their fingers on their trousers to wind him up. He looks ready to blow.

Perfect.

Willis spots us coming and ups his volume now that he has a bigger audience. He really makes me want to vom all over him – he's so stuck up his own bum.

I give Jericho a sneaky thumbs up, and him and Large go over to Willis. Badger and I hang back by the door.

'Willis?' says Jericho.

'What? Can't you see that I'm in the middle of something important?'

I notice Jericho take a quick breath. Getting angry won't help. 'I know. I'm sorry, it's just we don't know what to do.'

Willis pauses.

I can see Jericho's lip curl a little. Even though it's part of my plan, I know how hard the next bit is for him. He takes a deep breath and it comes out rushed and squeaky. 'We need your help.'

Willis grows by about five centimetres and puffs his

chest out. He turns his back on Flea's group and they take the opportunity to run for it. They dash past me and Badger, then through the door and off down the corridor. Badger smiles.

'And . . .?' says Willis expectantly.

'It's the foghorn pump,' says Jericho.

'What about it?'

'It may have had a teeny accident.'

'You what? What have you done?' Willis goes storming off to the engine room with Jericho and Large following right behind.

'This is far too easy,' Badger says quietly. We both go after them at a sauntering kind of pace.

★

Once they're in the engine room, we hang back at the door and peer round. It's hot and stinky. My mouth immediately tastes like it's been oiled.

Willis stands by the air pump as Jericho explains about the imaginary fight that him and Large had and how this imaginary fight means that the air pump got damaged and there's *no way* Cap'n can know about it. If only Willis can help, they'll owe him one.

Big time.

Willis is a fish on our hook and we're reeling him in rapidly. It's dead easy when you know which of his buttons to press.

He studies the pump and then starts wiggling different bits. Each time he touches something, Large says, 'Tried that already.'

By the fourth time Large says it, I've got my hands over Badger's mouth to stop her laughing. By the sixth time, she's slammed her hands over mine too.

'Basically,' says Jericho, 'we've properly broken it, haven't we?'

He looks like he may burst into tears, which Willis laps up.

And that's kind of true, except *we* know what's broken it: the missing valve sitting happily in my pocket.

'Yes,' Willis says with absolute glee. 'Yes, you have.'

I can imagine his little brain whirring about how he'll get to tell Cap'n how naughty Large and Jericho have been. What a hero he'll be for fixing it, and how he should be allowed to decide their punishment.

Willis kneels down and begins to wiggle parts of the pump again. The problem is, Willis thinks he knows everything, but actually knows very little, as is the case with most shouty people. We could be here all night.

I cough a bit and Jericho looks up at me. Willis is too intent on jiggling bits of pipe to notice. I mouth the word *kit* at Jericho.

'If only there was a kit we could use to fix it,' says Jericho.

I slam my hand on my forehead. Could Jericho be any more obvious?

'Ha!' says Willis, and completely skirts over the fact that he's just bashed his head on the underside of a pipe. The clang reverberates round the room and somehow both Jericho and Large manage to ignore it, though it does look like Large's shoulders are beginning to shake.

'You probably don't know this,' says a now upright Willis, 'but Cap'n keeps a spare set of parts in the tunnel that leads to the foghorn.'

He turns round and wags a finger at Jericho and Large, right up in their faces. 'Just in case something *ludicrous* like this takes place.'

Jericho and Large hang their heads in mock shame. Large's shoulders are definitely starting to go and he makes a sort of choked-down snort-cough.

'You also wouldn't know that I am one of only two keyholders. Cap'n was not enthusiastic about handing over a copy, but for health and safety purposes there must *always* be a second keyholder.'

Willis begins to sort through the keys that hang on a loop on his belt. He mutters under his breath. 'Just wait, just wait till I tell him I was right . . .'

I tap Badger on the shoulder. It's almost time for stage two where Badger and I get to sneak off and investigate. We'll find one of the following:

a) nothing
b) clues
c) my mam.

I can't work out which one I hope for more. That's a lie. I do know. It makes my heart race and I need to be calm.

Willis locates the correct key and unclips it. He goes to unlock the wooden door and Large steps up beside him. He taps Willis on the shoulder. Willis stares at him. Large holds out his hand and bows his head. There's a pause. A long pause. Then Mr Smug-face Willis hands over the key and allows Large to open the door.

It's thick and old. Heavy with iron fittings and whorls in the wood. It groans as Large pulls it back to reveal the tunnel beyond. A smell of off-green leaks out. Light from the engine room crawls into the first few metres of the tunnel so its damp walls and sandy floor are visible. Then the dark swallows the last of the light and the rest of the tunnel remains black.

Just a couple of steps, Willis. That's all you need to take.

He's stopped. I thought he'd barge through the two boys and march ahead. That was my plan – rely on bolshy, best-at-everything Willis.

'What are you waiting for?' says Jericho.

Willis pats his pockets. He looks smaller than before, like he's deflating. His puff has gone. 'Just checking I've got everything.'

Jericho looks at Willis. Looks at the tunnel. Then back at him. 'You scared?'

'Of course not,' Willis says. He shakes his head like he's dislodging a thought, then takes those precious steps forward and walks into the tunnel. 'Follow me.'

But no one does.

Large slams the door behind him and turns the key in the lock.

Chapter Fourteen

Badger and I are hurtling along the corridor and out into the darkening dusk air. As soon as we get outside, Badger nearly goes flying over a tabby cat sauntering in front of us. I grab her to stop her face-planting.

'We did it – we're free!' She's giggling and whooping in between her clicks. The cat gives us a look of sheer disdain and disappears into a bush. I try to join in with Badger's excitement, but all I can see is how Willis shrank when he saw the dark.

Badger notices I'm silent as we skirt the garden edge. 'You OK, Alph?'

'Yup.'

'Really?'

'It's just . . .'

'You can't be feeling sorry for him? Alph!'

'I know. But you didn't see his face.'

'Just think of all those times he's dobbed you in, made stuff up! And he's awful to Flea, always picking on him.'

'True.'

'We're out, aren't we? We're on our adventure. It's nearly dark. We're breaking rules. We did it. Flippin' fishfingers, we only went and bloomin' did it!'

Badger thumps me. I thump her back. She giggles and it's catching.

We descend into a play-fighting, giggling mess.

'Stop it!' I yell.

Badger has me in a headlock and won't stop tickling my sides, which she knows are my ultimate weak spots.

'STOP IT!'

She does, after one properly hard knuckle-gouge in my side. We both stand up and she links arms with me.

'Right,' I say.

'Right,' Badger says.

★

We head straight across the Leas to the pillbox. I still haven't told Badger who I think the glint might be, why I'm the only one that sees it. I should tell her, but I can't formulate it in my head enough to explain it out loud. She'll understand when we catch her. When we meet my mam. When I see her face.

When I get to ask why.

I forget to walk because of the thinking, and Badger tugs my arm.

Focus, Alpha. I shake my head to get rid of the thoughts. I've been doing too much thinking lately.

I'm so busy remembering not to think that I forget to knock twice on the whitewashed wall.

★

Badger and I race along the cliff edge and hide about twenty metres away from what should be the opening to the pillbox. Except now it has a door. A big chunk of driftwood, wedged in place. We didn't put it there. I tell Badger.

'How did we not know about this, Alph?'

I shrug, then say, 'Stay here.'

She pulls a face, but knows it's the right idea. Her clicks will be noticeable the nearer we get, and without those she'll have to rely on me for her eyes. Plus, she's the best sentry in the universe.

'What bird do you want this time?'

I think for a moment. 'Gannet.'

Badger smiles. '*Morus bassanus* it is.'

She drops her chin on to her chest and a burbling *krock* breaks free.

I giggle, and she shushes me and pushes me towards the pillbox.

★

At first, I think the sea is pounding, but it's the rhythmic sound of my own heart in my ears. The small frightened feeling is running up the back of my neck again.

I want to calm down, get focused, but the same thought keeps barging into my head. *Who put a door there?*

Holy seaweed.

The renegade commander?

OK, that's maybe a step too far. I'm always getting told off for exaggerating.

Maybe a Wreckling did?

My brain can't help frantically wondering if it's *her* inside. I want to be the one to find her.

No, we should go back. We must go back. There might be someone here who shouldn't be. They've broken through the Boundaries that keep us safe, and none of the adults or mermaids know that Badger and I are here.

But what if she leaves before we can return? What if I miss my only chance?

I cover the open ground low and fast. There's no light coming from the slit or round the edges of the makeshift door. Whatever caused the glint isn't doing it now.

Is my mam inside, waiting for me in the dark?

I slow my breathing just as Cap'n taught me on the nights when I was little and I woke up screaming.

In through the nose, out through the mouth.

Clear air in. Black smoke out.

I listen for the sound of other breath. Nothing.

I crouch low and crawl along the front of the pillbox. Underneath the slit, I sit on my hunkers with my back to the wall, waiting for the velvet clouds to pass over the moon.

When they do, I pull my dark hair over my face. I can see through it with my right eye, but I should blend into the night.

What are we doing? Why didn't I tell Ephyra when I had the chance?

I slowly raise myself up to peer through the slit.

Holy mackerel, it's changed since we were last here!

The rubble from the roof fall has been cleared. The bigger chunks are piled in two columns, and there's a piece of board over the top to form a desk covered in maps and books. I squint: some have titles about the sea. Some are written by people with lots of letters after their names: *Clinical Anatomy* by K. Prestwick MB BS, *The Doctor's Way* by N. Winkler MRCGP, *The Abdomen and Pelvis: Anatomy for Students* by S. Sillington MB ChB.

My heart hammers. She's training to be a doctor! Why else would my mam bring so many heavy books with her?

Maybe she just loves books as much as me. Do I get that from her? I look around further, eager for more clues.

There's tarpaulin stretched to cover the hole in the roof and a hammock in the opposite corner with a rucksack underneath. I wonder if she knows about sleeping diagonally? I could teach her.

There's a photograph frame on the desk, but I can't make out the picture. *Does she look like me?*

Before I enter the pillbox, I make my noise to let Badger know I'm OK. Two cries of the black-legged kittiwake, *Rissa tridactyla*. (It's an in-joke with Cap'n. Try to imagine the sound of cats trapped in a box – it sounds exactly like that.)

Krock krock calls in return.

The driftwood door is lighter than I expect it to be, and it throws me off balance. My still slightly wonky ankle bends the wrong way, which makes me do a swear under my breath.

Krock kroooock?

'I'm OK,' I whisper, knowing that no one but Badger could possibly hear my response. I slip inside. On my way over to the desk, I pass a bucket in the corner. The tarpaulin has been rigged to filter rainfall, and next to it there's a folded flannel and a bar of soap. I pick it up and sniff it. The smell is not of flowers like I'm expecting. It's musky. The bar is smooth, pure, perfect. We don't have anything like that at home. I run my nail through the middle, leaving a gouge, and place it back on the flannel.

Everything here is orderly and methodical, a world away from the chaos at Old Ben. It smells of ink and Brasso. It's new and strange. I like it.

I move to the makeshift desk. There's an open book with a picture of a person sliced in two, showing all the bits our skin keeps hidden. I pick up the photograph frame and hold it in a sliver of moonlight that has pierced the cloud blanket and is shining through the slit in the wall. In the photo, a man with a handlebar moustache and lots of medals on his jacket stands with one hand on the shoulder of a woman. She's sitting, staring straight at the camera. She does not look happy.

Does she look like me?

The man's other hand is on the shoulder of a young boy with short trousers and socks so long that there's just a little gap of knee-skin in the middle. It makes me giggle. *Do I have a real brother?*

Shut up, brain! It's hope and fear and panic-head muddle and that never leads to anything good. What would Ephyra say? *Get back to Badger. Ring the 'emergency use only' bell.* That's the sensible plan now.

I place the frame back down and that's when I see the smooth leather cover of a diary next to it. This will tell me everything I need to know. I'll just have a quick flick through, then I'll go . . .

<u>1st April</u>

Brought before HCT and his cronies. How was my father ever friends with him? Was given my mission — locate a mermaid

specimen, give the signal, await its capture. I laugh. April Fool!
No one else laughs. Is he really serious? Who cares? At least it
gives me a chance to get away.

<u>*6th April*</u>
Slept in an old fisherman's hut by the lighthouse at Redcar. Can
see over the River Tees towards Hartlepool. Dropped binoculars
quickly when spotted someone looking right at me with a
telescope. Will pack up and move on before dawn.

<u>*14th April*</u>
Nights are getting colder the further I head up north. Spotted
nothing until today when three dolphins broke through the waves.
Need a roof for the night. What would my father make of all this?

<u>*21st April*</u>
Passed a shabby allotment and falling-down buildings around a
lighthouse. Not marked on my map. Found an old army pillbox
on the headland to the north. Roof caved in, no sign of use.
Will rest here, keep watch, read.

<u>*23rd April*</u>
Who are these people? Felt like I was being watched today.
Must keep up my guard.

<u>26th April</u>

They all went down to the bay at nightfall, elaborate claps and flashes. Something happened, I know it did, but I can't remember the details.

<u>30th April</u>

Still haven't given the signal. They'll wonder why I'm not moving on if I don't leave soon. Don't know what to do . . .

<u>3rd May</u>

Getting to know residents better. What is this place, so full of invalids? Feel sure Fried looked up at me from the beach. Must stay hidden. Must move on! Wheelchair-bound one seems to manage fine. Hadn't realized Fried's mate was blind until today – I've been calling her Batty in my head because of those clicks she makes. Can't tell what's wrong with Moonface yet. They'll gather on the beach soon. Will write as it happens so I can't forget.

Midnight: The kids are looting ships with help from MERMAIDS!

I don't know how much time has passed, and I don't know how long Badger's gannet has been calling, but I know I'm white-heat furious. How could he call us by those names? Write about me like that? My friends?

This proves that Outsiders don't belong here.

Fury shifts to terror.

This was never my mam. Of *course* it wasn't. Why would she ever come back for me? What the seas was I thinking?

No Outsider has broken through the Boundaries before. We shouldn't be here at night. Not alone. We need to get help.

A specimen? Ephyra! What have I got Badger messed up in?

I fling the diary on the desk, sending a torch rolling on to the floor and spilling a glass of water. It pools on the beautifully formed words and makes them blur into an inky puddle, then streams across the desk and drips on to the floor.

The gannet cries are frantic and now I can hear footsteps. There's nowhere to hide and no time to get out, so I dash to flatten myself against the wall. I almost believe I can make myself invisible behind the door.

I forgot to knock twice on the wall, I think. *I forgot to knock twice on the wall.*

I've been so stupid. *Why did I—*

There's a man at the door.

The man who wrote the diary.

He comes closer. He smells of the musky soap and the ink and the Brasso that made his belt buckle glint. I can see the shine of it approaching.

His footsteps are nearer now, on the hard mud near the doorway.

On the concrete step.

Step up one foot. Step up the other foot.

I can see him. He's looking straight at me. I close my eye.

There is screaming.

Is it mine?

Chapter Fifteen

I need to run or punch or do *something*, but my mind has gone blank and I can't move.

This is not my mam. This is a man who's been sent to destroy us all. The renegade commander is real.

Badger's noise has stopped. Badger? Is Badger OK? Has he *murdered* Badger?

That thought slams my brain back into life. I open my eye. He's still there, staring at me. I think he's as shocked as I am.

He's taller than me and dressed in faded camouflage. No wonder I couldn't see him when I first spotted the glint: he's the colour of the clifftops. Why did he wear his belt? That's what the light hit. He's a twit.

I'm so much better than a twit. No one's going to take this away from us. Everything we've worked so hard for. *Our world*.

He knows about the mermaids, Ephyra. He knows about everything.

I take a step towards him.

'No,' he says. Just one word. The word doesn't make me stop.

The gun in his hand does.

My head goes light and airy, and I dig my nails into the palms of my hands to make sure I don't float away.

He takes a step towards me.

Is this it? *Oh, Neptune.*

I close my eye.

I don't want to see. I don't want to see. I don't want to see.

THWACK

There's a hand on my arm and I'm screaming, screaming, screaming –

★

I open my eye. It's Badger's voice and face that I come back to.

'Alpha, Alpha, stop. You've got to stop screaming. It's me. Stop, please stop.'

I focus on her voice and I come back to her and the screaming in my ears stops. Why was I screaming?

The man.

The gun.

'There was a man here. He pointed a gun at me. Where is he? What happened?' I ask Badger as I grab her and squeeze her tight. 'You're not dead!'

Badger extracts herself from my hug, takes my hand and steps to one side. The man is lying on the floor. Blood seeps from a gash on his head. There's a big chunk of dead branch next to him.

'I hit him,' she says. 'Hard. He's not a Wreckling.'

'I know. Is he dead?'

'I don't know.'

Her voice is as small as I've ever known it. Her bottom lip begins to tremble and then that tremble rolls out over her whole body and she starts to shake. I can hear her teeth clattering. 'I thought he was going to kill you.'

I pull her towards me into the biggest hug I can do.

'It's OK,' I say. 'It'll all be OK.'

I glance at the man over the top of Badger's hair. I can't tell if he's breathing.

I recognize him. 'It's the boy from the photograph,' I say.

'Who?' Badger pulls away from me.

'On the desk, there's a photograph. Of a boy wearing long socks and shorts. It made me laugh. I thought it might be – never mind. It's him.'

'I killed a boy?'

'No, Badge. I . . .' I run out of words for a moment, then really quietly I say, 'What have we done?'

Badger not-looks at me. I look at her.

'I'll sort it,' I say.

She takes my hand. '*We'll* sort it,' she says.

'He deserved it,' I say.

It's true. He was sent by the renegade commander. He came to finish us.

So why do I not feel proud?

★

I try not to look at the blood. I think Badger is lucky that she can't see it, but her sense of smell is better than mine and the air is filled with rich iron red.

'I need to check if he's breathing.' I say it to myself as much as Badger.

She hangs behind me and clings to the back of my jumper.

'You need to let go of me, Badge.'

'I don't want to.'

'I know.'

There's a pause and then she lets go.

'Tell me what you're doing,' she says.

'I don't know yet.'

I look at the sprawled man, the blood, and I try to imagine that we're in one of Maura's stories and that this is all make-believe. If I was the hero in Maura's story, what would I do?

I pick up the branch.

'What are you doing?' says Badger. 'Tell me what you're doing!'

'I'm going to prod him,' I say.

'Oh.'

'Oh? That's helpful. Got a better idea?'

'No.'

'Shh then.'

There's a pause.

'Have you done it yet?' asks Badger.

'No!'

'Oh.'

'Stop with the oh.'

'Oh,' Badger says. Then she giggles and it turns into a sob.

I take a step forward and hold out the branch. My heart is yammering in my throat. I keep expecting him to spring up and grab the branch out of my hand. I prod him, at exactly the same time that Badger yells, 'TELL ME WHAT YOU'RE DOING!'

I drop the branch on his head. *Doink*. Well, if he wasn't dead before, he is now. I gaspy-giggle snot.

'Check his pulse,' says Badger.

'You do it,' I say.

'Nah, I can't see.'

'You're going to pull the blind card now? Charming.'

I move fast. If I don't, I'll chicken out. I plonk myself down and sit cross-legged beside him. The gun is still by his hand. I use my foot to carefully push it out of his reach. It's heavier than I expect.

'What are you –'

'Shh, Badger,' I say. 'I'll tell you when it's done.'

I don't want to touch his skin. His wrist is poking out from his sleeve so I don't have to pick his hand up. I just have to touch it. I take a deep breath.

'Don't use your thumb.'

'Badger, man! If you don't shut up, I'll –'

'What?' she says. 'Kill me?' She snorts.

'That's not funny.'

'I know.' She does the laugh-cry thing again.

I think of postcards, cheese-and-pickle butties and cats, then I firmly grasp his wrist in my hand. It's warm.

I do a bit of sick in my mouth and swallow it down.

I place my index finger and middle finger on his wrist. Nothing.

Too close to the bone. *Think, Alpha!*

I pretend I'm in class and we're taking our first-aid refresher test. I space my fingers correctly and then place them on his wrist. I press firmly. I wait.

'Badger?'

'Yes?'

'He's alive.'

Chapter Sixteen

Once we realize he isn't dead, we also realize we can't leave him here. The pillbox is too far away to go and ring the EMERGENCY USE ONLY bell to raise the alarm and then get back here. What if he's gone by the time we return?

Is Willis still in the tunnel? Are the boys in trouble? No time for those thoughts. They eat up my brain and I need it for planning.

My brain says we're in the biggest doo-doo ever, probably never to be let out again until we're thirty. All the fun things will be over by then and we'll be proper old and have to do knitting.

We decide we need to get the man closer to home

and somewhere he can't hurt anyone if he wakes up, become heroes, leave the rest to the grown-ups.

It's a win–win situation.

'What about Cave Four?' says Badger.

It's in the cliffs underneath the lighthouse so nice and near, and it's like a maze in there if you don't know it as well as we do from our mapping project. He'll never get out. Perfect.

I fill Badger in on what Ephyra told me and what I read in the diary. It says this man was sent to find us by someone called HCT. *That* must be the renegade commander. The diary says our prisoner hasn't dobbed us in. Maybe there's still time? There *has* to be.

I haven't told Badger about any of that stuff he said about us; that makes me feel sick. Why was I was worrying he was dead? Maybe I should tell Badge; she'd finish him off.

I wish he'd been my mam.

★

I stay with the body, the not-dead body, while Badger goes to fetch the wheelbarrow from where we keep the horses. Badger thought of the wheelbarrow as well as the cave. I'm usually the ideas person. My head feels useless.

I hate the silence with the not-dead man. Even unconscious, I can feel the power of what he might do to us. If he *has* told anyone, it's over.

For us, that means back to the world beyond. The world I've never known. Where Outsiders talk about us like he has. Where they don't understand, or even try to. Where they don't just see us for us. I can't be made to go there!

For Ephyra and the mermaids, that could be the end.

Suddenly I'm freaked out because I realize that if he isn't dead, which he isn't, and just unconscious, which he is, then at any time he could wake up.

I yank out some of the bindings from his hammock to use as rope. Tying his legs together is easy. I don't have to touch skin. I can *tralalalalala* and pretend he isn't real.

His right hand is at least easy to get to, but he's fallen on his other arm so it'll need yanking out. What if that wakes him up?

I can be ready. I move the branch closer to me, well within grabbing and thwacking distance.

I grip his upper arm and pull. It shifts and I yelp and reach for the branch. But he doesn't stir. I tug, and his whole forearm and wrist and hand pop out all at the same time. Then I just need to tie his hands together. I have to use my teeth to hold the rope, and kind of ruffle and scuffle it under his arms.

I get scared that he might be able to undo it so I use all the rest of the rope to do half hitch on top of half hitch, which probably isn't necessary, but makes me feel better.

The man doesn't move. The man. The man has a name. What is it?

The diary.

I move to the desk and pick it up from the puddle of water. I turn to the front. It says:

This diary belongs to Able Rate Robert Glass

Robert. He has a name. So do we. Not the names *he* chose to call us.

I look at him tied up on the floor and decide I liked it better when he was just a not-dead body.

★

'I'm back!' Badger startles me. 'The wheelbarrow stinks.'

'I don't think he'll care.'

I fill his rucksack with things that look important, like his diary, the photograph and the books. Then his clothes, the gun and anything that could identify him. I kick sand over the blood on the floor.

Have you ever tried to lift and fold an unconscious body into a wheelbarrow?

You get very, very sweaty.

I pick up the handles of the wheelbarrow and Badger holds tight to its side to steady it. Both of our hands have white knuckles. Not just because of his weight, but because of how late it's got, how much time we've taken. Come bedtime, we'll be missed. Then there'll be a search party and then there'll be trouble.

'We're actually doing this, aren't we?' says Badger. 'I mean, this is actually happening, isn't it? Hit me. Then I'll know it's real.'

I put down the handles of the wheelbarrow and thump her arm.

'Ow,' she says. 'Thanks.'

The good thing about it being dark is that everyone's inside, which makes getting to the lift and down to the beach easy.

We have to abandon the wheelbarrow halfway into

the cave as we can't keep it upright with all the rocky bits. Instead, we drag and heave him to the section right at the back where noise can't escape. We know about that bit because Jericho got stuck once and he was yelling for ages and was furious when we just came sauntering in – proper radged.

It feels like it takes forever and, by the time we have Robert out of the wheelbarrow and seated with his back against the wall, neither of us can speak.

All of me aches, my ankle especially.

Badger wedges his head on a jutting-out rock to stop him keeling over to one side. 'He doesn't seem particularly comfy,' she says, and then giggles.

'It's not funny, Badge.'

'I know.'

She's laughing really hard now. I can't help but laugh too, even though it's the most unfunny situation in the world. It's like that moment where someone goes all serious and says they're going to tell you some really bad news and then you get the nervous giggles.

'Have you got a vest on, Badge?'

'Yes. Though that's a bit of a random question, Alph.'

'We need to gag him.'

She takes off her baggy jumper, slips off her vest and hands it to me.

I tie it tight round his mouth while she puts her jumper back on. I make sure that his nose is free and he can breathe. Then I hide the rucksack behind a ledge, out of his reach.

We both stand there. Me watching him. Badger listening to him breathe.

This is *not* the night I planned. I thought we'd find: a) nothing; b) clues; or c) my mam. Hadn't thought of option d): discover a disgusting diary, get a gun pointed in my face, nearly kill a man, tie him up, wheelbarrow him to Cave Four.

The Wrecklings are together people. We didn't do this right.

I suddenly go cold, the tiredness hits me hard and I need to sleep right now.

Why didn't I tell Ephyra? On the beach, I had the chance. She asked. Again and again. I didn't want to worry her.

That's not the whole truth.

I didn't want to upset her, didn't want to make her think that, by hoping for my mam, she wasn't enough. She's everything. I don't need another mam.

I wanted Ephyra to be proud of me too – to know that, even though I'm not properly hers, I'm a warrior just like her.

I don't feel like a warrior. I feel cold and small.

★

'Wish I'd told Ephyra now,' I say.

'Me too,' says Badger. 'Me bloomin' too.'

We turn to leave.

'Wait,' I say, and go back to the rucksack. I root through it until I find the diary and shove it down the waistband of my trousers and pull my jumper over the top to keep it hidden.

'What are you doing?' asks Badger.

'Just checking his knots,' I say, and I take her hand again.

We walk out of the cave together, leaving our prisoner behind.

Chapter Seventeen

We take the lift Up Top. Badger and I are holding hands, which is really babyish and I should let go, but I don't. She doesn't either.

We'll get Jericho and Large, let Willis out of the tunnel, then do our grand reveal.

But when the lift doors open, I'm not prepared for the mass of swarming Wrecklings that greets us.

We're in trouble. A hot, stinking mess of it.

Peter comes dashing over and signs frantically at me. I sign for him to slow down – I can't keep up.

'Seen who?' I sign back and say out loud for Badger's benefit.

Peter signs 'Snot' and then fingerspells WILLIS.

'No.' I shake my head and tug at Badger. I drag her out of the lift so we can't be ambushed again. She stumbles and lets go of my hand, linking arms so I can guide her.

'I'm tired, Alph.'

'Me too.'

'What the heck is going on?'

'I have got no idea. We need to find Jericho and Large.'

★

We eventually find them in Maura and Laura's kitchen, which is the final place we think to look after I pegged it right to the top of Old Ben's tower and Badger scouted the Leas and the outbuildings.

Large has a pinny on and is wiping down the benches, the sight of which would usually be hilarious, but it's not very funny right now. Jericho is at the table, folding the cloth.

'Where in the holy high seas have you been?' says Jericho when he sees us. 'And why do you look so gross?'

I peer in the mirror above the fireplace. I've got sand stuck all over me. My jumper is torn and mossy. My jeans are filthy. I sniff myself. I stink. Badger looks no better. She has a smear of blood up her arm. I shudder.

'Long story. What the absolute Neptune is going on with everyone?'

'Willis is missing. We had to cover,' says Large.

'But you know he's not missing,' I say. 'He's in the tunnel.'

Jericho just stares at me.

'You didn't tell them he was in the tunnel? Just tell them he's in the tunnel! There's more important stuff going on now!' I roll my eye. I don't understand why there's all this fuss over snotty Willis.

Badger is slumped in an armchair in the corner. She doesn't seem to have any words left.

'Why do you think we're here?' says Jericho. 'We *did* tell them. We got an absolute rollocking and now we've been banished. Probably forever.'

Large takes off the apron and hangs it on a drawer knob and then pulls up a chair and sits at the table. Badger doesn't budge.

'When we looked in the tunnel, Willis was gone,' says Large.

'How can he be *gone*?' The tight feeling in my chest intensifies. It's dark out. There's a man in the cave who's been sent to destroy us. That's enough to deal with, even without my brain obviously thinking it isn't and trying to make me cry because it wasn't my mam, though I'm not completely sure I wanted it to be.

I look at Large, but he just shrugs and then slumps his head on to the table, resting his chin on his hands.

'How?' I ask again.

Jericho shoves the cloth to one side and folds his hands. 'You were gone for ages and we didn't know what to do. We hadn't worked out anything beyond shoving him in a tunnel, had we? Your plan was rubbish.' Jericho seethes. He hates being told off, probably more than me. His hands shake. I don't know if it's anger or fear. When I stare at them, he moves his hands under the table. I look at mine. They're trembling too.

'I just thought you'd let him out after we'd gone. Then he'd be so peed off with you he'd forget about me and Badge,' I say.

Large lifts his head, stares at me and says, 'You didn't say that out loud though.'

I don't say anything.

Jericho sighs. 'Willis banged on the door for ages, yelled at us. It was kind of funny at first, but then he started to cry. Large wanted to unlock the door . . .'

Large nods.

Jericho continues: '. . . but I wouldn't let him. Do you know how many times that slimeball has made other people cry? Then he went quiet. We heard Cap'n shouting for Large, so Large left.'

'And then you opened the door?' I ask.

Jericho shakes his head.

'Why the hecky thump not?'

Willis sucks. But the thought of him crying . . . The thought that he was so terrified in the tunnel that being outside, at night, alone, was a better option . . .

I was out there, but I had Badger. Not having a Badger? It doesn't bear thinking about.

We're going to be banished here forever. And they don't even know about the man in Cave Four yet.

Jericho is silent for ages. I'm about to ask again when he finally speaks. He's so quiet even Badger shifts in her chair to hear properly.

'First night I arrived, you were all so kind. You made sure I had everything I needed. Cap'n spent most of the evening with me. The wheels on my chair were knackered so I had to be pushed, which I hate, but Cap'n said it was no bother and he'd fix them in the morning.

'Cap'n introduced me to Willis and you know he was

all right? Bit straight-laced, but we got on OK. Talked about geeky stuff, trains and the like. He knew things that I didn't and that was cool. I *liked* him.

'Then at supper Willis went off to get us both a cuppa and you three came over while he was gone. I saw him stood there with the cuppas, watching, and I waved him over, but he pretended he hadn't seen and walked off.'

This stops my brain going into overdrive. I didn't know any of this. None of us did. I sit down at the table, quietly, so Jericho doesn't clam up.

'I didn't think anything of it really, thought he must have got distracted by something. Then later on I shared his room. Cap'n had seen how we'd got on OK and thought it'd be good for my first night. I thought it would be too. But Willis just grunted if I asked him stuff. Even when I talked about trains, he just stared at me and rolled his eyes.

'In the night, I needed the loo, but because of the broken wheels on my chair I couldn't get there by myself. Willis wouldn't get up. I knew he was awake. Just ignored me.'

Jericho looks down. Embarrassed. None of us know what to say.

'Anyway, in the morning, Willis just got up, got

dressed and left me there like that. Maura found me and got me cleaned up.

'When he was crying in the tunnel, all I thought was, *Serves you right!* Payback time. But, when Large came back, and we opened the door, he was gone.'

'I still don't get what you mean by *gone*,' I say. 'There's no way out. That was the whole point.'

'There is if you smash the window in the foghorn,' says Large.

There's a pause. My brain fills with fear.

Why didn't Ephyra tell Cap'n what she knew? He'd have put us under immediate curfew, then none of this would have happened. It's all her fault.

But I didn't tell her about the glint. It's my fault too. Willis is out there, alone, and there's an Outsider in our midst.

My heart stops for a beat.

What if our Outsider isn't the only one?

'We thought he'd be in a heap halfway down the tunnel,' says Jericho. 'He wasn't and, like Large says, the foghorn window was put through and there was blood on the edge of the glass and on the ground inside and out. The twit didn't realize that you have to brush all the glass out first.'

I wonder how Jericho knows to do this, but I don't ask.

'Large went straight to Cap'n and fessed up. They formed a search party straight away.'

'Don't worry,' says Large. 'They don't know you and Badger were in on it. Thought you were searching.'

It goes quiet. They've nothing left to say. But we have.

'There's something Badger and I need to tell you . . .'

★

The hours tick by. Time goes wrong, the clock on the wall dawdling at midnight, then speeding up. Still no word.

Jericho and Large fall asleep, Large still with his chin on his hands. As soon as we'd finished speaking, Large had stood up straight away to go and tell Cap'n what we knew, but Jericho hauled him back down, said we were in enough bother already and it wouldn't help the adults focus on finding Willis. Besides, what harm can the man do when he's all tied up in Cave Four?

I don't know why I don't tell them that I'm scared there could be more Outsiders here. To protect them?

Large mumbles, gets upset in his sleep.

This is all my fault. I go to Badger and sit at her feet.

'You awake?' I ask quietly.

'Yup,' she says.

'What do we do? Think we need to tell Cap'n?'

'Yup,' she says again, but doesn't move.

'Willis is out there somewhere. They've got enough on their plate looking for him,' I say, trying to make myself believe it by saying it out loud. 'Would what we tell them help? Or make it worse?'

There's the bit of me that overrides everything, that makes me ashamed. Will it make it worse for *us*?

'Do you think he's OK?' asks Badger.

'The man or Willis?'

Badger looks like she's going to cry. 'Either? Both? Mainly Willis,' she says.

There's a pause. Then she says, 'Can you remember why we hate Willis? I can't. I just do it because that's what we do. Actually, it's because it's what *you* do.'

I don't have anything to say to that.

'Holy mackerel,' says Badger and I jump.

Large lifts his head with a jerk and Jericho wakes.

Badger stands up. 'I know where he'll be.'

Chapter Eighteen

It goes really fast after Badger lets off her bird call.

Yammer. Yammer yammer krock squeak. Yammer. Yammer yammer krock squeak.

The sound of the albatross. The bird that holds the souls of lost sailors, the bird that it's bad luck to kill. The sound Badger only makes in a pure full-on emergency.

We joke about loads of things. But you do not joke about the albatross. Not ever. It makes toes icy and Wrecklings come running.

Large carries Willis from the boiler room where Badger somehow knew he'd be, and brings him to the porch, me and Badger on one side of him, Jericho on the other. I try to ask Badger how she knew where to find him, but she just shakes her head. It seems we all had our own histories with Willis that we kept hidden from each other.

The shouts of the other Wrecklings attract Cap'n's attention and he stands in the doorway of Old Ben as we carry Willis towards him.

'Bring him straight in,' Cap'n says, and Large takes Willis inside.

We all try to follow. Cap'n stops us.

'You three to Maura's cottage. You *do not* budge until I come and get you. Understand?'

Badger, Jericho and I nod.

He looks at each of us in turn and then his eyes rest on me and he slowly shakes his head. 'I thought better of you.'

I've never been on the receiving end of a look like that from Cap'n before. This is worse than bread buttering, potato peeling or manure duty. I wish he'd shout and get it over with. Cap'n looked at me like that, *said* that, and he doesn't even know everything. I bow my head and hold back the tears.

This is too big for us. There's a man tied up in Cave Four and he had a gun and he's on a mission to destroy us. I'll take the consequences. It's all my fault anyway and the others are standing there silently, taking the blame for me cos they're my friends. You don't leave your friends in the poop.

I can't think how to begin.

Maura appears at the end of the path. 'You're needed, Cap'n.'

He looks up at her.

'Now,' she says.

I can hear voices behind me and one of them is Ephyra's. I go to turn round.

Cap'n places his hand on mine, not the way he did in the classroom. This is firm and cold.

'Stay here,' he says to me. Then looks at the other two. 'All of you.'

He walks towards Maura.

I can hear that Verdigris, Henrietta and Ephyra are with Cap'n and Maura. We often see Ephyra on the beach, but never here any more, never Up Top. And never, ever, ever Verdigris and Henrietta, who don't even like being on the sand.

Whatever was holding my tongue finally snaps.

I go running towards them. Badger shouts after me, but I don't stop.

'I told you to say there!' I've never heard Cap'n so

angry. I didn't know he could shout like that, look like that. His face and voice are all hard angles and spikes.

I keep on running towards them.

'Alpha, I'm warning you!' Cap'n shouts at me.

I'm crying, and there's tears and snot muddled with the sand and muck on my face, and I'm ripped and torn, and I just need Ephyra to hug me and Cap'n not to shout.

I bundle into her arms, and Ephyra has no choice but to grab me to stop herself falling over.

'That's it,' says Cap'n. 'I've had enough of this tonight.'

He grabs my arms and tries to haul me off Ephyra.

'You stop right now,' she says. Her voice is the sea when it's icy-lake calm. 'Take your fingers off her and step back.' Ephyra bares her teeth at Cap'n.

'Stop fighting! Stop shouting!' I sob at them. 'It's not helping!'

I can't stop crying. Ephyra holds me close. Cap'n takes a step back.

They're both shocked by the state of me. *I'm* shocked by the state of me.

I'm shocked by Cap'n, and the mermaids Up Top. By what we've done. By everything that's happened since that glint on the clifftop.

Ephyra kneels in front of me and turns my head so I'm looking only at her.

'Forget them,' she says. 'Pretend it's just me and you floating In Deep. I will not be angry. I promise. No matter what it is you want to say, I'll make it OK.'

'Promise?' I say.

'I promise,' she says.

I lean away from Ephyra, wipe the snot from my face with my sleeve.

'You need to read this,' I say as I pull out the diary from my waistband and hold it out to them. To Ephyra, who's still kneeling, to Henrietta and Verdigris behind her, to Maura and to Cap'n. Cap'n takes it from me and goes to walk away. Ephyra grabs him to make him stay.

'There's more,' she says to him. She looks at me. 'There's something else. What is it?'

I take a deep breath. 'I need to show you something.'

Chapter Nineteen

The grown-ups take over once I tell them about the man tied up in Cave Four. Badger can't stay awake so Maura puts her to bed in her cottage and stays with her, the toddlers, Jericho and Large.

Norma is standing guard outside the cottage with Malcolm. She gets me out of my manky jumper, then bundles me into an old yellow waterproof. I now smell faintly of fish, but it's no worse than I smelled before, just a different sort of pong. Norma grabs my arm too tightly. I try to wriggle out of her grasp and she goes to say something to me, but Cap'n shouts, which distracts her, and I wriggle out of her grip.

★

Cap'n and the mermaids follow me into Cave Four, their torches blazing. Cap'n grabs me when my tired legs stumble, then he doesn't let go.

I stop before we reach the bit of the cave where we hid the man, the bit where all the noise gets stolen.

'He's back there.'

My legs won't go forward.

'Stay here,' says Cap'n. 'Leave it to us.'

Cap'n helps me to sit down because all of a sudden my body doesn't seem to be under my control.

'I'm so sorry, love,' he says. 'I really didn't mean to shout. I was scared.'

Then he hands me his kitten and the four of them leave me. I can't hear anything.

I fall asleep.

★

I wake up under a duvet, and light is dancing behind the curtains.

Curtains?

I wiggle and I don't move. I'm in a bed, not my hammock. I must be at Maura's.

I sit up, but I'm not in her cottage. I'm in Cap'n's room on a camp bed. He's snoring in a chair opposite.

And on Cap'n's bed is Willis. He's awake too and staring at me.

My whole body aches, especially my ankle. I swing my legs out of bed and wince as I stand up. I pad quietly out of the room and, before I can close the door gently behind me, Willis comes out too.

We don't speak. He shuts the door behind him and then walks to the window seat on the landing and sits down. I don't know what else to do, so I follow and take a seat next to him.

The silence kills me. His breath is snotty and I want to hand him a tissue. Or punch him. Punch, then tissue. His hands are bandaged up. That makes me feel rubbish and want to hug him.

I remember his face when he saw the dark.

'Why are you such a fish-head, Willis?'

'Why do you hate me, Alpha?' he counters.

'Hate you? I don't flippin' hate you,' I say as I suddenly realize it's true. I don't. I can't really remember why I hated Willis any more. I remember the man in the cave. Hating Willis seems so pointless after everything that happened last night. 'You just completely do my head in – all the rules and the grassing up. You're so mean to Flea. To everyone!'

Willis is silent for a while. I am too. We don't look at each other.

We stare out of the window. From here, you can see the whole world, our world, Haven Point. But it isn't safe any more. I shudder.

Willis watches me. 'You do,' he says. 'You hated me from the day I arrived.'

I think back to then. He came in beautifully dressed. Someone cared enough about him to do that.

Why didn't I like that? Was I jealous? That's not a nice feeling to sit with.

'I tried to be friends,' Willis says. 'You didn't want anything to do with me. You're so popular, aren't you, Alpha? If you didn't want anything to do with me – well, then neither did anyone else.'

'That's not true,' I say, and then I think about it. 'So not true,' I say quieter.

But was it? *Is* it?

'Everyone goes on about this being the best place ever. An inclusive community where we're all accepted exactly as we are, no matter which bits of us don't work.' Willis knocks on his fibreglass leg to highlight his point.

'But if your personality doesn't fit, or if the favourite

one decides to take the hump, that's it – game over for you.'

I'm really quiet now. I want to argue back, but I can't. I'm desperate to change the subject.

'Why are you scared of the dark?' I ask.

'You think I'm going to tell you that? So you can take the pee out of me later with your mates?'

I suck in a deep breath and tell him something I haven't told anyone, not even Badger. I feel I owe him, and this is all I have to give.

'I'm scared of the dark because that's where fire lives. I went to sleep in the dark and the flames came and I melted and my whole body was needles and pain. And I'm scared of the dark because my mam's face hides there and I can't see it. I'm terrified I never will.'

I've never said my everything like that before, out loud. It makes it real. My shoulders slump and it feels like my whole body has caved in on itself. I really thought it was going to be her in the pillbox. I was going to find my mam, that she'd come back for me. She was going to tell me everything and hug me and I'd get to see her face. She would look just like me.

She'd probably be terrified if she saw me. But she's never coming back.

I feel like I've been abandoned all over again. Silent tears run out of my eye and along the hollows that the burn carved out of my cheek.

Willis doesn't say anything.

But then he nods. He understands what I've just handed over. He doesn't hand anything back in return, but I'm OK with that.

'Why did you do that to Jericho on his first night here?' I ask.

Willis sighs. 'He told you?'

'Only last night.'

'Because you stole him. It was better for him to properly hate me. At least that way he wouldn't have to pretend to be nice to me.'

We sit in silence for a bit longer. His sniffing still makes we want to thump him, but in a less mean way. I pick up a doily from under a lamp on the table next to the window seat. I dry my cheek with it first. 'Here,' I say. 'Use this.'

He takes it from me and blows his nose with a massive honk. 'I hate bloomin' sniffing all the time.'

'Why do you do it then?'

He half smiles. 'Because I know it does your head in.'

'Slimeball,' I say, and he half smiles a bit bigger. I do too.

'What am I supposed to do with this?' he says and holds up the balled-up, snot-filled doily. 'I don't think Cap'n will want it back.'

I look at him. Is he being serious? Then he half smiles again and it looks really weird on his face.

Nice weird though.

'Chuck it out the window,' I say.

Willis looks mortified. Then he opens the window and flings it straight out before he has time to think about what he's doing.

I'm gobsmacked. He is too. He laughs at my face.

Cap'n walks out of his room and sees us both. 'What are you two up to?'

'Nothing,' we say at exactly the same time, and then catch each other's eyes and giggle.

Cap'n smiles.

'This has been one helluva night, and I don't mind telling you both that the most frightening bit of it all is seeing you two sitting together.'

Cap'n looks at me and I daren't answer back, remembering how he was when he yelled at me last night. That he had good reason to. 'You are officially grounded forever, Alpha, but it will have to wait. You're *required*.'

He sets off down the stairs. 'Fifteen minutes and

we're meeting in the War Room!' Cap'n yells back up to us. 'Get a wiggle on.'

Willis gives me a puzzled look and shrugs his shoulders.

'Where's that?' I call after Cap'n.

'Cave Four!' he yells back. 'Where else? Though I wish you'd hurry up with that project and give it a better name.'

Chapter Twenty

Norma and Malcolm stand guard at the entrance to Cave Four, holding fishing spears.

Norma whistles and Large comes to the entrance to get us. She looks questioningly at me and Willis. I shrug.

Large goes to lead us inside, but Norma grabs my hand. 'You OK, Alpha? Did he –'

'Of course she is,' says Malcolm. 'Proper hard, this one!'

Willis grins and Large drags us both inside, but not before I hear Norma grumble, 'Can't ruddy let me finish one sentence, can you?'

★

In the third chamber of the cave, they've added furniture. In the centre, there's a table. Ephyra and Cap'n sit at the head, Henrietta to Ephyra's side, Peter next to Cap'n. Kelvin is opposite them with a pad of paper in front of him and a coot-quill pen in his hand. Sitting round the rest of the table on the spare foldy seats we usually keep in the outhouse are mermaids, including Verdigris, some of whom I've never seen before, and the ones I do know I've *never* seen on land.

Jericho and Badger are to one side of the chamber. Badger is leaning against the shale wall. Jericho looks startled when he clocks me with Willis and I see him whisper something to Badger.

Willis stops suddenly.

Large puts his hand on Willis's shoulder and walks him towards Jericho and Badger. I follow. They're already discussing stuff at the table so we just quietly lean against the wall next to them.

'You OK?' I ask Badger. She nods and shushes me.

'Where's the man?' I ask Jericho. He points to the noise-eating section of the cave, then he shushes me too.

'Following analysis of both his diary and his belongings, what conclusion do we reach?' asks Cap'n.

He picks up a mug and drinks from it. The kitten

mewls as a drop lands on its head. Cap'n takes it out of his beard and uses his jumper to dry it, then places it gently back inside.

One of the mermaids I don't recognize speaks up. 'Shelly. Southern Clan, guardians of the Seaweed Scrolls. As requested by Henrietta, we have consulted the scrolls. Unfortunately, in this instance, guidance is unclear. Something is clouding them, making them hard to decipher. That aside, the diary confirms our fears after the Central Fins vanished. We know his mission, that he's been here for almost two weeks, and has been recording your every move.'

The anger I had when I read the diary in the pillbox floods back. How dare he come here to ruin everything we've worked for? He doesn't know a flippin' thing about us and he made all those judgements. He didn't know our names; he could have made up some nice ones. Instead, he chose the easiest thing in the world – to label us by our impairments.

I spit on the floor, wishing it was at him. We can choose our nicknames. Our friends can. Not him.

Shelly continues speaking. 'This tallies with the rumours we'd been hearing about the commander. It takes them out of hearsay to as close to fact as we can ascertain right now. Someone is hunting us. How near they are, and why? That's what we need to find out next.' She licks her teeth. 'By any means possible.'

I don't realize I'm gulping breaths until Badger puts her hand on my arm.

I still haven't told my gang about what he said about all of us in the diary. That's the sort of stuff that breaks people here – not our bodies or brains but the way Outsiders think about them.

'Has he given the signal and reported us?' asks Cap'n.

'At this present moment, we think not,' says Shelly.

'But we would be wise to assume the worst,' adds Ephyra.

Shelly nods. 'Indeed. The diary indicates that he travelled for a considerable time and came here with no inkling that he would find anything. We won't know more until we decide whether to give him what he wants.'

'The interrogation has completely stalled?' asks Cap'n.

Henrietta nods and spits out some fish bones she'd been chewing. 'He was not for answering, no matter what I did . . .'

Those words hang in the air.

'Time to vote,' Shelly says. 'All those in favour of sending in Alpha, raise your hands.'

Shelly puts her hand up. So do those of the mermaids I don't know. The Wrecklings are slower to move. Ephyra and Cap'n have not raised theirs. I'm too stunned to run.

'Tied,' says Henrietta.

She looks at Ephyra and Cap'n. 'We must call on you both for your decision.'

Ephyra shakes her head. 'I can have no part of this.'

Cap'n doesn't look over at us. He studies the faces round the table. 'For the greater good,' he says, and raises his hand.

Badger turns and hugs me.

Ephyra comes over to where we're leaning. She reaches down and places her hands on either side of my face. 'Be brave,' she says, kisses my forehead and leaves.

The other mermaids follow.

Cap'n comes over and holds out his hand to me and I take it because I don't know what else to do.

Badger won't let go of me. Peter has to prise her off.

'Peter,' signs Cap'n. 'Take this lot Up Top and don't lose them.'

Cap'n pulls my arm through his and walks me towards the noise-eating bit of the cave. 'I had no choice, pet. He says he's not speaking to anyone until he speaks to you. You made quite an impression, it seems.'

My legs go wibbly and my head kind of floats and I want to sit down.

'Easy,' says Cap'n. 'I've got you.'

★

The man sits in the centre of the cave, where the rock dips down to the floor like the middle bit in the letter 'M'. He's got his hands tied behind him, and the rope loops round the rock column so he can't wiggle it up or down to free himself. Me and Badger didn't think of that.

There's lots of stuff we didn't think about. He doesn't have Badger's vest as a gag any more because they realized he didn't need it. That's why they put him here, where the noise gets stolen. His belongings have been removed. He has a big plaster on the side of his head, above his left eye, and a bandage that covers the edge of the plaster and most of the rest of his head. Some bits of hair tuft out at the sides. The bandage he needs because Badger whacked him with a branch.

To save me.

Because he had a gun.

His nose looks broken. Badger didn't do that.

He says, 'Hello.' Like this is normal.

'You stay right there,' says Cap'n as he sits me down on a smooth boulder that is thigh height. 'Whatever he says, you do not move.'

'OK,' I say, then Cap'n begins to walk away.

'Where are you going?' I shout at his back.

'I'll be just there. Right there.' He points beyond my section of the cave.

'Ten minutes,' he says to the man. 'Not a second more. Then you talk.'

The man nods.

Cap'n leaves me alone with Able Rate Robert Glass.

★

The boulder I'm sitting on is cold and slightly damp. That's what I try to concentrate on, not the man opposite and the fact that Cap'n has left me with him. Alone.

I don't look at him. Not directly. I stare at my hands, but sneak peeks upwards through my fringe. He's not sneaking peeks. He's staring.

I sit upright and stare straight back at him.

He smiles. 'Hello,' he says again. 'We haven't been properly introduced. I'm Bobby Glass. I'd shake your hand, but . . .' He shrugs.

'Robert,' I say. 'You're Robert, not Bobby.'

'Bobby comes from Robert. It's a shortened version, a nickname.'

'I know that. I'm not thick. But you're starting out in a lie. With a friendly name. I'm not calling you that.'

'Touché,' he says. 'I like you.'

I have no idea what *too-shay* means, but, having told him I'm not thick, there's no way I'm going to ask.

'Well, I don't like you.'

The conversation stops. He looks confused as to what should happen next.

I'm not sure he's had any dealings with children in real life, never mind been trapped in a cave with one.

He's out of his depth here. I like that.

'Why are you here?' I ask.

'Walking holiday.'

'With a *gun*? I've already told you I'm not thick.'

'Well, if you're not thick, you tell me why I'm here and I'll tell you if you're right. Deal?'

'I'm never making a deal with you. Never.'

'OK. Understandable. No deal, but the offer still stands.'

His clothes are filthy. Especially the backs of his trousers where Badger and I dragged him into the cave. There's the faintest tang of manure in the air.

'Do you know how we got you here?' I ask.

'No,' he says. 'Enlighten me.'

'In the poo-barrow,' I say.

He looks puzzled. Then sniffs his arm. Then winces.

I continue. 'I think you're here to destroy everything. I think you're cruel and heartless and you work for your boss, the commander, who's even more cruel. I think you're good at watching, but I don't think you've told anyone about us yet. They all reckon you have.' I nod behind me. 'But I don't and I can't work out why.'

'You're good,' he says. 'Very good, much cleverer than that lot out there. Some of that is right. Most of it.'

'Which bits?'

'That would be telling.'

He wriggles and tries to get comfy. He looks like when you get Flat Bum if you've been sitting for too long. Flat Bum comes just before Dead Leg.

'What's your name?' he asks.

I stare at him. How dare he ask my name? I touch the melted side of my face, the eye that popped and ran and then sealed right up.

'Fried,' I say. 'My name is Fried.'

I keep on looking at him. I'm angry, never been so boiling, roiling angry. I want to shake him by the shoulders and scream in his face. I want to scream that it's people like *him* that make us live here.

I wish I had his gun.

He has the courtesy to wince. When he speaks, his voice is quieter and he sounds less like a robot posh person, more like a human.

'You read my diary?' he asks.

'It's your bloomin' diary that got me in this mess in the first place,' I tell him. Except I don't say bloomin' and I don't care. 'What right do you have to call us by those names? What right?'

'I'm sorry if I offended you.'

'If? That's not an apology. "If" makes it my fault. You're either sorry or you're not sorry. Either way, I don't care.'

There's a long silence. It lasts until it passes out of awkward, until it's just how we sit.

The man – Robert, Bobby – he looks like someone's taken a cork out of him and some of his innards have whizzed out.

'I am good at watching,' he says after what feels like an age has passed. 'Very good at it. I can be still for long periods because my dad used to take me twitching.' He sees my puzzled look. 'Twitching? Birdwatching.

You're right – I was sent to destroy everything. You're right – I haven't told anyone. And *I* don't know why either.'

After a pause, he continues. 'You're wrong about one bit. Up until this moment, I'd never thought of myself as cruel.'

'That's the problem with Outsiders,' I say, the rage in my voice making it come out all cracked. 'Outsiders *don't* think.'

Cap'n comes in. 'That's it – time's up. Come on, Alpha, let's go.'

I stand.

'Alpha,' says the man. 'Alpha, I'm Bobby, and I *am* pleased to meet you.'

I follow Cap'n out.

Just before I take the last step before sound gets swallowed, I hear him say, 'I'm sorry.'

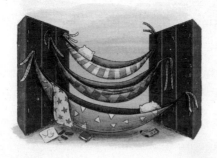

Chapter Twenty-one

This is the busiest I've ever seen it before a wrecking. We didn't even have time for our Sunday nap.

Five days since we found him, and everyone knows about the man in the cave. And that he works for the commander. We stand to lose everything. Our home, our mermaid friends. Everything will be destroyed. No one has been told what we're going to do next. What the plan is. Not even me. Not even after they left me there with him.

There has to *be* a plan, doesn't there?

And, most urgent of all: *how did he get through the Boundaries?*

Everyone's gathered in the lighthouse, and it's not just

because tonight we're on alert and will double up for the wrecking. It's in the hope that Cap'n will make a speech and we'll find something out.

Fear does strange things to people and the Wrecklings have reacted in very different ways. It doesn't help that we've had all this time without being told the facts so we're coming to our own conclusions.

Hattie has written a song, a terrible song, about Bobby Glass. She sings it when she's baking. It's a love song. It's creepy.

Rupert has started a 'Ban the Bobby' group. He has a petition that he tried to get me to sign yesterday. Norma's name was right at the top.

Kai is terrified of the commander. We found him in a cupboard, which he refuses to leave except to go to the loo, so we've started delivering his meals to him in there. Malcolm's set him up a reading light, and Willis found him a blanket and some comics. Jericho has even called off their wheelchair warfare – that's how bad it's got.

Any Wreckling who's lived outside our borders has told us what it's like beyond Haven Point. Their stories are all I've heard since they found out about Bobby Glass. It's like their old nightmares about being bullied and excluded, everything that ever brought them here and we've worked hard together to heal, has all come bubbling back to the surface. Their memories really hammered home what we have to lose.

And that's just the by-product of his mission – which was actually to seek out and capture a mermaid.

That's the huge threat hanging over our friends.

Over the last few years, we've all gradually taken over the wrecking roles from the grown-ups. Kids are just as good as adults at stuff if they're given the chance. Spot a skill – use it. You've got one leg or you're a wheelchair user and you want to push a handcart? We'll make it work. As we do make it work we'll discover solutions we didn't know existed that make other things work better too. You're blind and you want to be on watch? Let's get your ears so fine-tuned that they pick up on everything better than your eyes ever could.

We make the jobs ours.

I look out of the window and a cloud glides across the moon, darkening the sky. Right on time.

We're so dependent on the weather here. It can *whoosh* and rain so that even with your hood up it comes in horizontal and drenches the top of your head. You get the food ready for bonfires on the beach because it's been beautiful all day, then, just as soon as you're set, sea fret descends and you can't see your hand in front of you.

But for one night only, every single Sunday without fail, the sky is just as it needs to be.

We always get a perfectly black night for a wrecking.

Whenever I ask Ephyra or Cap'n about it, they wriggle out of a proper answer. But I know they've fixed it *somehow*, that it's part of the sea-magic. That's one for me and Badger to get back to investigating later.

My tummy goes woozy. Me and Badger will never be allowed to investigate anything ever again. Not after Bobby. And that's why we're all crammed in Old Ben tonight. Everyone who can be here is.

We've managed to bagsy the prime spot right near the gong.

'Who's with the toddlers?' I ask Badger.

'Laura.'

'Is she well enough today?' I ask.

'She says it's worth the energy,' answers Badger.

Laura gets knackered easily. Not a bit tired, but some days noise or even light is just too much. She says it's like her battery doesn't get as full as mine, even when she sleeps and sleeps; it's always flashing to say it needs a recharge. So she has to make choices, sometimes between big things like a party, or watching a film, and sometimes between brushing her teeth or sitting up. She says she's a life in balance. She pulls her weight as much as anyone else, but on her own terms like we all do; we measure worth differently here.

Cap'n doesn't need the gong tonight, which due to our close proximity is lucky for our ears. Although it's heaving and we're squished together, there's actually very little noise, and no football being kicked about.

We're all waiting. We want to know the plan.

'May I have your attention?' says Cap'n, and the little bit of noise that there was fades away. Maura stands by his side, translating his words with her hands.

'You will all by now be aware of the ongoing situation, which was brought to light in the most efficient manner, involving not the smallest bit of skulduggery, by some of our younger members.'

Pretty much the entire lighthouse turns to stare at me.

'He said "members",' I say. 'Not just ruddy me. Stare at them too.'

'Don't bother,' says Badger. 'I won't be able to see.'

Jericho snorts and starts coughing so Willis slaps him

on the back. Jericho gives him such a death stare that Willis stops and steps away.

Cap'n shakes his head and carries on. 'The situation is currently under control, watches are in place and we're working hard to solve the mystery of why he's here.'

'Why aren't we being involved in this mystery-solving?' yells Rupert, who usually works in the kitchen. 'Leave him alone with me for five minutes and that would sort it.'

Some of his mates cheer. Other people tut.

'You elected members of this community to the board. They are making the decisions, which are therefore yours. We're filtering down the information as we gather it,' says Kelvin.

Kelvin's calm makes me feel calmer. I make a mental note to find him some coot quills. He says they're the best sort. I'll just give them to him this time, not barter. I'll make sure he knows that's a one-off, mind. Can't have people thinking I'm going soft.

Rupert does not look happy, but he stays quiet. So does everyone else.

Cap'n looks round the room. 'Thank you all for making yourselves available to be here. I know that some of you were shocked by my decision to proceed with tonight's wrecking and I would rather have cancelled it, but needs must. We're running low on vital medicines and equipment, which the mermaids tell me are on the ship that's about to sail past our bay.'

Cap'n continues. 'It will be much busier on the beach tonight than you've been used to. We must ensure that the noise is kept to a minimum, and that those of you offering assistance –' he stares at Rupert as he says this – 'do so in order to speed up the job at hand, not in order to take over. The young people are in charge. You are merely backup.'

I look over and Rupert is rolling his eyes. He waits until Kelvin has his back to him and sticks two fingers up. I'm glad Rupert's not helping me.

Cap'n continues. 'Once you leave here, control passes to Large and Ephyra. You do exactly what they say, when they say it. Let's keep this speedy and safe. Fair winds and following seas.'

We all repeat it back to him. 'Fair winds and following seas.'

★

Large moves quickly towards the door and, after a brief hushed word with Cap'n, he puts something in his coat pocket and then leaves for the beach.

Willis, Jericho, Badger and I are all in the same crew so we linger by the gong until we're called.

The atmosphere is decidedly iceberg. Jericho growls if Willis looks at him. Badger is trying to pretend nothing's wrong and I haven't got the energy left to be bothered. Malcolm and Norma have finished their watch at the mouth of Cave Four, so they join us. They'll be with us on the wrecking.

Norma beckons to me and we sit down so we're on the same level. 'I hear you were in the cave with *him*,' she says.

It's not the first time this has been said to me. I thought I'd enjoy being a celebrity, but actually it's tedious. No one cares what I did. They just want gossip from me that they can take away and twist.

'What did he say?' she asks. She looks around to see if anyone's listening in, then stares right at me and waits, biting the edge of her lip.

I don't want to talk about it. I haven't been able to put it right in my head. That, despite everything, there was something about him I liked. Especially after what he wrote in that blasted diary.

Luckily, Gordon comes over and I say hi to him instead of answering Norma. She goes to speak again, then her nose wrinkles and she slips off the seat and takes a step away. Gordon's been pulled out of retirement to assist Badger, much to her disgust. 'He smells, Alph. How am I supposed to concentrate with him making me want to barf?'

Gordon keeps ferrets, which are eye-wateringly pungent. Even though the lighthouse is busy, he has space around him.

'You'll manage, Badge,' I say.

'Thanks for that, great help.'

'Come on,' says Malcolm. 'It's our turn.'

We all move over to the table by the door where Maura is ladling out the soup made from the razor clams Ephyra and I caught the other day. Bloomin' heck, that feels like absolutely yonks ago.

I take a mug and drink a mouthful. It's sweet, not very salty, or even fishy.

'Oi,' says Badger. 'You forgot to clink.'

I cheers her mug against mine. Then Jericho's. Then I hold mine out to Willis. He looks unsure, but I hold my mug out steady. He clinks it and grins. He holds his mug out to Jericho. Jericho just shakes his head.

'Too soon?' asks Willis. I nod and push him out of the door.

★

It takes longer to reach the sand than usual. So many people are waiting for the lift that, by the time we get down to the bottom, chattering has broken out and the urgency of Cap'n's speech has worn off.

Badger doesn't bother going over to the Needle. 'No point yet, Alph. I can't hear above this racket.'

CRACK. The air fizzles and I slam my hands over my ears.

Large stands at the tideline with an air gun. He shakes his head at all of us and puts the gun in his pocket. Enough of us could hear it to shut everyone else up. He lifts both hands up to his temples and then, keeping them the same width apart, pushes them forward towards us.

'Concentrate,' he signs and says.

'Mwah,' says Badger as she blows me a kiss and scurries off to the Needle.

'Fwah,' I reply.

Large pauses. We watch. He claps. Light flashes. We begin.

★

We're racing with our carts; we can see the ship; the mermaids are leaping; their song is building. It's all clockwork and everyone's a team.

Boxes and crates, person to person, moving up the beach. The human chain is chaining. Up to the Knot Crew, hauling, hauling –

It happens so fast.

I hear a whipping noise with a *whoosh*, then a massive sickening thud.

I hear Badger – *Yammer. Yammer yammer krock squeak. Yammer. Yammer yammer krock squeak.*

The albatross. Twice in two days.

Then the silence is broken by screaming.

Large yells and signs, 'HOLD.'

Everyone does.

Everyone knows to fight their fear and stand still. The only thing worse than the sound of that screaming would be chaos.

Large begins to run up the beach towards the cliffs. As he passes me, he taps me on the shoulder and nods. I run after him.

Chapter Twenty-two

Large and I reach the base of the cliff. 'What happened?' he asks.

No one answers.

I try to piece it together from what I can see.

One of the knots must have come loose. A crate has plummeted down the cliff and landed on Kelvin.

Oh my seas, *Kelvin*.

I get that bad-giggle thing, the naughty one that sneaks out at the wrong time.

Rupert is by the cliff, leaning right into it like he wants it to swallow him. He's shaking and there's sick on his chin, on his jumper. 'I only meant to . . .'

There's the smell of iron in the air, overpowering

the stench of stale seaweed and the ammonia of seagull poo by the cliff edge.

'Answer me,' says Large, turning to Henry who heads up the Knot Crew.

'Rupert sent it up before I'd checked his knot,' says Henry. 'He knows we do a three-person check. I told him once already. That was the second one he sent up without my permission.'

The screaming is awful. But at least screaming means breathing.

I glare at Rupert, then I kneel beside Kelvin.

The edge of the crate is wedged right along his chest. There's blood and he looks too flat. The iron smell makes me want to retch, especially when I realize it's coming from him. I don't think Ephyra's pine sap is going to be enough for this.

Wendy kneels beside me. 'I don't know what to do,' she says.

'Take his hand,' I reply. 'Talk to him.'

'About what?'

'I don't know – it doesn't matter,' I say. Then I think maybe it does, especially if these are the last words . . . I can't finish that sentence. 'Birds. Law. Postcards.'

Wendy looks blank. Nearly cries, says, 'I don't know about birds. I don't know about any of those things.'

'Something you do know then. Make it up!'

Wendy begins to talk about her BMX, asks Kelvin if he rides. I imagine Kelvin on a BMX. It would be funny if Kelvin didn't keep screaming.

I stand back up and look at Large. 'We need Cap'n,' I say.

Large shakes his head. 'He won't –' Large checks himself. 'He *can't*. He's done so much this week. Don't think he could help down here anyway. Need to get Kelvin Up Top to surgery.'

We needed the medical supplies from that ship! My heart thumps. Got to hope we have what we need Up Top. 'Do you think he's OK to be moved?'

Large pauses and thinks. I wait.

'No,' he says, shaking his head. 'But we don't have a choice.'

We stand together for a moment, then Large turns to give instructions.

We are so isolated here. That's a good thing, that's the best thing, but since Able Rate Bobby Glass arrived everything is different.

We're all bloomin' broken, but I've never seen anything so final, so scary as Kelvin just lying there –

Then the thing that's been scratching at the inside of my brain, trying to make itself heard, shoots into focus. We do have a choice.

I can't believe I'm about to do this, but all the rules have changed and it's the only chance we've got to save Kelvin.

'No! Don't move him,' I say to Large. 'Not yet. Give me your torch. And the gun.'

Chapter Twenty-three

The inside of Cave Four is not friendly at night and especially when lit only by weak torchlight.

The beam swoops in crackly angles and makes shadows where they shouldn't be. It isn't strong enough to light all the way to the back and, although I know nothing is lurking, my body doesn't seem to realize.

The books on Bobby's desk.

I stumble over a rock because I can't work out the best way to hold the torch for maximum foot visibility and minimum fear.

People don't carry big fat books about bodies with them for no reason. Those books are special to him. Why?

I slip and make a 'whoa' noise and flap about a bit. I stop. Breathe.

When I begin to walk again, I deliberately slow down otherwise I'm not going to make it to him without breaking a bit of me.

I peer round the wall and he's looking straight at me.

I forgot he can hear me; it's just that I can't hear him.

So that's the surprise gone then. I wonder if my 'whoa' sounded really wussy or maybe a tiny bit cool.

There's a small lamp just out of his kicking distance so I turn off the torch to conserve its battery.

'To what do I owe the honour of your company?' Bobby says to me.

'Shut up,' I say. 'Just shut up, shut up, shut up.'

He does.

I crouch next to the lamp and my fretting hands twiddle with the metal handle. I see him watching me and I put my hands behind my back. I'm sick of them giving me away.

'Why do you have those books with you?' I ask him.

He just looks at me.

'The ones of the bodies.'

'You mean my textbooks?'

I nod.

'Because I'm studying to be a doct–' He pauses. 'Because I *was* studying to be a doctor.'

'Did you hear the scream?'

It's his turn to nod.

'If you're a doctor, you have to help. It's the law.'

'I'm not a doctor,' Bobby says. 'And it doesn't work like that.'

'It does. The Hippocampus oath.' Yet another thing to tell Kelvin if . . . *when* he gets better. That something else of his came in useful.

'The hippocampus is located in the medial temporal lobe of your brain. The Hippocratic oath, which I have not taken, does mean one should treat those that are ill to the best of one's ability.'

I shake my head. I have no idea what he's just said.

'Right,' I say. 'So can you?'

'Can I what?' he asks.

'Help.'

★

I point the air gun at not-quite-doctor Bobby Glass as he walks in front of me.

He has the torch in his mouth because his wrists are tied behind his back. I'm not sure this is a good idea –

the torch and him in front, not the wrists. Keeping his hands behind him is definitely a good idea, but without the torch he kept falling over because he couldn't see where he was going, and I didn't want him behind me because then I had to walk backwards to keep the gun focused on him and *I* kept falling over.

After I freed him from the column, and untied his feet, it took a bit of ironing things out to get this far.

Luckily, his wrists had been tied together, and a separate rope attached him to the column. Wrecklings are very good at knots so I know his hands are staying put.

My elbow knacks from where I clonked it when I fell.

Torch in his mouth, him first, was his suggestion. I just pretended it was mine and waved the gun a bit more.

★

The screaming is like background noise. The loud comes when the screaming stops.

Bobby pauses, then picks up his pace.

Near the mouth of the cave, starlight creeps in where the ground becomes less rocky. I take the torch out of his mouth, grab his wrists, stand behind him and place the barrel of the gun in the small of his back. We walk out together.

As soon as Large spots us, he comes straight over and grabs Bobby by the upper arm. I feel safer now Large has him.

Bobby looks scared. Then concern takes over as he sees Kelvin under the crate.

Kelvin who isn't screaming any more.

Bobby goes to move towards him, but Large won't let him.

'I need to get nearer,' says Bobby.

Large looks at me and I shrug. 'He's sort of a doctor,' I say.

It turns out that was the end of my idea. I have no clue what I'm doing now.

Large drags Bobby over to Kelvin and pushes him down beside him. Wendy shuffles over to give him space.

'Is he breathing?' asks Bobby.

Wendy just looks at Bobby, in awe, like she's met someone famous.

Bobby speaks again. 'Since he stopped screaming, has anyone checked if he's still breathing?'

Everyone shakes their head.

I kneel down by Kelvin and bend forward. I put my ear over his mouth.

'He's breathing,' I say.

'Good. That's your job now,' Bobby tells me. 'If he stops breathing, you tell me immediately. He'll have passed out with the pain.'

Bobby shuffles to try to get a closer look at where the crate is stuck in Kelvin. He teeters because having his arms tied behind his back makes him unbalanced. Large has to grab him before he headbutts Kelvin.

'I need my arms free,' says Bobby.

'No flippin' way,' I say, then go back to breath-watch.

Large picks up the gun from where I've laid it beside me. He walks back over to Bobby and with one hand drags him to his feet. Large grabs the top of Bobby's shirt, just under his neck, and balls the material together in his fist. Then, with ease, he lifts him off the ground and points the gun between his eyes.

'Hurt anyone. Try to escape. I will kill you,' says Large.

Bobby nods.

Large places Bobby's feet back on the ground, but doesn't leave go.

Bobby nods again.

'Untie him,' Large says to Henry.

Henry does as he's told and hands the rope to Large

who puts it in his pocket with one hand, all the time keeping the air gun trained on Bobby Glass.

Bobby wiggles his wrists, rubs one then the other, and then begins shouting orders at the Knot Crew.

He checks Kelvin's pulse, gets Wendy to raise his legs, keeps asking me about the breathing and I keep saying it's fine. He examines the line along Kelvin's chest. Then looks at Large.

'There's nothing more I can do without moving the crate, which I don't want to do, but we don't have a choice. I need a stretcher to carry him on. I need blankets to stem the bleeding and to keep him warm. If he isn't already in shock, then he soon will be once we take that off his chest. It all needs to go fast. It all needs to go calm. Then we all need to get him somewhere clean and with medical supplies. Everyone got that?'

Large stares, allows it all to sink in. My hands clench. I feel panicky again – will we have enough supplies?

Bobby is about to speak again, but I catch his eye and shake my head. 'Give him a mo,' I whisper.

Then Large begins calmly but firmly giving tasks to the Wrecklings. They run off to carry out his orders.

I keep on monitoring Kelvin's breathing. I measure it in Mississippis. I've only ever used them on razor clams. I never thought I'd need them in a situation like this, with Large pointing a fake gun at a prisoner who's helping a crushed Wreckling.

I go back to doing Mississippis. It's better than thinking.

Some of the Hauling Crew arrive back with a surfboard to use as a stretcher, and loads of towels from the hut.

'Will this do?' asks Large.

Bobby nods. 'Good work.'

He pauses, loses his doctor face for a moment. I find myself smiling at him even though I don't mean to. Just to will him on, like.

'Right, we're doing this,' Bobby says more to himself than anyone else. 'We're doing this,' he says again louder, like he means it.

'Ready?' he asks Large.

'Ready,' Large says.

'On three. One. Two. Three.'

Large, Henry and the others heave the chest off Kelvin. I have to duck so they don't barrel it into my head as they sweep it away.

Kelvin's eyes open wide and his head shoots up so I have to grab it. He begins to scream for about two of the longest seconds ever, then his eyes roll back in his head and he flops back down.

Bobby is pressing more and more towels on to the wound and they're immediately going red then black.

'Is he still breathing?' he asks me.

'Still breathing,' I say.

Large is back and takes a corner of the surfboard, so does Henry and two of the others.

'You there,' Bobby says to Wendy. 'Keep a hold of his feet.'

Bobby grabs Kelvin's shoulders and I struggle to my feet. My legs have gone to sleep so I bounce to wake them up.

'On three,' Bobby says again, and this time on three they drag Kelvin on to the surfboard stretcher. On the next count of three, the surfboard is lifted up.

I stay at the head to check Kelvin's breathing. Bobby stands by his chest and presses the soggy towels on him. He keeps getting handed more and the blood keeps soaking through.

'Move,' says Bobby, and we do, straight towards the lift. The rest of the Wrecklings leave the positions they've been waiting in since Large yelled at us all, forever ago, after we first heard Badger's albatross and then the screaming.

They form a silent column that follows in our wake.

★

In a déjà vu scene from when we found Willis, Cap'n is standing in the doorway of Old Ben and shepherds everyone inside. This time I'm allowed to enter and I'm not shooed away.

We go straight into the cold room, which is all tiled and mostly used for storage, but it's our surgery in emergencies. They've been busy Up Top. The room is clear apart from a table for Kelvin and a trolley with our surgical kit laid out on it. The room stinks of bleach.

Cap'n looks at Bobby, then drags him to the sink, turns on the tap and starts squirting soap into his hands. 'Can you talk and wash at the same time?'

Bobby nods and doesn't move his hands. Cap'n yanks them under the tap. 'Can you?'

Bobby looks a lot younger under electric light. I've only seen him in darkness before now.

'Yes,' he says, and begins scrubbing his fingers.

'Fill me in on what you know.' Cap'n starts scrubbing too.

Chapter Twenty-four

Five hours have passed since they closed the door and began to work on Kelvin.

Jericho, Willis, Large, Badger and I are curled up together in the old fishing hut. The floor is strewn with beanbags and blankets and we've got a fire going. Jericho keeps prodding it with a stick and giving orders to Willis to get more wood or damp it down or do whatever. I told Willis he didn't have to, but I think he figures that being shouted at is one step better than being ignored.

Badger is eating her third Belgian bun in the way you have to do it, following the swirl from the out to the in, cherry last. We had to teach Willis because he just took a big chomp out of the side. He's got a lot to learn.

'Dyo fink heesa-addy-en?'

'Want to spit that at me again, Badge?' I say as I wipe my face.

Badger swallows the piece of bun she was chewing. 'I feel sick. Shouldn't have eaten so much.'

'Yup,' says Large. 'You ate mine.'

'Soz, Large. You snooze, you lose.'

'What did you say?' I ask her.

'Oh yeah. So, do *you* think he's a baddie?'

This is what we've been going back and forth with all night.

I don't know the answer about Bobby Glass. All I'm sure of is that Kelvin would definitely be dead by now if it wasn't for him.

'Well, he helped,' I say. 'He didn't have to.'

'Maybe he only came out of the cave to spy on us. Learn more about how we operate to tell the commander,' says Jericho.

'Or to escape,' says Willis.

'But he didn't, did he?' says Large.

That's the thing that we've been circling round all night, in between dozing and eating cake. Bobby had the chance to run, and he didn't take it.

Chapter Twenty-five

There's black again, and the smell of charred flesh – She has her back to the door. I try to call out, but I can't because I'm a baby, and there's shadow behind her and ahead of her – and the smell makes me retch and then all of me, *all of me,* is aflame, and there's a bright white light –

'Wake up, Alph! Please, you're scaring me,' says Badger.

I'm awake but not, can hear her, but can't quite leave the dream behind. I can feel Badger prodding my arm, then splatting her hands on my face, trying to open my eye. She accidentally sticks her finger up my nose, which makes the dream retch a real retch.

When I open my eye, she's wiping her finger on her jeans.

'Yuck, Alph. Next time I'm leaving you to it,' she says.

'Taking one for the team, Badge. Full marks for effort.'

Badger giggles.

I look around the hut. It's empty. 'Where is everyone?'

'Gone to find breakfast, mainly because I may have accidentally eaten all the buns. You were sleeping; they didn't want to wake you.'

I sit up and stretch. There's an awful smell in the room: stale sweat, iron, fish and sleep breath. I sniff my T-shirt. It appears to be mainly coming from me.

'I stink.'

'Yup,' says Badger. 'You stink *bad*. But I do too, so at least that's something.' She smiles and holds her hand out to drag me up. I take it and haul.

My body does not want to move. It objects strongly and every single bit of me, bits I didn't even know I had, aches. My ankle hurts.

The glint.

It's like the pain brings back everything that's happened since I first saw it and it's overwhelming and I forget how to move.

Badger keeps hold of my hand.

'Everyone's OK,' she says. 'They are, Alph. They're all OK.'

'Kelvin?'

'Even Kelvin.'

'How? I've never seen anyone look that . . . broken.'

'Have you met the Wrecklings before?' asks Badger.

I smile, but it's not touching my eye.

'They fixed him up. They've had to take out some of his insides, not actually sure which bits . . . He won't be properly better, not for ages, and he might not stay better, but for now – well . . .'

'He's alive,' I say.

'He's alive.'

I put on the yellow waterproof and muddle fastening the zip. My hands are shaking and I'm glad Badger can't see it. 'How do you know all this stuff?'

'Maura called in to check on everyone – Large mainly, I think. She said they were making breakfast and told us then.'

'What about Bobby?'

Badger shrugs. 'That was definitely left out.'

'On purpose?'

Badger shrugs again.

'I'm not having that,' I say. 'We found him. He's ours.'

'And she's back in the room,' announces Badger.

I grin and open the door.

★

There's a quiet, orderly queue by the breakfast table. It feels wrong. It's felt wrong ever since we found Bobby. I'll never moan about our chaos again. I *really* want it back.

'I can't hear Cap'n,' says Badger. I look around and she's right. He's not there. Neither is Maura.

'This is most definitely not where the party is at,' I tell her. 'Let's go.'

'Where?'

'I'm guessing they're all in Cave Four. If they're making plans, we deserve to know about them. And if they're not? Well, then *we* need to be making them.'

'What are we missing?' asks Jericho, who rolls up behind me with Large and Willis in his wake.

'We found Bobby,' I tell them. 'Me and Badger. It's not on if we're not involved in whatever they're coming up with.'

'Darn right!' yells Willis and shoots his hand up.

'Are you asking to come or summat?' asks Jericho. 'And who says "darn"?'

Jericho waits for us to laugh. We don't. He has the decency to let his cheeks go red.

Willis goes quiet and drops his hand, then his eyes. It's like Jericho has popped him. We don't know where to look.

'I didn't say you *couldn't* come,' says Jericho.

Jericho looks really serious and Willis like he wants to cry. I'm about to say something, but I don't know what when Large bangs Jericho on the back.

'Great joke, mate. One of your best, that was.' He links his arm through Willis's. 'Let's go.'

Once again, Large has it completely sorted.

★

No one bothers us as we leave Old Ben, which I find weird because someone is nearly always telling us off or making us do stuff.

It feels like someone's watching us. Hairs rise on my arms, my neck. My ears ache. It feels like that uncomfortable being-watched feeling on the beach when I thought it was my mam, all that time ago. And I was right, wasn't I? Maybe not who I thought, but someone *was* spying on us. I look around, but I can't see anything.

Everyone in front of me comes to a stop and I walk into the back of Jericho's wheelchair.

'Darn it,' says Jericho, but he's not taking the mick out of Willis.

'What?' asks Badger.

'Norma and Malcolm are on guard,' says Willis.

The watching feeling is still there. I rattle my head to shake it off.

'Darn it indeed,' says Badger. 'That's that then.'

'Darn it,' we all say at the same time and half-heartedly smile, though it was worth at least a group snigger. We reverse and hunker down behind the wall where the mouse lives before they spot us.

Only Willis stays standing, undeterred. 'No, it's not "that's that then". Darn it. Nope. No, sir.' He flings back his shoulders. 'Jericho, you're with me.'

Jericho looks startled and is about to say something, but bites it down and wheels towards Willis.

'You three, wait for my signal – you'll know what it is – then race to the steps by the lift. You can use them to get down to Cave Four.'

'They're out of bounds,' says Large. 'Dangerous.'

'They are, yes,' says Willis. 'Have you got any other ideas?'

We all shake our heads.

'Ready?' asks Willis.

We nod.

Willis gives us a little smile, oomphs himself up into old-Willis mode and goes stomping off to Norma and Malcolm, Jericho following behind him.

We stand and wait, ready, knowing that at some point we have to run. The steps aren't far from here, but it's impossible to get to them without being seen. And Large is right: they are out of bounds.

We can't hear what Jericho and Willis are saying, but they seem to be working as a team and there's lots of arm waving. It's weird seeing them next to each other. Nice weird.

'Badger,' says Large. 'Make your ears work.'

'I can't,' she says. 'The wind keeps snatching the words away.'

There's a sudden movement from Willis and it looks like he's lost it with Jericho. He's running and pushing Jericho towards the cliff edge. Jericho is screaming, and Norma and Malcolm are yelling and running after them.

Large and I look at each other in disbelief and then we're running too – right towards Jericho to save him.

Jericho sees us coming, shakes his head and frantically points towards the steps. We turn in the opposite direction and slam straight into Badger.

We need to get better at telling each other the plan.

Luckily, no one's looking at us because all eyes are on Willis and Jericho and my eye is on them too, until Large grabs our hands and yells at Badger and me to hurry.

We hurtle over the uneven grass and make it round the side of the lift to the steps. We begin our descent.

The steps are flaking with orange rust. It smells like old blood. They hug the cliff tight. There's a handrail, but it dangles. The sea air has battered and eaten the posts that hold it in place.

We race down, step by step, zigzagging the cliff, trying to cling as close to its face as possible to avoid going near the unprotected edge. I have to slow down because my eye can't keep up with my feet. Badger is ahead of me and has her hands on Large's shoulders. She's following him, trusting him.

I'm so focused on my feet that I nearly barrel into Badger's back and knock her and Large flying as they come to a dead stop in front of me. Large does this comedy, not-actually-funny windmilling with his arms and eventually takes a step back from the edge. He stands on my feet. I don't even mind.

When we stop panicking, we look over the edge.

'What's up?' asks Badger.

There's a chunk of steps missing is what's up.

Large hasn't moved and I pat him slowly on the back. It probably soothes me more than it soothes him. 'That was close,' he finally says.

I feel real anger all of a sudden. *Bobby!* Bloomin' Bobby. If it wasn't for him, none of this would be happening.

Large crouches down and the step creaks.

I quickly take a step up, and then feel awful that I left them both on a creaky step. 'Sorry,' I say.

'Why?' asks Badger.

'Nothing,' I say.

Badger not-looks at me and shakes her head. 'What's the plan then?'

I peer over the edge. 'It's a big drop, Badge.' Which even for me is a massive understatement.

Still crouching, Large lets out a big huff. 'Nee bother.'

He turns round and shoves us both backwards up the

steps to give himself room. Puffs of white chalk come out of the bolts where the steps cling to the cliff. I don't tell Badger. I just stop looking at the dodgy bolts.

Large slowly and carefully gets on to his knees. He can't fit completely on the step and is at an awkward angle, half dangling over the edge.

My heart pounds in my teeth. 'Large, what are you doing?'

'Shh,' he says.

When Large tells you to shush, you shush.

The whole staircase groans and big clods of white drop down. They smash on the rocks below.

'What was that?' asks Badger.

'Nothing,' I say, but I take her hand and squeeze it.

Large wriggles until he's kneeling on the edge of the step, looking over. His toes and fingertips barely cling on. He pauses. Takes a slow breath. Then he lets go and leans forward into the void.

It happens before I realize what he's going to do, and before I can yell his left hand is sliding down the cliff face, his right suspended in mid-air, and he's dangling, falling until – *clunk* – his feet kind of catch him and get wedged up the back of the step.

'Ooof,' he says.

'What the heck just happened?' asks Badger as the steps bounce and clang.

I shake my head, which she can't see, so I shrug, which she can feel because my insides are now in my throat and I can't actually speak.

Large is dangling off the step, far above the beach below, held only by his feet, his toes squished between the cliff face and the step above.

'Quick,' he says.

'Quick what?' I yell at upside-down him. There's hysteria in my voice.

'I'm a ladder,' he says.

Badger giggles at how ridiculous this sounds and I do too because – oh my sails! – he is, and you can't let a human ladder just *dangle*. If he can be that brave, the least I can do is try to be a smidgen brave too.

I lean over, telling Badger where I'm putting my hands, and I begin to crawl down Large.

He groans and I get to his arms and close my eye because this is not fun and it feels safer not to see. I keep lowering myself down him until my hands are in his. He lets out a roar and then uses his whole body weight to swing from his feet. I open my eye just as he lets go of me and I'm flying from a human trapeze and my legs aren't going to reach the other step. I'm falling – *falling* –

– and then I'm there.

'I'm there!' I yell.

I'm there, on the next section of steps.

I'm alive and I'm breathing and, oh holy Neptune, that gap looks even bigger from down here, which is something I definitely do not tell Badger.

With us telling her where to stick her hands, Badger quickly makes it down to me. I grab her when Large lets go, and haul her by the waist on to the step with so much force that we both tumble together down a few steps.

When I look back up, Large is still in the same position.

'You OK?' I call.

'Yup. Just getting my wind back.'

'Sure?' He doesn't sound sure. Or OK.

'Yup.'

I watch as he very slowly kind of wiggles and jiggles and bucks a bit and uses his hand up the cliff to kind of backwards slide-walk himself up. When he finally gets on to the last step and upright, his face is the colour of a beetroot.

'Just going to sit for a while,' Large says. 'Nice view. Go!'

'Really?' I say.

'Go,' he says.

Badger places her hands on my shoulders and we go.

★

As we're running across the beach towards Cave Four, I look up and Large is beginning, very slowly, to make his way back up the steps. I can't see big chunks of cliff falling, but I still cross my fingers and think of knots to be on the safe side.

'Alpha!' Badger yells as we run. 'Wouldn't it have been easier if Large had dangled by his hands?'

'Never, ever tell him that!' I yell back, and we save our lungs for running.

Chapter Twenty-six

Nobody is guarding the entrance to Cave Four. They obviously thought that having Norma and Malcolm by the lift Up Top was enough.

The prickle of watching is still round my neck, but it's probably just all the 'upheaval' as Norma would call it. She likes to play things down.

We slow to a walk and stick to the wet seaweed bits. Slippy but quiet.

'Have we actually made a plan?' whispers Badger.

'Nope,' I reply. 'But we found him – it's our cave, so we get a say in this too.'

★

The entrance to Cave Four is dark. The sun is at the wrong angle and I can't see beyond the opening, so we hug the cliff wall and peer round the edge. I'm about to step forward when Badger grabs my arm and yanks me back.

A few moments later, I hear what Badger heard, and out into the light storms Henrietta. She's sheathing her razor-clam blades and muttering to herself. She marches to the sea on shimmering legs and dives straight in.

I take this to mean that things aren't going marvellously in there.

Badger cocks her head, then takes my hand, and we walk into the cave.

★

We stay in the shadows before the light from the lamps on the table can reach us and give us away. Cap'n, Peter, Ephyra and Shelly are at the table. In fact, bar Henrietta, they're the same faces from the other day. Minus Kelvin.

Bobby sits there now too.

He makes me feel weird, all jumbled up in my head. He said sorry to me. I heard him. Then he helped Kelvin and he didn't run away. But that's exactly what a good spy *would* do if he'd been discovered. But getting found makes him a pretty rubbish spy. The diary said he'd been here for yonks, watching us. So he could have given the signal and told the commander about us before we even found him and he didn't.

Badger nudges me. I grab her hand. 'Close enough,' I spell into it. She nods.

'What is the process of informing the commander that you'd found mermaids?' asks Cap'n, and my ears perk up.

But what if he lies?

Bobby's voice is rich, with longer vowels than mine that slip and slide like they're made of cream.

'The dots and dashes at the back of my diary, that's the pattern.'

'It's not Morse code,' says Cap'n.

'I thought you would have tried that,' says Bobby. 'It's completely unintelligible. It means "mission complete".'

'You transmit it how exactly?'

I can't understand half the words they're saying, but I think I get the gist. Bobby's hands are bandaged now and he winces as he moves them. Cap'n is making notes, his head down, and he's kept it out of his voice, but I can tell he's tense by the way he's gripping his pen. He'll make holes in his paper like that and have to mark himself down a grade.

'It's simple. Find a high spot, like the pillbox, wait for darkness, use a torch and begin the pattern.'

'How do you know it's been received?'

'I don't.'

Cap'n looks up from the table where he's been scribbling. 'You *don't*?'

'I'm nowhere near important enough to get a signal back.'

Cap'n asks more questions. Bobby says he doesn't know.

Central Fins disappearance? Don't know.

Commander's plans? No.

'Give us *something*!' yells Ephyra. She slams her fist down on the table and bares her teeth.

'I don't owe the commander anything,' says Bobby. 'I'd give you something, anything, all of it! If I had it.'

Cap'n places his hand on Ephyra's fist until it softens. I'm glad he does that. I would have done that.

'Tell us about the commander,' says Cap'n. 'Begin there.'

Bobby's frown deepens, then he makes an effort to drop his shoulders. He goes to speak, and then stops.

Ephyra stalks towards him. 'You held a gun to my Alpha's head. Want to keep up the same old not-telling-anything game? Go right ahead. See what these teeth can do to flesh.'

It's like Bobby's trying to weigh up the odds, who he's more scared of – the commander or Ephyra.

He swallows, hard, then begins to speak. 'The commander's name is Toombes – Horatio C. Toombes. Somehow he knows details about this place that he shouldn't, things that I haven't reported to him. I think he was watching you long before I got here.' He shakes his head, doesn't want to carry on.

He's terrified. So am I.

Ephyra takes another step closer to Bobby, who speaks just above a whisper. 'I don't think everything he knows could be from just watching. I think someone here is passing him information.'

Cap'n stands up with such force his chair flies out behind him. 'You have the gall to try to turn this back on us? To deflect suspicion away from you!'

Ephyra doesn't attack Bobby like I thought she would. She tilts her head to one side and steps away, as if she's trying to figure something out.

It's like Bobby's relieved to have finally said it cos all this other stuff comes out in a blurt. How things he overheard before he left that made no sense make sense now: the exact number of ship-breakers at a lighthouse. A kitten in a beard. How would the commander know details like that if he didn't have a spy? Then stuff about his dad serving with Toombes and how he never trusted him. About Toombes building his own squadron. How dangerous he is. I try to process what Bobby's said by counting pebbles larger than my big toe.

We've got a spy at Haven Point.

'There's a rumour that Toombes met a sea creature when he was a child,' says Bobby. 'No one believed him and he's been holding a grudge ever since.'

I wonder if that was one of the mermaids I know. Could it be one of the gaps in Cap'n and Ephyra's story?

We've been here for ages now and my back is beginning to ache from all the skulking.

'I need a break,' says Cap'n.

Everyone stretches. Peter goes over to the little stove and lights it. Ephyra begins to walk towards the cave entrance.

I shove Badger back and we hide in the shadows. She passes us by. She takes one more pace and then stops. She doesn't look at us, but speaks in a tiny voice only meant for our ears. 'Alpha, Badger, I could smell you both from over there. Leave. Now.'

She carries on walking.

Badger takes my hand and tugs. She's had enough.

I want to know everything, but no matter how much I adore Ephyra there's also a bit of me that's scared of her. I know what those teeth can do.

Chapter Twenty-seven

It's one of those rare blue days. The ones that make you dance even though you don't feel like it. Where breath matches sky matches chest, and your shoulders pull you taller. But, right now, the rare blue light is burning through my eyelid and it's 5 a.m., which is an inhuman time, and I can't get back to sleep.

I sneak out of the dorm, pulling on a baggy, snuggly jumper as I walk. It's got cats on it, three of them brushing their teeth. It's a hand-me-down from Laura, a bit too pink for my liking, but it's got fluff on the inside that feels snuggly.

I grab an apple from the windfall basket in the kitchen

and head to my bench in the garden, checking the apple for wormholes as I walk.

'What's worse than finding a worm in your apple? Half a worm,' is Large's favourite joke. When you've just found half a worm in your apple, it becomes less funny.

★

The bench is my unofficial thinking spot. It's always better to keep your thinkings a bit hidden; it makes sure you stay mysterious and unthreatening. I learned that from Ephyra.

Things have changed since Ephyra made me and Badger scram from Cave Four a week ago.

Bobby's still our prisoner. He's still being interrogated, monitored, under lock and key at night, but it gets a bit less official each day. The fear focus has shifted from him to the commander, and for me and my gang – who thus far have extraordinarily managed to keep it a secret – the possibility of having a traitor in our ranks.

Some Wrecklings believe that Bobby was never going to shop us. Other Wrecklings don't. A few think he already has, and that the commander will be here any moment.

The rest think Bobby's unwell, and made it all up, and that's how he got through the Boundaries. We should therefore look after him, just like we look after each other.

I think that the commander is watching and waiting for the right moment to strike, that the spy is feeding him information, that Bobby is somehow the only one who can get past our Boundaries. And then someone else talks to me and I forget my think. People have an opinion, then talk to someone and change it. Then change it back again. It makes my head hurt.

So do the arguments, which are spilling over into everything. Factions are forming; people are keeping secrets, hoarding things. It feels like it's all coming unglued round the edges.

Because of what happened to Kelvin, Cap'n just let us usual lot wreck as normal yesterday. It was successful – same old, same old. The wrecking was so routine it kept my mind clear, pulled me back into a time before Bobby. Almost as if the glint, and everything after it, never even happened. Until my ankle twinged and it was all helter-skelter in my head again.

It's in what happened to the Central Fins – or not knowing what happened – that the fear lies for a lot of us. The Wrecklings are terrified about how all this affects us, but I'm also scared about what it means for Ephyra and the rest of my mermaid friends In Deep. Even Cobalt.

I shake my head. This blue day, just for a minute, deserves happy thoughts. I think back to after the very first wrecking I took part in, when I was the only kid. I was wedged into the rock alcove at the base of the Needle and tied with seaweed so I couldn't wander.

But I didn't want to. I loved the bustle and urgency. Everyone, Wrecklings and mermaids, knowing their jobs and doing them. All under a velvet-black sky. Every time we do a wrecking now, I get that feeling. That being-a-part-of-something feeling.

But at the wrecking yesterday I didn't.

★

The only one of us who steadfastly believes in Bobby's innocence is Kelvin. I think, once he's well enough, he'll start making Bobby Fan Club badges.

Understandably, mind, cos he's not dead.

I'm still in the camp of don't-really-know. I'd like to trust him, but that's a big ask, and what if he's just a very good liar? It messes with my head that I even *want* to trust him. It would be much easier to hate him. Especially after everything he wrote – never mind about me – about my friends.

Friends always come first. That's the law.

Norma and Rupert are leading the anti-Bobby camp, which some people thought was weird as Malcolm is on Bobby's side and people thought that Norma and Malcolm would stick together. I guess they haven't heard the arguments I have, or watched Norma go storming off along the clifftops, leaving Malcolm looking lost.

Cap'n and Ephyra, they're the ones I trust. I always have and always will. Ephyra thinks Bobby's OK, just an unwilling pawn in a much bigger game. Cap'n doesn't know, so is deploying worst-case scenario procedures for the good of us all.

So that's helpful.

It doesn't help that we've been excluded from the interrogations. After the steps incident, they placed guards on the cave too.

I breathe and look out over the Stacks towards the horizon. Blue sea meets blue sky and it's hard to see where they separate.

I suck the blue into my lungs to make me feel lighter. My apple is sweet, I've got a fluffy jumper on, and life in this moment, if you get rid of all the thinking, is good.

I do a massive stretch, one of those where you don't realize how long you can make yourself and then, when you've finished, your body feels new and bouncy. I put my apple core in the hole in the wall where the mouse lives and leave through the gate.

There was another bloody shark tooth on my pillow this morning. Ephyra is up to something.

This time, I remember to knock twice on the wall before I leave.

★

Ephyra meets me at No Entry. I give her a hug and she swings me round and round. When she puts me down, I totter to the left because I seem to have forgotten where right is.

She giggles. I've missed her laugh. I've missed *her*. Bobby business has stolen her away. Now it feels like she's back and mine again. I don't tell her I love her and I've missed her and I need her to tell me what to think. Instead, I take her hand. I thought we were going In Deep, but she leads me into the mouth of Cave Four.

'It's looking good,' I say.

'Looking good? Is that all you have to say?' Ephyra pulls a mock-shock face and I laugh.

'It's divine, delightful and, holy Neptune, AWESOME!' I throw myself back and yell the awesome bit up into the rocky ceiling. 'Will that do?'

'Cheeky beggar,' says Ephyra, and prods me in the side.

'Oi. In all proper seriousness, it looks bloomin' beautiful.'

Ephyra gazes round the cave. 'It does, doesn't it?'

That's what I mean about things changing. This time, nearly a fortnight ago, I didn't know I was about to come face to face with a man holding a gun and then transport him in a wheelbarrow and keep him prisoner here. That Kelvin was about to be squashed by a crate, have surgery, be on bed rest for a month and lose an organ, but I still haven't remembered to ask which one.

Today Cave Four is being dressed up for Maura and Laura's wedding.

There are candles everywhere, ends melted to make a waxy glue and then stuck on to rock shelves. There are curtains of dried seaweed that glisten with iridescent fish scales. The shiny insides of mussel shells arc in patterns across the rock faces. Snail shells have been strung to make bunting that hangs over every available surface and in tumbling rows from the ceiling. It is stunning.

I hear a noise further back in the cave.

'Who's there?' I ask Ephyra.

'I've been putting the prisoner to work,' she says. 'May as well get something useful out of him while he's here.'

'How long *is* he here for?'

'I don't know, my sweet. We just don't know.'

'I thought he was with Kelvin?'

'He was, he is, but now Kelvin's getting better he doesn't need to be closely monitored all the time. I figured if I brought Bobby here we could talk to him, find out more. I know a certain someone was getting annoyed that they hadn't seen him properly since they were told to leave . . .'

Ephyra stares at me until I have to look away. She never blinks first.

'I thought this might help you make up your mind about him. Are you any good at weaving?' she asks. 'It's just that I've got a man back there who may be medically trained, and quite possibly a top-grade spy, but is seriously rubbish at making rugs.'

★

I surf, rock-climb and capture prisoners. I fly on hillsides and hurtle down quarries on tea trays. I come up with fiendish plans. I punch people when they're mean. Well, I haven't yet, but I would.

I'm really terrible at talking to new people.

Ephyra has to take my hand and drag me over to where Bobby is sitting on the floor. I pull my hair forward and over the side of my face. Ephyra notices and she tucks it behind my ear and then pushes my shoulders back and up. By the time I get to him, I'm hunched again and my face is re-covered.

'Hey, Alpha,' he says when he looks up and sees us both. 'It's really good to see you.'

I mumble something and Ephyra kicks me. I eventually say, 'Hi.' It comes out squished.

'I am close to admitting defeat,' Bobby says, and holds up a piece of knotty material. 'I can't work out where I'm going wrong. Care to offer any advice?'

Ephyra tuts and takes it out of his hands, then sits down cross-legged beside him. The edges of her land legs above the sand are shimmery, like they're not in focus.

I can see that Bobby has spotted it too. He's definitely taking it all in. *As a spy?* I still don't know.

I should have sat down straight away. Now too much time has passed and I feel silly. My limbs don't appear to belong to me and I can't remember what I usually do with my hands. I don't normally have to think about them, they just hang there, but now they're really heavy and awkward. I watch as Ephyra looks at Bobby's weaving and I try to pretend that I'm standing for a reason. This is awful.

'OK up there?' ask Ephyra.

'Yes,' I say. 'Fine, thanks.'

Fine, thanks? Now I'm stuck up here like a razor clam. Brilliant. Just flippin' brilliant.

Ephyra reaches up, grabs my arm and yanks so I sit down next to her. She looks at me and rolls her eyes. I pretend not to notice and then stick my tongue out at her when she looks away. Bobby sees. I think I should just go and swim out to sea now and never come back.

'How are you today?' asks Bobby.

I shrug. Small talk is rubbish. I wish I was back in bed.

Ephyra passes me a long strand of material and I begin to wind it up into a ball.

'What happened to your face, Alpha?' Bobby doesn't look at me when he asks the question, keeps his eyes on his awful weaving.

I ignore him. Asking that straight away when you don't even know someone? Not on.

'Sorry,' he says. 'I get awkward, and inappropriate things come out. Please forgive me.'

'Not the best of questions to lead with,' I say. It's my turn to not look at *him*.

'You're right. I'm learning – I'm trying! I promise I'll remember. I'll do better.'

I understand the awkward blurting thing. If he hadn't done it, chances are I probably would have – it was next on my list after forgetting how to have hands. I make sure my hair is still covering my face. 'I was a baby and there was a fire. That's all I know.'

'How did you get here?'

'Like I said, that's all I know. Cap'n found me in the Lux Soap Flakes box. He could go outside more then.'

'Wow,' says Bobby. 'Do you know how you got here? Of course you don't, sorry. You just said you didn't know. Do you know?'

I giggle even though I don't want to. We haven't had anyone new for ages. All the folk here have heard everyone else's stories countless times. It's nice having someone who's interested.

We sit in silence for a while. Ephyra hums, which she does when she's concentrating, like I poke out the tip of my tongue.

'Would you have actually shot me?' I ask Bobby. 'When you found me, I mean.'

He puts down his weaving and looks at me, but I carry on with what I'm doing. You can't have conversations like this *and* eye contact. That's far too much.

'I'm very sorry about everything that happened, Alpha. I can't begin to tell you how much.'

'That's not an actual answer,' I say.

'No, you're right, it's not. Of course I wouldn't have. I had it with me to shoot rabbits. I wasn't expecting anyone to be there and before I had time to think about it I'd drawn my gun and it was in your face.'

'Then Badger whacked you out.'

'She did indeed.'

'She's dead chuffed about that, like.'

Bobby smiles and touches his head. 'She did a very good job.'

He pauses for a while and the silence is less scratchy. 'It scared me. Not just you being there, but the speed and ease with which I grabbed the gun. If I'm being very honest, Alpha, and I think I owe you that, I don't really know whether I would have shot you. And it terrifies me.'

I nod. I'm not sure what to think about this bit of information so I store it away for later.

'Tea?' asks Ephyra. Bobby says yes and I nod.

'I'll be there,' says Ephyra to me. 'Right there.' She pushes herself up and goes over to the little camping stove.

I carry on winding the material. Bobby picks up the end and makes sure it's unravelled for me. I watch him from under my hair.

His eyes are very blue and his hair is more red in this light and it still doesn't know which direction to go in. His nose is OK, and his hands have healed; Ephyra must have used the pine sap on him. I wonder what swears he said. His stubbly beard is ginger and grey, but he doesn't have any wrinkles. I can't tell how old he is so I ask him.

'Twenty-three,' he replies. He strokes his beard and smiles. 'Hard paper round.'

I have no idea what that means so I ignore it. 'Nearly the same as Ephyra. She'll be twenty-four next spring. Or at least she will be in human years.'

I can tell that Bobby has lots of questions about that because his face kind of chomps. I ask him another question, one that's been bugging all of us. 'What's an Able Rate?'

'The lowest of the low.' He smiles. 'My turn.'

I think he's going to ask me how old I am, but then he

comes up with a question that I definitely wasn't expecting. 'Are you happy here?'

I don't know what to do with that, so I don't say anything. Of course I'm happy here – it's my home. What a ridiculous waste of a question.

'Why did you do it?' I ask him back.

'I was sent by Naval Commander Horatio C. Toombes to discover a mermaid colony and to return with a specimen.'

Hearing him say the word *specimen* out loud makes my insides go cold. I look over to Ephyra, and then back to Bobby.

'You thought that was OK?' I proper stare at him.

'OK? I thought he was deluded! It was an excellent excuse to get away from everything, grab a rucksack and tramp up the coast. For the first time in forever, I felt free. Of course I wasn't going to find any, never mind bring one back. Mermaids don't exist.'

Bobby looks at Ephyra too. She's humming again as she adds sugar to her tea. Mermaids don't usually have a taste for sweet things. They live on raw fish, algae, seaweed, seals. Or at least they do if they don't have a child in their care who loves cake. It rubbed off on Ephyra and now she has very sweet, very sharp teeth.

Bobby shakes his head. 'This whole thing was –' he searches for the word – 'unexpected.'

'Anyway,' I say, 'I already know that. What I mean is, why did you join up, or whatever you call it?'

'Ah,' he says. 'That's more of an interesting question. Well done.'

Ephyra comes over with our tea and we take our mugs, then she sits back down again.

'I asked Bobby –'

'I heard,' she says. We both look at him, her full on, me through my hair.

'My family are important. Well, their name is, and that means a lot to my mother.'

'Is she the grumpy one in the photo?' At least he now knows it's not just him that does the awkward blurt. My heart catches a little as I remember who I *thought* it was.

'Yes,' he says. 'That's her. The boy with the dreadful socks is me, and the man with the medals and the moustache is my father. He was also Robert, but never Bobby.' He sips his tea but puts it down straight away. I bet it burned his tongue. Then he picks his weaving back up.

I blow on my tea to cool it, and the waves get a bit too choppy and some slop over the side. I lick the bottom of the mug so I don't waste any drips.

'My mother married my father thinking it would give her the chance to mingle with the higher echelons of society.' Bobby pauses as I throw up my hand and stare at him. 'Ranks,' he says. 'Or groups. Groups of people!'

I roll my eye and nod. *Don't you try to bamboozle me with your big words.*

He carries on. 'She did not count on Papa having a troubled mind. His head was broken by the things he'd seen during the war. He was a kind and gentle man with me; we spent lots of time together, just the two of us.'

'Twitching,' I say. He smiles and nods. Ephyra looks confused. 'It means birdwatching,' I tell her.

'We did indeed. Happy times. Then I went to Oxford. I was in my third year of medical training when I received the call to come straight back home. Papa had taken his own life, and with it my mother's good name, and her income.'

'I'm sorry to hear about your father,' says Ephyra, and puts her hand on his. I'm not sure I like that. It means trust. It means *closeness*. What does Ephyra know that I don't?

Bobby's eyes are a little bit watery, so we both look away to give him a moment. 'There was no money for me to continue at Oxford. We moved to a small house. Mama became more bitter and spent the money we did have on fancy clothes to keep up with her so-called friends who now shunned her. Papa had served with Toombes. Mama called in a favour and, with no real choice in the matter, I was signed up to the navy under his command.'

'Then he sent you to find mermaids?'

'Yes.' He smiles at me. 'And I only went and – how would you say it? – bloomin' found 'em.'

'Your accent is rubbish!' I can't stop laughing. Ephyra gets the giggles too.

I watch them both. Ephyra doesn't giggle like that with me. I've never seen her like this before: it's new and soft.

'Is it better than my weaving though?' Bobby holds up what could most definitely be the worst rug, part-rug, meant-to-be rug in the entire universe.

'Where've you been?' asks Badger as I come through the gate.

They're there with hot buttered toast. Large is sitting with his face up towards the sun. He tries to make a new freckle for every sunny day. Willis and Jericho are chatting like that's really normal.

I don't want to tell Badger where I've been. I can't unravel it for myself, never mind try to explain it to her.

'Just for a walk, couldn't sleep.' The lie pops out so easily it shocks me.

'Nightmares?' Badger pats the bench next to her and rips her toast in two, handing me the bigger half. I take a bite so I don't have to answer and I'm glad she can't see my face. She's just given me toast. She's worried about my dreams. I am awful.

'Anyone for tennis?' says Willis.

Large gets up and swoops his imaginary tennis racket. 'Oh yes. Oh yes indeed.'

'Darn it,' says Jericho, and this time everyone laughs. Except me.

Badger nudges me. 'You OK?' she asks quietly.

I ruffle her hair so I don't have to lie again.

She leaps up. 'Last one there is a shrivelled sea lettuce!'

They all go shrieking up the path, Jericho making Large yell as he rams him aside and overtakes him.

★

That night when I'm back in the dorm I can't sleep. Again. It's becoming a habit.

We've hung an extra hook for Willis and since he

now blows his nose he doesn't snore so bad, so I can't blame being awake on him.

I've been thinking a lot about Bobby and what he said this morning in the cave. Is any of it true? I think of how Ephyra touched his hand. How I lied to Badger. The main thing I'm thinking about though, and the bit that keeps waking me up when I'm about to drop off to sleep, is the silly question he asked.

Of course I'm happy here.

Aren't I?

Chapter Twenty-eight

It has been sixteen days since me and Badger found Bobby. It has been three days since I lied to Badger. I've been spending most of those three days with my ear pressed to a door, or trying to hold completely still and pretend I'm invisible. It's nice to go up to the top of the tower to escape the whispers. You can taste the fear in the air down there, the hushed voices, the overpolite and the fake happy as we all try to pretend we're not terrified of what might happen.

'You comin' to help?' Badger asks me. She dangles upside down off the railing that runs round the balcony. Her toes are hooked in to stop her falling. She now calls this 'doing a Large' in honour of his cliff-step heroics.

'Badger, man! If Cap'n sees you doing that again, you'll be forrit.'

She reaches up and grabs on with her hands, then yanks herself round until she's sitting upright.

'He won't see me, will he? Cos he's never here now.' She links her arm with mine and plops off the railing. 'Laura and Maura have given us a pile of material to cut and string. There's a fruit flan in it for us if we finish by lunch.' She gives my arm a tug.

I extract mine from hers. 'I can't, Badge.'

She cocks her head to one side. 'Can't? Or won't?'

'What does that even mean?' I ask.

Badger shrugs and heads off down the stairs, muttering.

'What did you say?' I yell after her, but she pretends not to hear or ignores me, or maybe both.

I watch her circle all the way to the bottom of Old Ben where she's met by Jericho. They talk and then both look up at me. I wave. They don't. Then they head out.

My tummy feels funny.

I did hear what Badger said. She said, 'Whatever,' which isn't a swear, but hurts more than one.

★

By the time I make it to the meeting room halfway down the tower, the door is already closed and I don't know what to do. It's not like I've been told not to come, but I haven't exactly been invited either. Over the last few days, I've been getting round that particular issue by arriving first and sitting really still and trying not to be noticed. I swallowed down four sneezes yesterday and haven't felt right since.

I put my ear to the door and hear nothing. I wouldn't, I suppose, because it's super thick, and I think maybe you need a glass tumbler to make that trick work. I haven't trained as a spy and now I'm thinking that would have been much better than geography and volcanoes. Who here *did* train as a spy? That's what's scaring me. And everyone else now. Secrets don't stay secrets for long round here.

There is a keyhole though. I try with my ear, but again there's nothing. Then I have a go at looking through the keyhole. I can't work out the perspective and then realize it's the far end of the big table I can see. The one we made from bits of ship. If you run your hand along it the wrong way, you're picking spelks out for a week.

Ephyra is there. I can't see her face, but I recognize her hands.

It's weird to think she used to hate coming Up Top; she's part of the furniture up here now.

Another arm comes into view – Bobby. I can tell by the watch. It has a moon and a sun on it that rise and fall depending on the time of day. He showed me the back of it. You can see all the workings, the rubies, the weight and the hairspring that tightens as you wind. That's now on my list of things that I *covet* along with Ephyra's saltwater charm.

Bobby puts his hand on top of hers. I expect her to move it away, but she doesn't. There's a pause and then she laces her other hand on top of his. Then takes it off again.

'Alpha,' she says without looking at the door. 'Either come in or go away. We are not here to be gawped at.'

I flinch and step back.

Yesterday the three of us were hanging out in Cave Four. I thought I already knew all the bird names, but Bobby told me some new ones. Ephyra watched and smiled. It felt, well, normal. Nice. For the first time in ages, my gut said it was right. That was unexpected.

It's like that when Badger practises her bird calls and I just sit beside her and it's OK. Except it's not OK with Badger right now and that's why I'm hanging out here and that's why I've been caught.

This is *so* Badger's fault.

'Alpha!' Ephyra says. 'In or away.'

I sigh and turn the handle and enter the room.

'Busted,' says Bobby.

I stick my tongue out at him. He sticks his out. I stick my thumb on the end of my nose and waggle my fingers at him; he does it too.

'Stop copying,' I say. Bobby goes to speak and I say, 'Don't you dare,' at the exact same moment Ephyra puts her hand over Bobby's mouth.

Bobby laughs and Ephyra pulls her hand away and wipes it on the table. The right way so she doesn't get spelks.

Bobby looks at me and smiles. I don't think I should like it the way I do.

'What are you up to?' asks Ephyra.

'Nowt,' I say.

'OK, rephrasing, what should you be doing?'

'Making bunting with Badger.'

'That sounds like fun.'

I roll my eye at Ephyra and walk to the window.

'I've just remembered. Cap'n asked me to check on Kelvin.' Bobby stands up. He thinks I'm not watching, but I can see in the reflection of the window as he quickly kisses Ephyra on the top of her peacock hair. 'See you in a bit, Alpha. More weaving lessons later?' Then he's quick out of the door and closing it behind him.

Ephyra comes up and stands behind me, puts her arms round my waist and rests her chin on my shoulder. 'You're always comfy.'

'I know. I'm talented like that.'

'What's up? And no "nowt". That's not the correct answer.'

'Just friend stuff,' I say.

I change the subject to avoid having to answer her. Then realize I really want to know the answer to my avoidance question. 'What's going on with you and Bobby?'

It's Ephyra's turn to sigh.

'No "nowt",' I say. 'That's not the correct answer.'

Her sigh changes into a giggle and she bites my ear. 'Cheeky whelk!'

I rub my ear and stay quiet. I'm not going to help change the subject back to being about me.

'It's complicated. It's uncomplicated. It's . . . it's really hard to explain . . .'

'I am old enough!' I say.

'Thanks for yelling, Alpha – didn't need that ear. I

wasn't going to say that. It's hard to explain to someone when you don't know yourself.'

I know that feeling. But I'm not letting her off that easily. 'Try,' I say.

Ephyra moves to the windowpane next to mine. We both stare out at Marsden Rock. The seagulls argue over the best spots, pecking each other and turfing a different bird out of their place.

'Remember when Badger arrived?' Ephyra asks.

Of course I do. Four years ago. She came over the Boundaries and walked right up to Old Ben.

'You absolutely knew she was OK, didn't you? Because the Boundaries let her in.'

'That's how you know he is?' I ask her. 'Because the Boundaries let him in? But he's not wonky! He's not a *Wreckling*.'

'No,' she says. 'But maybe he could be. He *was* lost and lonely. When I looked at him in Cave Four the day he told us he thought there was a spy here, it just all made sense. It's so simple. Look, sea-magic, the Boundaries, they aren't tricksy, are they? In or out. *They let him in*. I believe we should trust them.'

I think for a while. It's the most sense I've heard since he arrived. 'Me too,' I say.

We continue to stare out to sea, then a little thought gnaws at me. 'Ephyra,' I ask. 'Bobby hasn't gone In Deep, has he?'

She moves her hands to hold my face. 'No,' she says. 'That's ours.'

I smile.

Maybe he could though, one day.

If the three of us went together.

Chapter Twenty-nine

Ephyra is happy and it's catching. I know it's still danger time. The commander is out there, and we need to be alert. There might be an informer in our midst and that's terrifying, but I also know now that Bobby was telling the truth about not ratting on us. Ephyra's right: the Boundaries don't lie. *Can't* lie. It makes me feel light for the first time since he arrived.

I need to explain to Badger the same way Ephyra just explained it to me. That Bobby isn't the threat. Then Badger can move past that and help me unmask the spy. She signed Rupert's 'Ban Bobby' petition the other day. We've been really niggly, trying to bait each other into fights. I hate it, but don't seem to be able to stop.

Spiralling down the lighthouse stairs, taking them two by two, I decide to be the bigger person and forgive Badger for what she said earlier, the *whatever* that still makes my tummy funny. It's not my fault I'm needed in the meetings and she's not, but that probably feels rubbish for her, makes her hate Bobby even more, when it's really not his fault. Jealousy can be a *very bad thing*.

★

I head off at full pelt towards the fishing hut, the one we camped out in the night Kelvin was hurt and Bobby saved him. That's where they'll be doing the bunting; it's become our spot now. Well, a bit more *their* spot cos I haven't been around much.

I pull up just before the door to the hut. Badger is outside, trying to prop open a window. It gets proper steamy in there otherwise. The chimney's partially blocked so if you don't open it you choke on smoke and end up leaving looking like you've been working down a mine.

I know she can hear me, but she doesn't turn round. It's going to be like that then. This is worse than the fallout when there was only one free toy on a magazine that came from a wrecking and we argued until Cap'n took it off us. If I still had it, I could hold it out as a peace offering.

'Hey, you,' I say. Badger acts like she hasn't heard me. Am I meant to pretend I don't know that I know that she has? Do I walk away? I feel like it.

The window that she's trying to wedge open with a rock suddenly drops, then there's this pause and she yelps.

I rush over. Her finger is already purple and looks like it wants to get bigger than it can.

'Shove it in your mouth,' I say. 'Quick.'

I balance the rock so the window stays open this time.

'Does it look bad?' she asks, though it's hard to tell what she's saying because of the finger in her mouth.

'Yeah,' I say. 'Well bad.'

She smiles. There's no point in having an injury around here unless it's gruesome. Too many people have too many broken bits and bits missing to get het up over a paper cut. If you're going to do something, got to do it properly. Wrecklings are still telling Kelvin he could have made a better go of it.

Once we've sorted her finger, it's a bit awkward. We both have lots we want to say. Neither of us says them.

Badger traces her toe in the dusty ground, making

trails round grass tufts. I look out to sea and watch the wind catch the waves and shift the foam. The pause grows bigger until it nearly swallows us.

Finally Badger says, 'Coming in?'

I say, 'Yes,' and we go inside.

★

We're in full conveyor-belt mode, cutting, stringing, piling, pinking, getting the bunting sorted for Maura and Laura. It's fun. And there's fruit flan on offer, so that's dead good.

'Tell us it again,' says Large.

Me and Badger capturing Bobby, well, it's become a Wrecklings legend. I begin with finding the door over the pillbox entrance, and then, 'There was no way he was going to take out me and Badger.' I look over at Badger, knowing she'll be loving this, but she's quiet. I make sure she knows I'm bigging her up. 'That's right, eh, Badge?'

There's this moment where I think she's not going to say anything, so I go to tell the next bit, then she stands and slams her fist on the table.

'No, it's not bloomin' right.'

We all stop what we're doing and stare. She has scissors in her hand and they're pointing towards me, maybe not on purpose, but they are.

'You're telling this story like you're the big I am. Everyone thinks you're this hero and you're waltzing off to all these meetings and we know you're not even invited! But we don't let on because we're not mean. It's all me-me-me-me – how *you* defeated him and *you* tied him up. Did that solo, did you? Give it another week and I won't even feature in it any more!'

All eyes in the room – Jericho, Willis, Large – move from Badger's face as she rants to my face that stays still and takes it.

'Well,' says Willis.

'Don't you bloomin' dare even *think* about defending her.' The scissors point in his direction now. 'Even you were saying she's got too big for her boots and we never see her any more.'

Willis turns to me. 'Alpha, it wasn't quite like that . . .' He can't look me in the eye and his head drops.

I'm bewildered. 'I came here to make up and this is the thanks I get?'

Badger laughs. 'See, it's *still* all about you! You froze

in the pillbox! *I* was the one that clobbered Bobby. It was me! I should be the one waltzing about. But I'm not. Because I know who my *real* friends are.'

I'm about to fight back when she says, 'You keep putting *Bobby* first, after everything we've been through! After everything he's done.'

She spits on the ground like she needs to get rid of his name. Her tone lowers, her face is all scrumpled up and she says through gritted teeth, 'When were you going to bother telling us what he wrote in his diary, eh, *Fried*?'

She crosses her arms and not-stares at me.

How do they know?

'Jericho?' I say. 'Large?' They both look at their hands.

Willis still won't meet my eye.

'Right,' I say. 'Right then.' Because I don't know what else to say. 'Right then!' I yell it this time and fling the bunting that we'd made across the room. It glides and gently tumbles, not the boom and crack into the wall that I needed. That makes my bottom lip begin to tremble and my eye leak. I furiously rub it.

No one's looking at me, apart from Badger who is still not-staring at me. She yells at me. 'Going to cry now, run off to your little Bobby, are you? Tell him Batty, Wheelchair-bound and Moonface said hi. He hadn't had time to come up with a name for Willis. Shall we christen him Peg Leg and be done with it?'

I heave open the door, and then I run and run.

Chapter Thirty

I don't know where to go. I only know that I don't want to think, that I want Ephyra, but she's busy. She's always busy.

I want Badger, but I don't want Badger because she's horrible.

I climb to the very top of Old Ben's tower where the lamp sits. From the platform, I go up the spiral stairs, tight and narrow by the wall. They slope, worn by feet and age.

There's the winch-and-pulley system so anyone can get up here, but I like the round and the up, the tightness, the need to think about placing feet and hands safely.

I grasp the brass rail and haul myself up the last step.

I'm on top of the world.

I walk around the glass edge, where there's barely room to fit another person passing you by. The lamp takes up all the room in the centre. It weighs the same as an elephant, yet because it rests on mercury I can spin it with just one hand. I do so and watch little rainbows of light dance round the window frames. I walk behind the towering lamp to the tiny green door that has a fist for a handle. I give it a fist bump. That usually makes me smile. Not today.

I stand up straight and then step on to one of the little wooden boxes so that I can see through the window. I stare down across the grass to the foghorn and beyond that to the sea. Norma appears in the distance. I watch her glance over her shoulder and then stride over the Leas and into the main door below me. She must have been at the pillbox. I think she still feels the watching feeling, just like I do.

I've told Cap'n I think the spy is Rupert. I've got it all worked out. Rupert is doing a double bluff with his *fake* hatred of Bobby and starting the petition, and that's why he squashed Kelvin and pretended it was an accident, to get Bobby out of the cave and divert attention from him, so he could do secret spying.

He's just not clever enough to get it past me.

Cap'n said, 'Duly noted, but you do know that an accusation without fact is slander? Kelvin would tell you that,' and then moved on.

I thought being up here would soothe me, but it doesn't. Badger and I don't row. I'm upset and angry and *not* thinking about the fact that I may also be a little bit ashamed.

There's no point in hanging about up here if it's not fixing my head.

★

I'm kicked out of the kitchen for loitering near the buttercream and it's absolutely chucking it down so my bench isn't an option.

Hallway it is then.

'What are you doing hiding here?' asks Malcolm. 'No use pulling your legs in – we've spotted you.'

I push the sou'westers to one side and shuffle forward so that they can both see me.

'Can't be particularly comfy there,' Norma says. I show her the cushions I've pinched from the springy sofas in the rec room. 'I take it back – astounding level of ingenuity. Room for two little ones?'

I shrug. They'd shout at anyone who called them little, but *they're* allowed to make a joke about their height. Just like I can say I have a flame-grilled jellyfish for a face, but if someone else did I'd thump them.

Malcolm puts down his toolbox and clambers over the shoes. 'Budge over then.'

I make room for them and Malcolm sits on one side of me, Norma the other. 'Do we need to sou'wester ourselves back up? I haven't read the hallway-seating guide. Is it published annually?' He wrinkles his nose. 'What's that smell?'

I point to the shoes.

'Ah,' he says. 'I'd suggest that slight kink needs ironing out before you moot this as a worldwide initiative.'

They get themselves settled, then Norma pulls the sou'westers back into place and they lean against the wall. Malcolm folds his arms and closes his eyes. 'Begin at will. Or don't. Either way, we'll be sitting here a while.'

I glance at Malcolm and he has his eyes closed. Norma is fiddling with the hem of her jeans.

'Badger hates me,' I say.

I expect a reply with a variation of *no she doesn't*, so

Norma's 'Why?' surprises me. It makes me sad because maybe she thinks Badger does too.

I'm glad no one's looking at me as I say quietly, 'I guess I've been a bit of a rubbish friend lately.'

They don't say anything.

'Are you going to help?' I ask. 'Or just sit there?'

Malcolm opens his eyes and looks at me. 'It's all a matter of expectation, Alpha. Badger expects you to be there because you always are. Something has cropped up that has taken you – lots of us – away from her, from our regular routines.'

Norma continues. 'When you feel frightened, it's even more rubbish if your best mate has dickied off.'

'Will that do?' asks Malcolm. 'I'm sure you knew that already so we can hardly profess to filling you with some new-found, hard-won knowledge.'

He closes his eyes again and I wait for him to say more. He doesn't. After a few minutes, his mouth drops open a bit and he starts to snore. Norma gives my hand a squeeze, then she closes her eyes too.

★

I leave Malcolm and Norma snoring together and make my way towards the fishing hut.

I'm sure the lobster crates weren't stacked like that when I left. It's not just the feeling-watched thing any more. I swear things are out of place that shouldn't be. It's like they've been knocked over and stacked back up by someone who doesn't know how to do it properly. I'll tell that to Cap'n too. No more bloomin' secrets.

Everyone's knackered from being on watch. We haven't been this alert for years, not since the mermaids thought another clan was trying to muscle in on their turf. Nothing came of that apart from more people falling asleep in their food at teatime. This though, this feels different, like when a storm's brewing. I used to think nothing exciting ever happened around here.

Ha!

★

I walk hunched over, trying to keep the worst of the rain off the bowl of buttercream I've nicked from the kitchen as a peace offering for Badger and the others. Five spoons, one for each of us, clang in my pocket. It's like déjà vu, but at least this time I come bearing a gift.

Now I get that it's just because Badger misses me, I know we can sort it out. We *have* to sort it out. I can explain about the diary, why I didn't tell them. I just didn't want them to be hurt, and Bobby really *is* sorry – he's learned. Isn't that what Haven Point is all about? Then we can work together to unmask the traitor. That's the bit that's really messing everything up here. They'll help once I tell them what Ephyra told me about the Boundaries.

The hut's curtains are half drawn and the window is still open even though the weather is officially nasty. They've still got the bunting conveyor belt going. Large and Jericho are cutting out triangles with pinking shears so the edges are like teeth. Willis is folding over an edge of each triangle and sticking it down, then Badger is poking the cord through the gap.

'She's so licky-lick with Bobby,' Badger spits. 'I just can't stand being around her right now.'

I have my hand curled ready to bang on the door when I hear the next bit.

'Should you be saying that about your best mate?' It's Willis's voice.

'Who says she's my best mate?' asks Badger.

I freeze.

Willis looks puzzled. 'Um, well, everyone?' he replies.

'Nah, best mates don't leave you to watch Ephyra go all gooey-eyed over some disgusting sailor who's going to dob us in.'

Jericho stops cutting. 'That's a little bit harsh, isn't it? She found him. She's just helping out.'

Badger stops what she's doing too. '*She* found him? Really, after all that's happened, you still think that? *I* was the one who clobbered him!' She picks up another triangle and tries to thread it, but can't find the hole. 'That's another thing,' she says, tossing the triangle and the cord on the floor. 'She thinks he actually *likes* her.'

Badger laughs and flops on to one of the chairs. 'Likes her! Can't even tell he's making it up about there being a Wreckling spy, that he's just using her to get the information he needs before he gives the signal and destroys everything.'

I prepare to burst through the door and launch myself at Badger. That's so not true!

And then she says, 'Thinks that him and her and Ephyra are going to be some soppy little family. She thinks she's keeping that hidden, forgets that I know her better than she knows herself.'

The rest of the group are silent, heads bowed. They

don't say anything nasty about me, but they don't stick up for me either.

I want to barge in and scream at her and tell her she's wrong, but my legs are jelly. The bowl slips out of my hand and smashes on the floor.

'What was that?' I hear Large ask, but I run away before they can find out.

Chapter Thirty-one

I run and run. I don't know where I'm going.

The seagulls shriek overhead and at first I think it's Badger because she's so good at seagulls, but then I remember it's her I'm running away from. I slow down because it turns out that it's impossible to run really fast and cry at the same time.

I find I'm up on the edge of the quarry and looking out towards Camel's Island. The rain's eased now. I can see the black clouds floating out to sea, ready to make someone else miserable.

Ephyra is a dot on the beach, working the salt beds. I trace a path from her to the horizon, my eye taking in beach, then wet bit, then wave-lap, then just sea, sea, sea meets sky.

It's so big it helps.

Another dot catches my eye. Wild red hair – it's Bobby. He moves towards Ephyra. She hates being disturbed by anyone that's not me.

I pick a purple flower and pull the tiny petals out. I suck the ends for the taste of honey and then spit them out.

I use my sleeve to wipe my tears and snot just in case anyone sees me. Though I don't know who would apart from a seagull, and that makes me cry a bit more.

The Bobby dot is not sent away by the Ephyra dot. They hold each other so they're one dot.

Why is everything so complicated? It's too much. It was so much easier before.

I pull up a handful of the flowers and rip and rip until the pieces are tiny and scattered. *That* feels better.

Malcolm and Norma are right. I have been a rubbish friend, but that's *harsh* what Badger said. Not my best friend? She said that. I actually heard her. That stuff about Bobby using me and Ephyra? That's just wrong! And I didn't get a chance to tell her *why*. How did they find out about the diary? Bet it was Rupert.

I was only trying to protect them.

I let out a huge sigh, lie back and watch the clouds.

They amble along, lazy in the breeze. I half-heartedly try to spot things in the shapes they make, but my heart's not in it.

I can't stop thinking about what Badger said. About me and Ephyra and Bobby being a family.

In the sky, there's a cat curled up. It overlaps a ginormous puffy cloud that eats its head and blocks out the watery sun.

Badger knows that what I secretly want, above everything else, is to have my own family.

To use that against me . . .

Ephyra isn't scared of Bobby. She's scared of the commander and for the mermaids, about what happened to the Central Fins, about keeping me safe. But she isn't scared of Bobby.

He's not going to dob us in. Badger doesn't know what Ephyra told me about the Boundaries. And she hasn't spent loads of time with him like I have. Which is also my fault too because I kept them all to myself. But we share *everything* here – isn't it OK to just want to have one thing that's mine?

I'll get Ephyra to explain it to everyone, then instead of all the fighting and bickering it can go back to how it was before. Almost.

But it's not going to, is it?

Ephyra and Bobby sometimes hold hands when they think I'm not looking. His hand brushes against hers like it's not on purpose and then it just stays. I like it.

I sit up quickly. Badger's jealous. That's what it is. Of course that's what it is!

She feels left out – fair enough. But she *could* come too. She just chooses not to.

I'm growing up and want to hang out with grown-ups. I want to have responsibilities and go to meetings. I don't want to play any more. Well, she can have 'em. Willis and Jericho and Large. She can keep 'em if that's what she wants. I don't need 'em.

'I DO NOT NEED 'EM!' I yell out across the quarry.

I can teach Bobby to fly up here. I bet he's better than Badger.

I make sure I've wiped my face properly, then I get up and march down through the quarry back to Old Ben.

★

I hold my head up and keep on marching right up to the gate, then I peer over to make sure that they're not all at the bench. I wouldn't want it to be awkward for them.

Coast clear. I head up the path and in through the

front door. No one. Good. The hallway is empty, but I can hear noise from inside the base of the lighthouse and I need to be in there to get up the stairs.

I duck in the nick of time. 'Oi, Flea, man!'

'Sorry, Alph.' He runs past me to collect his football. 'Know where Badger is?'

'No,' I say. 'Why would I?'

'Cos you always do?' He looks at me like I've grown another head. 'Anyway, I was only asking.'

He hoofs the ball to his mates and runs back to them, shaking his head at me while he goes.

She's not here then. At least I don't have to worry about seeing her and making her feel bad. Though I don't know why I care.

I set off up the stairs. When I get halfway, I slow down so my lungs don't evacuate out of my mouth. This should get easier and never does. The wall cabinets are empty. That's weird. I keep on climbing. When I see Cap'n, I'll have to tell him someone's nicked his ships. I add that to the ever-growing list of stuff I need to tell him.

★

I press my ear to Cap'n's door. Nothing. My eye to the keyhole. Nothing. What is wrong with everyone?

Why can't just one person be where I need them to be right now?

I knock. No reply.

I press on the handle. I don't expect the door to open so when it does it gives me a fright and I tumble inside.

There's a Persian cat under the window on a cushion. She knows I shouldn't be in here without Cap'n, so she gives me a haughty stare. I should leave, but I don't. I make my way over to his desk. Being in this room always calms me. If Cap'n isn't here, being where it smells of him is second best.

I run my fingers along the edges of the books on the shelves as I pass them and they go *duh-donky-donk* as I hit all the different levels their spines make. Cap'n says he doesn't need to go out in the world any more: the world lives in books.

On Cap'n's desk, among all the papers and charts and a big bag of kitten food, sits Bobby's diary. I pick it up and flick through. There are the names he used for us. Badger's right: they are cruel, inexcusable, but he's said sorry and I know he'd never do that again. Doesn't that make it a little better, that he's learned? We locked Willis in the tunnel. That was inexcusable and he's in our gang now.

Am I still in the gang?

I turn to the back and there are the dashes and dots that mean mission complete. The signal that he never sent. I read through the pattern: *dee dum, dee dee dum, dum dum dum.* It keeps on going. It's really long. I put the diary back down.

There's an open drawer in the desk, really skinny. I never noticed it before. It kind of sits inside the one below so it's hidden when that's closed. Whenever I'm in here, the drawers are always closed.

I shouldn't look. But of course I do.

The big drawer is full of junk. Lots of ashtrays and books of matches from places like 'The Anchor's Rest' and 'The High Winds' – port mementoes from when Cap'n sailed round the world, perhaps? I don't know why he wouldn't let me see these. I put them back.

Inside the skinny drawer there are just two things: a teeny little sprig of dried lavender, so old that the colour has faded, and a hand-embroidered handkerchief. The threads are colourful, but the stitches are uneven and somehow that makes me like it more. The pattern begins down one side with flowers, then there are clumsy ships and fish and something that

I think is trying to be a compass. There are letters sewn in one corner – M.G.E.

I hear Cap'n's footsteps. Being here alone is *bad*, but being here alone with the handkerchief is worse. I quickly put it back and grab the diary instead and open it just as Cap'n walks in.

'Hi,' I say.

'F . . . lippin' doubloons!' yells Cap'n. The kitten dives out of his beard and lands on the beaten-up chesterfield sofa by the door. He looks at me and I smile. I don't know what else to do.

'Why are you in here alone, without permission?' asks Cap'n.

I mean to say I was looking for him because I needed a hug, and the door opened accidentally, but I don't because he looks like he could do with a laugh, so instead I say, 'Why? What are you hiding?'

Cap'n doesn't laugh. His face hardens. 'What's that supposed to mean?'

'Nothing,' I say.

'What were you looking for?' He strides over and yanks the diary out of my hands.

'This,' I say, even though I wasn't and that's another lie.

I can feel my eye fill, which makes me cross because I

hate it when tears sneak up on me. Cap'n sees them, but doesn't stop being angry.

'Time to leave, Alpha. You're pushing it. There's so much going on and you're not making it easy!'

'Like what? Why won't anybody tell me anything?'

'Because sometimes, Alpha, it's not all about you. It's about keeping *everyone* safe. It's about sending out patrols because we're seeing shadows that *may* be real, but it *may* just be that we're beyond tired. It's about logging the possibly real or possibly imaginary sightings and not knowing what to do about them. It's trying to stop everyone being scared, everyone arguing, everyone taking it out on each other. It's about trying to work out how to keep this place going if we have to abandon the wreckings. It's about working out if someone we love has betrayed us. We're on the brink of destruction, and you have no idea.'

'I could help,' I say.

'Like you've helped so far?' he says, laughing. 'You were the first, Alpha, but that doesn't give you privilege, make you better than anyone else.'

'I know,' I say. I push my pet lip out because that always makes him stop being angry.

'Time to stop being a baby and grow up, Alpha.'

I gasp even though I don't mean to. His face crumples and he goes to grab me as I run past. He misses and I race out of the room.

'Alpha, wait –'

I'm already flying down the stairs by the time he gets to the door.

Chapter Thirty-two

I reach the lift and Malcolm's there. Norma's not with him. Probably had another argument. No wonder if the kind of advice they gave me in the hall is anything to go by. Malcolm doesn't stop me going down. He doesn't stop anyone any more so I'm not sure why he's still there.

'You OK?' he asks.

I ignore him, press the button for the lift and wait.

'Alpha?' He reaches for me, but I pull my arm away.

'I'm fine,' I say, and the lift doors open so I step inside. I turn round and face him. As the doors close, I hold up my thumbs. 'Brilliant chat we had. Perfect. Life couldn't be better.'

★

I just need a hug. I don't think that's too much to ask. To have someone who'll always hug you when you need it.

That person is Ephyra. I thought it was Cap'n and Badger too, but obviously not.

I can see inside Cave Four. The last of the evening sun pours in and glints off the shells that stud the walls, making an arch of pearl. Chairs lined up in rows.

The wedding is tomorrow. Despite everything, we're still trying to pretend that this is all normal. I've never felt in such a *not*-celebratory mood. Everyone's getting ready and being happy except me. I should be with Badger and I'm not because she hates me and Cap'n hates me and Malcolm probably hates me now too.

I go to sit on one of the chairs, wiping the seat of my trousers first because I don't want to get quarry mud on the cushion, when I see a silhouette on the cave wall. Then I hear the two separate voices that match the entangled shadow and my shoulders relax. It's like all the horrible stuff disappears. If it was just the three of us, I wouldn't need anyone else. Ever.

I think I might yell 'Hi!' but that didn't work out well the last time I tried it on Cap'n, so I figure I'll wait until they come out and pretend I've just got here.

Which is kind of another lie, but that's obviously what I do now.

I try not to listen, but bar sticking my fingers in my ears and humming, which would give me away, I haven't really got much choice.

I look out to Marsden Rock and try to concentrate on counting the seagulls fighting over where to sit, but the voices keep floating in and I count to twenty, then have to start again because I realize I'm eavesdropping. I do the tune-out malarkey until I hear my name, then I can't even pretend to not listen any more.

'Alpha adores you, you know that, don't you?' says Bobby's voice.

'I know.'

'It's more than that though – she idolizes you.'

'Well,' says Ephyra, 'who wouldn't?'

'Come here, you!'

There are sloppy noises, which I try to tune out. I don't try very hard just in case they keep talking about me. I don't have a good track record at being talked about right now so this is a chance to even things out. An ant climbs across my knee. I flick it and watch it scurry away in the sand.

'She's a funny thing,' I hear Bobby say. 'I've never met anyone like her before.'

'She's an original, all right,' replies Ephyra. 'That spike and grit. There's something soft and broken underneath it. You've got to find it and tease it out. Trust doesn't come easy. Understandably.'

'Understandably?' says Bobby.

The Bobby shadow sits, then so does Ephyra's. The shadows become one, so I think she's on his knee.

'Your *mam* should be the one you can trust. She never had that.'

'I know how that feels,' says Bobby.

'No you don't,' Ephyra says. 'Your mam may be a selfish woman, but she was there. She didn't abandon you when it was difficult. If anything, it was the opposite: she called you back.'

'Hmm,' he says. 'Not entirely buying that, but carry on.'

'The worst thing happens – your baby is hurt – and you don't accept them. You don't stroke their new ridges and skin and love them with all your heart, finding the patterns in their new beauty. You dump them and leave.'

I knew this, I suppose, but I've never heard it said out loud by Ephyra. Why did I ever wish for my mam to come back? Everything I need is here.

'But she brought her here, somewhere safe.'

'She left her. That's what she did. *Before* this space was safe.'

There's a big pause. I've never heard Ephyra talk about my mam with venom like that.

'Maybe she had her reasons,' I hear Bobby say.

'Have you learned nothing from this place? They're not reasons to leave. They're reasons to love harder! They're reasons to stay.'

I see shadow-Ephyra try to stand. Their together-shadow almost rips in half, but Bobby pulls her back. 'You're right. I didn't think. Again. Sorry.'

Ephyra sits back down.

'How come it's you and Alpha?' he asks.

I love it when Ephyra tells our story. She'll say how there were no other Wrecklings, how I was the first. How she kissed my face. How I toddled beside her In Deep. How she taught me to swim, to catch fish. How she showed me how to catch the razor clams, then how to teach Wrecklings to catch the razor clams; how that's my job now. She'll tell him about us riding with the seahorses, catching moonbeam pearls underwater, how I caught my first eel.

'Cap'n and I go back a long way. We've got history. So when Alpha came – well, I owed him one.'

Something happens to my insides: they go liquid, fast. That is not our story.

'You've got history with Cap'n?' asks Bobby.

No, I scream inside. *That's the wrong question to ask. Ask about me!*

Why hasn't she told our story?

Am I just a favour?

'A long time ago, Cap'n and I had a, let's say . . . encounter. And during it, well, it could have been the end of me. Thanks to him, it wasn't.'

'That's why you live here?' asks Bobby.

'One of the many reasons, but yes. We work well together. It makes sense for him, for me, for now.'

'For now?'

Bobby asks the question my heart is screaming. For now? *For now?*

'I never say forever. It's hard to live up to.'

'What about Maura and Laura tomorrow? They're saying yes to forever.'

'Which is beautiful, if not bizarrely timed right now,' says Ephyra. 'But my forever is a lot longer than theirs, which makes it more complicated.'

'Is this complicated?' asks Bobby.

There's a long pause. The seagulls caw like the world isn't changing around them.

'Let's not talk about it. Maybe that's what makes things complicated,' says Ephyra.

'What, just do?' asks Bobby.

'Yes,' says Ephyra.

There's a pause, then Bobby continues. 'There's nothing here to make me stay; there's no home that I want to go back to. It's time for me to move on. Maybe it's time for you to move on too?'

I wait for Ephyra to say she'd never leave me. She doesn't. She just sighs.

Her shadow stands and pulls him to his feet. I see them on the wall, towering, facing each other. She reaches into the net bag and pulls out a thin, barely-there strand. I automatically touch my neck, feel the missing, see it in her shadow-hand.

She promised he wouldn't go In Deep, not without me.

There are tears running down my cheek and I don't really know which bit of all the horrible they're even for. I don't wipe them away.

I ditched Badger for this – for them – for a *favour*.

She was right. They don't care. They made me lie to Badger, fight with Badger.

Lose Badger.

The tears still come, but they burn now, angry and embarrassed.

Ephyra, my not-mam, my everything. She's fallen for *him*, over me. Over us.

He was sent to capture her! She's forgotten that and she's there, girly and floaty, with the stranger. He's a liar. Badger is right. He'll wreck it. He'll wreck it all.

He *has* wrecked it all.

I realize I'm waiting for something. For Ephyra to say no, that she can't leave me, she can't leave us.

She doesn't.

I run.

Chapter Thirty-three

Snot, so much bloomin' snot and tears, which I keep having to wipe away as I run. Dusk is tumbling down. The sea cracks as the wind picks up the waves and dashes them on the rocks below. I keep on striding along, hoping that my legs will pound it out of me.

When I finally look up, I can see the pillbox ahead. The place where Bobby – I spit as I think his name – hid and it all began.

Badger was right about him. So were Norma and Rupert. We were taken in by his charm. We thought he was one of us, that it was our duty to protect him. He took full advantage of that. He made me think Rupert was a spy. I even told Cap'n that! Made us suspect each other, fight among ourselves. *He* was the one passing information to the commander; there never was another spy. Of course there wasn't. How could we even think that?

Badger knew he was here to destroy everything we've worked so hard for. For this place where we can be completely *us*, our way, with no one here to call us names or build steps instead of ramps.

Why didn't I believe Badger?

Bobby knew what I wanted more than anything – a family of my own. He worked it out, and he used it against me.

I can't go back there, to Badger, with just something like buttercream in a bowl. I need to prove my friendship to her. She clobbered him to save *me*.

More than anyone else has ever done for me.

★

I wrench open the door to the pillbox, so hard it bounces off the wall with a crack and splinters. All Bobby's stuff is gone. Just the desk he constructed still remains under the window.

I see if I can find the place on the floor where I kicked the sand over his blood, but I can't. It feels wrong that there's no trace of what happened here, of Badger's bravery.

It's getting dark now. I'm cold.

What can I do to make everything OK?

The desk has a faint inkstain from where the words ran from his diary when I knocked over the water. It poured down the back under the window. I look underneath to see if there's any trace, knowing there won't be if the blood has disappeared, but I want something to touch to make it real.

There's something at the back, right against the wall.

I crawl underneath and reach. The torch. I remember it rolling off the desk when I spilled the water. I sit under the desk and hold it. It's heavy, but it balances well on my open palm. I press the switch, not knowing if it will work.

I have to shut my eye – it's as bright as Old Ben's lantern. I blink a few times, trying to get comfy with the dark again. There's another smaller button, round and spongy. When I press this one, the light appears for a brief moment and immediately disappears. If I squish it a bit harder, it stays a moment longer before disappearing. I jab at it a few times, hoping that I might break something that belonged to Bobby, taking my anger out on him.

Bobby's going to dob us in! Everything else is cleared

out of here but the torch. That's no coincidence. He's made sure it's here so he can make the signal in secret. Badger's right and everyone should know it.

Everything is electric in my head. It's like my anger has caused my brain to spark.

I know now what I have to do.

★

I sit cross-legged on the desk, the torch balanced on my calves, pointing out to sea, my fury making me bounce up and down like Flea. I can't contain it.

'This is for Badger!' I yell to no one but the gulls.

I think I remember the pattern from the back of the diary. I try to remember the dots and the dashes. I know how it begins: *dee dum, dee dee dum, dum dum dum*.

I press the button over and over and over. Stabbing it violently again and again.

Bobby, the piranha, playing us all off against each other like that! He'd have given the signal eventually. It was just a matter of time. It would have been a nasty surprise though, an ambush. They would have caught us unprepared and off-guard. This way, we can be ready for the commander. This way we can be in charge. This way we can be in control.

Badger and I can trap Bobby and save the Wrecklings and the mermaids. Haul him in front of everyone and show them what he's really like. I'm doing this for Badger. For Ephyra, though she doesn't deserve it. So I can scream 'I told you so!' right in her face.

Over and over and over again, I press the button and the torch flashes.

I jerk awake when my chin jumps. I start again. I don't remember the pattern. I just write out the beat of my heart.

When the battery dies, I curl up under the desk and go to sleep.

Chapter Thirty-four

I wake up in the pillbox the next morning, bleary-eyed and panicky, not quite sure why I'm there. Then I remember, and I know there are going to be battleships outside, and *it's all my fault.*

I dash outside and over to the cliff edge. I quickly scan the horizon.

Nothing.

There's nothing but clouds and seagulls and Marsden Rock. Nothing there that shouldn't be there. I'm so relieved. No one came.

How did trying to signal to the commander ever feel like a good idea? I had no right to endanger us. I could have broken *everything*. Our safe haven came about because of me and I was nearly the one to destroy it. That's what anger does. It sticks its nails in your eye and into your brain and makes you behave like a complete fish-head.

I am so lucky I couldn't remember the code. We all are.

I stretch and look towards Old Ben. I can see the Wrecklings dashing about, getting everything last-minute in place.

Maura and Laura have got another rare blue day for their wedding. Nothing less than they deserve. Some lazy clouds don't realize they're not required, but a seagull caws and the clouds putter away.

I spy a glint on the horizon and shake my head to clear it. I'm not going to see shadows, not going to cause any new fuss, not today. It's tiredness playing tricks on me, wanting me to mess up. I will not do that again. Cap'n's right: I need to grow up.

The anger, that's still there. I'm hurt beyond belief by Ephyra, and bottom-lip wobble over Badger and Cap'n. So that's a full set.

The sun glides over me and in the warmth is relief. I can feel how much I love it here: our bay, the sea caves, In Deep, Old Ben. The whole of Haven Point. I will do anything to keep it safe. Anything.

That's why Bobby needs to go. I don't know what's real any more, what are lies, but I do know he's trouble. Since he got here, our world has imploded. We can't afford to be on edge like this.

Also, he's stealing my Ephyra.

Wedding first. I mean, this stuff's important, but Cap'n, Badger, they both said I'm always all about me. Me, me, me. So today can be about them, them, them. About Maura and Laura, about love and a party. They deserve a good 'un. Then tomorrow I'll fess up about attempting the signal. Clean slate. I'll put it right with Badger and bite my lip with Ephyra. Then me and Badge can make a plan, finally come up with a ruddy plan where we work it out right to the end and tell each other all the bits. It's less scary with two.

My bones still feel crunchy, and the sun isn't warming me up completely. A night of cold and tears can't quite be erased that easily. But I have a plan and that makes me feel a bit lighter.

I watch the Wrecklings for a while longer, but I can't stay up here forever because someone will come looking and I don't want to be any more hassle than I obviously already am. Especially not on Maura and Laura's special day.

See, I *can* think of someone else but me.

I blow a raspberry at the top of Old Ben where I bet Cap'n is, surveying his domain, getting himself psyched up for the wedding. Then I feel like a proper toad. He's been struggling too. We all have.

★

I haven't even got as far as the front door when Norma springs out and grabs me. 'I've been looking for you since yesterday evening. Where have you been?'

Her concern feels lovely; nice to know *someone* still cares. 'Willis said you were gathering some things for Ephyra, then staying with her. Should have told me yourself, mind. You know we're on alert.'

I must remember to thank Willis for covering for me, despite everything. That's canny, that is.

Norma places her hands on the backs of my thighs and shoves me inside. 'There's no time for a bath. We'll just have to do a spit and polish as best we can.'

Today is looking up.

★

'There now. Just look at you.' Norma stands by my side as we both study the mirror. 'Aren't you a picture?'

'We both are.' I sit down on the edge of the bed and smile at her. I'm wearing my best jeans with thin bits on the knees but no rips. I have a shirt on. I don't know who it belongs to, but I can tell them Norma gave it to me if they spot it and tell me off. It has a white background and is covered in a gazillion tiny little forget-me-nots. It looks smart but not girlie.

'I do love you, you know,' says Norma. She gives me a smile, but it doesn't quite reach the edges of her mouth. Her eyes have tears in them. 'I'm doing this for you.'

'I know,' I say. 'I look ace.' I don't know what else to say to make her face look happier. 'The clothes are brill. Erm . . .'

I'm saved from trying to think of anything else when Cap'n walks past the open door and spots me in the mirror. He smiles. More than anything in the whole world I want to smile back, so I do.

'Wait there,' he says.

Norma shrugs and makes me sit cross-legged on the floor in front of her so she can attempt to brush my hair. It does not want to be brushed and my yelling is a bit much for Norma apparently, so we compromise and settle on a half ponytail instead, using the bits we can get the brush through.

Cap'n reappears at the door. He seems shy so I say, 'Hi,' and this time he says, 'Hi,' back and it doesn't go wrong.

Norma leaves us to it.

His kitten has a turquoise-and-yellow ribbon round her neck, but Cap'n has brushed his beard so it looks like it's struggling to hold on. I cup my hands and he passes her to me. Her nose is bright pink and she yawns, which makes me yawn and then laugh, which gives her a fright. I hold her to my cheek to say sorry.

Cap'n doesn't hold me to say sorry, but he does make me stand up so he can have a good look at me and nods in approval. 'That'll do,' he says, and smiles. He looks tired, old. My insides feel a little bit less heavy.

'You're missing something,' he says. He takes a handkerchief out of his pocket and I realize it's the one from the skinny drawer. The one with the initials.

I desperately want to ask Ephyra about it. Even though I don't like her right now. Emotions are odd – the only person I want to tell is the person I love and hate most all at the same time.

Does Cap'n know I found it? How come I'm not in trouble?

He folds it until it makes a neat triangle with the

compass thing facing out, then he places it in the top pocket of my shirt. He stands back and looks at me again. Nods. 'You are now wedding-ready.' He takes my hand. 'Tomorrow, after the shenanigans are over, I think it's about time you and me had a catch-up.'

He pats my head, takes back his kitten and walks out.

I check myself in the mirror again. I look weird.

I look complete.

Chapter Thirty-five

Cave Four is a triumph. There's no other word for it.

I have to stop at the entrance to let my eye walk over everything. It doesn't look like the same place we brought Bobby to, the night everything changed.

There are thousands of teeny shiny curled shells strung up and dangling from the roof. The faint breeze makes them sway and tinkle. There are streamers of iridescent seaweed and upturned crab shells with lit candles inside that make all the little bits of encrusted sand and salt on the ledges shimmer like they've been glitter-sprayed . . . It's pure magic.

The rows of chairs I saw yesterday have been covered

in material hand-embroidered with maps. When I look closer, I see names I recognize, then realize it's all of us, past and present. Every Wreckling there has ever been is remembered in the stitching. Laura will have asked the oldies who sew and sing on a Thursday for that, to make sure no one is forgotten.

It makes my throat lumpy, but I promise myself I'm not going to cry. Been doing far too much of that recently. It'll ruin my rep.

There are bright cushions on the floor at the front and along the edges, and gaps in rows for wheelchairs.

We're ruddy good at parties – just ask Large to tell you about his circus-themed birthday – but I've never seen us pull off anything quite like this before. And never under circumstances like these.

Jericho is in the corner, playing a lullaby on his guitar. One of the older Wrecklings, Hattie, the one who wrote the weird love song for Bobby, sings with him. She is so wrinkly you could stuff shells in her skin and you'd never find them again. Her voice is pure, swirling round Jericho's strumming, and the candlelight sparkles.

The Wrecklings are all here, except Norma, Laura and Maura. Norma will be doing last-minute touch-ups to their outfits. Everyone's scrubbed up and there's a hum of gossip as we wait. Hair has been brushed for the first time in a long time and people with partings look odd. Nice odd though. Everyone's really made an effort, not just with their clothes, but to put aside fear and arguments, just for now. To celebrate.

Cap'n stands at the front. He looks worried, but I think it's the people and the open space. He can rest afterwards. Sometimes it's worth it to push, if you know people will catch you once it's over.

It's balance. We do that really bloomin' well here. We do everything well here.

It makes me sad and happy all at the same time, and then I remember I'm here by myself because I broke everything – because *Bobby* broke everything – and that gnawing feeling in my tummy returns.

Jericho puts down his guitar, and Hattie gives him a right smackeroo on the lips. Then he makes his way over to sit with Badger, Large and Willis right at the front. Willis gives him a massive high five, which Jericho hits immediately.

I need to remember to say thank you to Willis for covering for me last night. Large sees me and waves me over, but I pretend not to notice. I'm not ready yet. Don't want Badger to ignore me in front of them all.

I'm so distracted with combining looking and not looking that I don't realize Ephyra has come up behind me.

'Hey, my sweet,' she says, putting her hands on my shoulders and swivelling me round. She looks me up and down and then her eyes catch on the handkerchief in my pocket. She reaches out to touch it and then stops herself.

'You look dashing.'

But I don't think that's what she wanted to say. It looks like a wasp has stung her mouth.

'I know,' I say. I don't smile, and I shrug her hand off my shoulder. 'I hate it when you call me that.' She looks confused.

'Are you coming to sit with us?' She points over at Bobby, who gives me a grin and a wave.

I don't spit because that's not fair on the floor for Maura and Laura, but I want to. I don't wave back.

'No,' I say. 'I'm sitting with –' I frantically scan the rows of people – 'Malcolm, and not because I owe him that.'

I turn round and walk off. I don't look back and I don't think about her face crumpling behind me because that's not my fault. I stalk over to Malcolm.

I'm angry and sad and I sit down quickly. I realize I

haven't really slept, I haven't eaten, and the world has gone epically wonky. It's all well and good working out what you're going to say in your head, and how you're going to feel, but seeing the people you've hurt, the people who've hurt you? Well, that's a different matter entirely.

Malcolm looks at me. Ugh. I was horrible to him too. This is all too big to solve.

'Sorry,' I say to Malcolm, and mean it.

'Nowt to say sorry about, lass.' He takes a paper bag out of his pocket. 'Looks like you could do with some of this. Take a big chunk.'

The banana toffee is sweet and absolutely rigid in my mouth. 'Ahnk-oo,' I say.

'Maybe all that shouldn't have gone in at once . . .'

I try to grin at him, but the wet mouth the sweet has made oozes out of the edges of my lips. He hands me his hankie.

'Ahnks.'

'Please, no more talking, or I'll be wearing that too.'

I peer through my fringe to look for Ephyra and Bobby. They're not sitting where Bobby was; they've moved back by the entrance, right out of the way. They whisper to each other, then Ephyra leaves. She must be really upset.

Stuff 'em.

Malcolm and I sit in silence, mine dictated by the toffee, until I've sucked it down to a still-not-polite-for-talking size that will have to do.

'Thank you,' I say again, this time with all the letters, and hand him back his hankie.

'I'd say keep it,' he says warily, trying to take it back without touching the sticky bits. 'But it looks like you've got a dazzler of your own.'

I'm about to ask if he knows anything about it when the music begins.

It's the sound of the sea, coming out in a triumphant march of waves and the place that we love, running through our veins.

It is salt and conch shells and singing. The crowd of seagulls outside on Marsden Rock joins in too. It makes my arm hairs stand on end.

Malcolm takes my hand. I stand up and he stands on his chair as we watch Maura and Laura come down the aisle.

They both wear dresses that have been dyed so they fall from the green of the Leas down to the deep navy blue of the sea, which then fades to white horses that gallop round their hems. They wear shawls of white lace. In their hair sit red poppies, the colour of the stripes on Old Ben. One in Maura's short hair, behind her ear, and hundreds in Laura's long curls. They are woven through the ivy that covers her wheelchair. I have never seen people look so right together.

Malcolm uses his sticky hankie to dab his eyes.

The toddlers follow in their wake, wearing little sailor outfits, throwing dried meadow flowers as confetti. When they reach the front, the toddlers plonk themselves down on cushions. There's a chair for Maura so she sits next to Laura, and now they're holding hands in front of Cap'n. He gives his kitten to one of the toddlers. We sit back down, then he begins.

'Wrecklings, we are here today because of love. It's that simple. That is the thing we must cherish and hold on to, especially now in the face of everything that's happening. We gather here together to honour two of our Wrecklings who have found each other, and are in front of us today to promise each other their forevers, however long, and however they may unfold.'

Malcolm does a huge sob and blows his nose into his sticky hankie. When he's finished, I pick a bit of banana toffee off the end of his nose.

Cap'n continues. 'Maura and Laura have asked me to

keep this short and sweet, and I am happy to oblige. We all know that this is just the bit we have to get through as an excuse for the party.' He winks and everyone laughs. Once it's died down, he straightens his shoulders and we know he's being serious again. 'Do you, Maura, promise to love Laura with all of you, share everything with her, and support her the way you would wish to be supported?'

Maura looks Laura directly in the eyes. 'I do.'

'And you, Laura, do you promise to love Maura with all of you, share everything with her, and support her the way you would wish to be supported?'

Laura grins and yells, 'I DO!'

We all cheer and Malcolm takes the opportunity to foghorn-style blow his nose. I check it for him, but it's fine – no toffee.

Cap'n lights a candle, then takes their right hands, places them on top of his weather-beaten atlas and drapes seaweed covered in tiny shells over their hands. 'With the power of the sun, the earth and the beating sea, I pronounce you both married. Fair winds and following seas.'

'Fair winds and following seas!' we all yell back.

There is cheering and those that can stand, stand and

everyone whoops and whistles and bounces, and does all the things that our different bodies do when we're happy. Those that find it too much are in quiet places with ear defenders and we give them the thumbs up so they know too and they can be happy in their way and we're all in it together, even me.

Badger looks at me and it's not quite a smile, but it's not quite a hate, and everything feels like it might just be OK, and then the first shots are fired.

Chapter Thirty-six

A series of bangs –
– and the happiness is gone. The air is sucked out of the cave.

What happened? I daren't look up. I daren't look up.

How did I get on the floor? *Malcolm dragged me.*

He takes my hand. He's beside me there. He's OK. Where's Badger?

Where is Badger?

'Everyone to their feet. Slowly. I said slowly! Up. Now.'

I don't recognize the voice. If you could tip into someone's throat the sound of the sea in winter when it eats the cliffs and we wake up in the morning and another centimetre has vanished – it would sound like that.

I look at Malcolm and he nods. We stand together. Everyone else rises as much as they're able.

I sneak looks and some people are crying. But there's mainly silence. People have their arms round each other. Rahul is with Hattie. I can see her shaking as he tries to hold her up. The cave is still shiny, but it now looks like it's accidentally got dressed up for a party no one else knew about.

With everyone up, I can't see Badger. Can't see any of the gang, or Cap'n or Maura or Laura. My heart is banging in my chest, making me light-headed.

Focus on the voice.

I stand on tiptoes, but I still can't see to the cave entrance to put the voice to a face.

'You are surrounded. The shots were a warning of what will come if you do not listen and you do not obey. You *will* do as you are instructed.'

Men in black wetsuits march down the sides of the cave. Instead of weights in their belts, there are guns and bullets and walkie-talkies. They hold more guns in their hands. They train them on us.

They don't look like air guns. They look real.

'Detain them,' says the voice.

There's a flurry of movement in two places in the cave at once. People cry out. There is a crack of gun hitting skull, and the thud of a person hitting the ground. I hear Maura's voice cry out, 'Peter!'

I go cold. My brain stops.

'I'm coming, I'm coming. Everyone, it's OK,' Cap'n says as he's marched up the aisle by two wetsuits.

The voice speaks again.

'You have seen and heard what happens when orders are disobeyed. You will leave the cave in an orderly fashion, one row at a time. Nice and easy, which it will be if you obey. First row, now.'

I hear people moving. There are no screams, but the sound of breathing in the cave is magnified. My chest thumps in time with all the breaths everyone is taking.

I still can't see in front. Can't see Badger. Where have they taken Cap'n? He said detain 'them'. They've got Cap'n. Who else makes it a *them*?

The rows in front file out. None of the toddlers are crying. That breaks my heart, how scared they must be to know not to make a sound.

The row in front of us leaves.

Our turn.

The wetsuit gunmen stand in front of us with one on either end of our row. Malcolm holds my hand tight. The wetsuit to our right nods. Our row moves towards him and he leads the way out of the cave and we follow.

★

Outside there are no clouds and baking sun. The breeze has left. I guess it got scared and scarpered.

I look over to Marsden Rock. There are no seagulls sitting on top of it. There are no seagulls in the sky and none on the clifftop. There's no sound apart from the waves.

We are alone and it's terrifying.

There's screaming as people are dragged away from each other. We're split up into smaller groups. I don't make a sound. I can't comprehend how quickly it all happened. Malcolm is in my group and he squeezes my hand. Malcolm doesn't have Norma, just me. I squeeze his hand back.

Where is Norma? She must have come in with Laura and Maura. How was it only a few minutes ago that we were cheering? I can't see Norma anywhere. Maybe she got away? Did she go to tell Ephyra and the clan? I feel awful that I made Ephyra leave by being rotten to her, but maybe that was a good thing. She'll hate me, but at least she'll be safe.

Please be OK, Norma. Please be OK, Ephyra. You both have to be OK.

★

They take Maura away from Laura. She cries out, arms outstretched. A wetsuit grabs her round the waist and drags her off. Maura quietens when she sees the gun to Laura's head. The wetsuit with the gun smiles.

Whoosh and I picture me sitting on the desk with the torch. My head goes light, floats upwards away from the rest of my body, and my hands go tingly. Malcolm grabs me, has to brace himself to keep me on my feet.

I caused this.

It was me.

Chapter Thirty-seven

We're all on the beach, the cave mouth behind us, Marsden Rock ahead. It's eerily quiet, just the occasional sob that is quickly shushed away.

We're in groups of about seven, each one with a wetsuit training a gun on us. Malcolm and I are sitting together. He has his arm round me.

He thinks I'm scared and that's why I nearly fainted. I feel such a fraud keeping his arm round me, but it might be the last time someone ever hugs me and I don't want to give it up. When they find out what I did . . .

I look around and I can see her. I can see Badger! She's there with Willis and Jericho and Large. Flea is there too, on Jericho's knee. Jericho holds his hands over

Flea's ears and presses his head tight against his chest, trying to make him safe. They're together. I'm glad they're all together. I wish I was with them.

I ache and miss them even though they're just there.

'Your attention, please,' says the cliff-eating voice.

I can't see who it belongs to at first because of the sun. When my eye adjusts, he comes into focus. Blue trousers and jacket. Crisp and smart. Medals, gun, flat peaked cap. He is chiselled, like a model from those catalogues that sell jumpers.

Behind him on the horizon is a modern ship, all shiny metal and angles, and on the beach five motor-powered dinghies that brought them all to shore.

'Hand over a specimen. Once the mission is complete, we will do you no harm and leave you in peace.'

At first, I don't recall what he means by *specimen*. Then I remember why Bobby was sent here. Sick rises in my throat. I did this. I brought the guns.

I thought the signalling didn't work. No one was supposed to come. I was just a silly little girl playing at being a grown-up.

Oh sails, this wasn't meant to happen.

Unless –

Did Bobby do it?

I can't see him.

But no. Bobby had no chance. He was guarded the whole time. Ephyra never left his side and – *of course* – that was part of the bloomin' plan. Someone was *always* with him. He didn't have a single opportunity to do anything. Why couldn't I see that? Why didn't they *tell* me?

Ephyra would never hurt us.

I don't have time to psych myself up. My legs know it's right before I do, so does my voice, and before I've properly thought it through I stand up and call out, 'It was me!'

Malcolm grabs my hand and tries to yank me back down, terror across his face. The wetsuit guarding our group takes two steps, so quick I don't see them until after he's done them, and his gun is to my head.

Like Bobby's was in the pillbox on the clifftop the night we found him. But this time it's touching the skin on my temple. Icy cold. Malcolm tries to take my hand again, but the gun presses harder, so he stops.

The man at the front looks confused for a moment, then he laughs. 'Bring *it* to me.'

Wetsuit presses the gun again and I walk.

I stand in front of him, with my back to everyone else. From the corner of my eye, I can see Cap'n and

Bobby. So Bobby was the other person that got taken when he yelled 'them'. They're both standing next to each other away from the groups, near the sea, with guns trained on them by two wetsuits.

Cap'n tries to move towards me, but just like they did to Peter the wetsuits hit him and he falls.

I cry out and try to run to him, but the wetsuit grabs me at the same time as the handsome man does. They're so strong that even though I struggle I don't budge. Bobby drops to his knees and holds Cap'n. *He's OK*, Bobby mouths and signs at me and tries to smile.

'Hey there, pretty thing,' the man says, and then he laughs and shoves me back at the wetsuit. He wipes his hand on his jacket. 'Let me see you properly. Glass named you Fried for a reason, didn't he?'

I growl at him.

'Easy, tiger. No need to take things so seriously. We're all friends here, just having a joke together. Now then. What do you think was you?'

Cap'n gets back to his feet with Bobby's help. I can't see Ephyra anywhere. Norma *has* to be with her.

The man looks at me, waiting for an answer. The handsome armour doesn't work, not when you get close up. He has frown marks on his face. Anger must permanently live in him if it's left its stain behind.

I need to fix everything, but I can't remember how this was supposed to work.

It seemed like a plan when I yelled out loud. I wasn't going to tell Cap'n until tomorrow. I didn't want to be the one to spoil the wedding. Which is almost a bit funny now the way it's turned out.

'I'm so sorry, Badge, for everything.' I hope she can hear me, even though I just think it and don't say it out loud.

'I'm waiting,' the handsome man says. 'The burnt bits affect your brain too?'

The wetsuit next to him laughs. I plump up my shoulders. Rage makes me brave.

'I summoned you,' I say. It doesn't come out as loud as I'd hoped.

'I can't hear her.' He calls over to Cap'n. 'Is there something wrong with her voice?'

'There is nothing *wrong* with my voice,' I reply.

'That's something at least. Speak up so we can all hear you. It's rude not to share.'

'You heard what Commander Toombes said. Speak up.' The wetsuit prods me with his gun.

'Now, now,' says the handsome man, who I now

know is the commander. He's right in front of me and I brought him here.

He continues. 'You can call me Horatio, see? We're friends.'

I can feel everyone looking at me. I suck in noisily and hoick a spitball at his shoe.

He leaps back, fear and revulsion on his face. He's scared of catching something from me.

The wetsuit grabs me tighter, shakes me.

'I said *it was me*. Leave them all alone. It's my fault, not theirs. I summoned you here.' My voice is much louder this time.

'You? *You?*' He looks at me then laughs. It's not funny. I don't know why he's laughing. Once he stops, he speaks again. 'You think you did this?' That laugh again. He nudges the wetsuit, and the wetsuit laughs too.

My face flushes even though I don't want it to and I think he can see it because he laughs even more. Then he takes a handkerchief out of his pocket, unfolds it, mops his brow and the back of his neck, folds it up again and returns it to his pocket.

'I can't even begin to imagine how you even think that and, quite frankly, it doesn't matter. Do you think we ever trusted *him?*' He points to Bobby. 'I served with his father.

A weak man. Weak men breed weak sons. We've been tracking him from the start. We've been monitoring you for weeks, way before Glass even arrived.' The commander looks over at Bobby. 'See, just like your father. Weak.'

Bobby goes to move, but Cap'n holds him back.

I can't keep up.

Where's Ephyra?

'We knew all about today and your pathetic little gathering. Knew you'd be at your most vulnerable, the perfect time to strike.'

He bends forward, stares right at me, then speaks so quietly only I can hear. 'How do you think we knew that? How do you think we know he called you Fried?'

My insides go cold.

It was in Bobby's diary. But Bobby couldn't tell anyone; he was monitored all the time.

The commander keeps staring at me. Keeps smiling.

Then he stands up straight and addresses all of us. 'Everyone, there's someone I'd like you to meet . . .'

I can't see at first because of the position of the sun. A figure walks up the beach from the dinghies. They're in shadow, I can't make out any features, but there's only one person it could be and my heart breaks.

Chapter Thirty-eight

'Why?' I ask quietly.

Norma tries to grab my hand and I push her away. I try to kick out, but the wetsuit yanks me back so I miss and just kick sand at her instead.

She smiles. 'Oh, pet lamb, none of this is real. Us, isolated like this? It's not good for you. Especially not you little ones. We should never have hidden away like this.'

I stare at her, my face all scrunched up, trying to work out *why*.

She must realize the millions of questions roaring through my head in waves.

'Did you think you were the only one to spot the glint? Oh, Alpha. I knew Glass had made it here long before you spotted him.'

The commander nods. 'We could have sorted this out far more efficiently if you hadn't got involved, Fried.'

'Because of my signal?' I ask. I don't understand anything any more.

'What is wrong with you?' the commander prods me. 'Are you stupid?' He turns to Norma. 'Why is Fried still talking about a signal? Sort this.'

Norma steps towards me and moves me out of his reach. 'I've known Toombes since we were children. Knew about his encounter with the mermaid, and how no one believed him. I ended up here with Malcolm because, bless him, he thought it was best for us, but it's so stifling, so fake! How can we make change if we hide away?

'The longer we were here, the more I knew we'd never leave. Then I remembered about Toombes and the mermaid.

'You weren't meant to spot Glass! No one was ever meant to get hurt. I managed to warn the Central Fins so they got out just in time. All I wanted was to make people see that we didn't have to hide! Toombes said he'd just disrupt the wreckings and, if we couldn't wreck any more, we'd have to leave. It made sense when I first thought of it. This? This doesn't make sense!' Norma turns to the commander. 'Toombes, you didn't say it would be like this. No one was meant to get hurt!'

'Well then,' the commander sneers, 'you should have kept your Wrecklings in line, shouldn't you?'

'Oh, Alpha,' Norma says to me. 'Everything would have all been sorted quietly if you hadn't got involved.'

There's a shout from behind me and I turn. We're all off-guard. Then Malcolm comes hurtling towards us, screaming, 'What did you do? What did you do?'

A single shot is fired and Malcolm drops immediately, like someone has cut his strings. I try to run to him, but I'm held back.

Wrecklings scream and attempt to move, but shots are fired into the air and people stop.

Norma rushes over to Malcolm, grabs him, cradles him in her arms. 'You promised you'd keep him safe!'

The commander smiles, shrugs. 'There are always casualties in war.' He looks at one of the wetsuits guarding Cap'n and Bobby. 'Take her to the ship.'

The wetsuit marches over and grabs Norma. She cries

and screams and tries to hold on to Malcolm as she's hauled away. We watch in silence. This cannot be happening.

Norma is dumped into one of the dinghies and handcuffed to the inside. The wetsuit pushes it off the sand until it floats and then he leaps onboard, starts up the engine and makes his way towards their ship moored by Marsden Rock.

There is silence. No one budges.

Malcolm lies curled up on the sand. Alone, unmoving.

The commander reaches out and grabs me. He lifts me up with one arm and holds me aloft. The wetsuit stands by his side, his gun pointed right at me. The commander is lean and strong.

My heart beats faster and faster until I'm sure it could explode. I am so sweaty.

'Who wants to do a swap?' he calls out. 'This *beautiful* specimen in exchange for one that we want. A fried Wreckling for a mermaid. Or is this offering too ugly to barter with?'

He begins to laugh and I just dangle there in the hot sun. My fight has gone. There's nothing left. It's over.

There's a cry from the crowd and Badger comes hurtling towards me.

I call out to her. 'Stop, please stop!'

They've got guns, I think, and *I love you* and *I need you to be safe*. But my words won't come out to warn her. She keeps on running and shrieking.

Then Willis stands up too. He yells and starts to run. Large follows, roaring and flailing his arms. Jericho begins to push, struggling on the soft sand. Flea leaps off his knee and helps. They're all coming to rescue me.

The wetsuits' guns are trained on Badger, and as soon as they move towards her some of the grown-up Wrecklings take advantage of the distraction and stand. The wetsuits begin to falter, not knowing where to point their guns.

I call out to Badger again. I kick and kick and the commander drops me. He tries to shout orders, but he can't be heard over the noise of my gang roaring as they come towards me. To save me.

The seagulls are back, circling and cawing. The waves get a sudden energy surge and they crack against the sand, white foam flying.

Badger can't see that the guns are raised and she's still running towards me and I make my kittiwake bird call, try to warn her.

Cap'n claps. Bobby signs. They have the other

Wrecklings' attention. Everyone except Badger and Willis and Large and Jericho and Flea, who are still hurtling towards me.

Cap'n screams, 'Now!'

The wetsuits' guns are moving wildly because everything happened at once and no one knows who to shoot first. *Oh my days!* Who *to shoot first?!*

The Wrecklings who stood up are taking bottles out of their pockets, and the wetsuits are yelling, and the commander is yelling, but he can't be heard over all the yelling. Bobby signs something towards them.

Badger reaches me and I hug her and it's the best feeling ever. I can feel her heart beating against mine, all *boom-boom-boom*. The others, they're racing towards us, yelling and cawing, making all their bird noises.

Over Badger's shoulder, I see Laura and Maura, Hattie and Rahul, Peter and Kelvin; they're in a line together. The distraction my gang has caused means they've been able to reach each other. I can see what's in their hands now, what they were taking out of their pockets. It's the bottles I thought had been stolen from the cabinets on the stairs.

They hold them out. They pull the string dangling

out of the bottle necks and the tiny ships inside fold and lie down flat.

Then they keep pulling the string and the ships are travelling through the neck of the bottles. When the tips of the boats leave the glass and hit the air, there's a deep gurgle from the sea, a hundred times louder than our foghorn, like someone has pulled out a massive plug. Everyone on the beach freezes.

Badger and I turn as the sea whirls and foams and crashes. Out of the crashes burst the ships from the bottles. But they're full-size now – galleons and the *Seahawk* with its three masts. They're all there, floating in the bay. Replica giant vessels on our waves.

Armed with sharpened razor-clam blades and harpoons, mermaids cling to the netting on the sides of the ships. Not just our clan, but Shelly and the Southern Clan too.

Ephyra! She's there! Balanced on the bow of the *Seahawk* with a harpoon in her hand.

Cobalt roars. I spot her leaning out from the mast, her poison-tipped cheek-wings standing to attention. The Wrecklings on the beach and the mermaids at sea roar in response. My gang caws, their noise swelling with the waves. Ephyra dives into the sea.

Bobby takes advantage of the gaping wetsuit guarding them and punches him. Then Bobby grabs Cap'n and together they run for the sea, the kitten in Cap'n's beard just about clinging on.

Henrietta and Verdigris leap out of the waves just as Bobby and Cap'n make it to the tideline. Henrietta and Verdigris grab them both and then they're all in the sea, the mermaids powering through the waves, dragging Cap'n and Bobby with them. In a matter of moments, Cap'n and Bobby are both climbing up on to separate ships.

Henrietta and Verdigris dive back under the waves and they're back on the shore, grabbing more Wrecklings to take them out to the bottle ships. Ephyra leads the mermaids powering on to the land, weapons raised, and I can see the sand through their shimmering land legs.

The commander jerks out of his stupor and he barks orders. 'No one leaves alive!' I'm close enough that his spittle touches my cheek.

He holds out his right arm with the gun in his hand. His face is pure rage and disgust. Then he looks at me and smiles.

I see him go to pull the trigger. It's pointing at Badger.

Badger, my best friend in the whole world, who's saved me twice.

I scream and shove Badger to one side so she falls into the sand and I run straight at the commander, straight towards the gun that's pointing at me now. I can't hear anything else any more; it's just me and him.

He doesn't expect me to run at him and it throws him off-guard just for a second and he stumbles backwards and falls, his feet sinking in the dry sand. It's just enough time for me to grab a rock and I smack it into the side of his head.

He's dazed and bloody, and I hit him again.

One of the wetsuits hauls me off while another grabs him and starts pulling him down the beach to a waiting dinghy. I kick out and make contact and the wetsuit yells and drops me to the ground.

Behind me on the beach, Wrecklings are fighting side by side with mermaids, and on the ships out at sea. There's a huge bang and then a massive explosion as one of our ships fires a cannonball into a dinghy and it bursts into flames.

They weren't expecting the ships. They're outnumbered.

Jericho and Flea are helping Badger get up. Willis and Large are charging down the beach after the wetsuits.

I pick up another rock, sharp to a point, and go racing towards the commander who's being dragged to a waiting dinghy.

'Retreat!' he's shouting. 'Back to the ship!'

He's not getting away from me. Coward. I run faster.

The gunshot is sharp like a whip. My ears ring and I'm thrown backwards.

Then it goes black.

Chapter Thirty-nine

I open my eye. My head hurts. I pat it and there's a lump on my temple. My side feels like it's been headbutted by a bull. I touch it. When I pull my hand away, there's no blood.

There's no blood.

My ears are still ringing and I can't really hear properly; everything is far away.

I'm lying on my back. I try to sit up, but Maura stops me. I can barely hear her, but I can read that her lips call for Badger.

Badger? Badger's OK?

Badger's head appears above me. I can see the white

streak in her hair covered in sand. Her smile. She splats her hand on my face.

'Not up my nose this time, please,' I say. Then she's hugging me so tight round my neck that I think she might actually pull my head off. Once she's stopped and I can breathe again, I laugh because she's OK and I'm OK.

Then I remember everything at the same time as I realize she's crying.

Badger takes my hand. She reaches for Maura and they both help me to sit up. They sit beside me, one on each side, propping me up between them.

I'm still on the beach. Most of the Wrecklings are here too, dazed, looking after each other, being tended to. One of our ships is still by Marsden Rock. The commander's ship is gone. As are the dinghies and the wetsuits.

The seagulls are back on Marsden Rock. Not cawing and scrapping. Standing to attention.

Badger is crying. Why is Badger crying?

My heart stops. I remember the mermaids ferrying the Wrecklings to the ships. The battle. So many wetsuits with guns. The look on the commander's face as I hit him. I can't believe I'm going to say this out loud, but I have to ask.

'Is Malcolm . . .' I can't finish the sentence. Maura squeezes my hand.

'I'm so sorry, darlin'. He won't have known a thing though; it happened so fast. That doesn't make it better, but it's all I've got for you.'

I begin to sob. Remembering him snoring beside me beneath the sou'westers. His banana toffee.

'We will mourn, I promise you that,' says Maura. She looks at me and squeezes my hand. 'But for now I need you to be brave.'

Somehow I know she's not talking about Malcolm. She means something else.

'Cap'n?' I go cold, filled with dread. I can taste it.

Badger moves to sit right in front of me so I can see her lips, which helps me hear her hazy words. My head's still ringing.

'He's fine,' Badger tells me. 'He's out at sea with some of the Wrecklings. Kelvin's with him – he's fine too. Shelly's clan are flanking them. They're chasing down the wetsuits.'

'Flea?'

'Flea's OK. And Large and Jericho and Willis. Though Willis will need us to build him a new leg. He used it as a weapon.'

'Wish I'd seen that,' I say quietly.

She half grins through her tears.

'Bobby then?' I ask. I can't see him on the shore.

Bobby. He *was* one of us.

'They took him, Alph,' she says. 'They sank the ship he was on. The commander captured him and Verdigris, then got away while everyone was fighting.'

I begin to cry.

The commander won. He captured a specimen; he got Verdigris.

I try to slow my breathing.

We'll find them. Cap'n will bring them back. And then we'll show Bobby that this can be his home. I'll teach him how to fly – me and Badger will together. And Jericho, and Large, and Willis, and Flea. We'll hold hands and make a rainbow of us in baggy jumpers along the quarry edge. He doesn't have to search for anywhere any more. We can help him belong.

There's a pause. Maura takes my hand again. She looks at me and her face crumples.

This isn't over. That's not it. Them being taken, that's not everything.

I can't keep playing this guessing game. It stabs my heart each time. Badger's still crying, mumbling that it's all her fault. She should never have wished for pirates.

'You need to come with me,' Maura says.

I look at her. 'No,' I say. Then, really quietly, even though I don't want to ask: 'Why?'

And in that moment I know.

Maura doesn't say anything else.

'Why?' I say again, even though I know, and my face falls and crumples just like hers. Badger squeezes my hand.

'Where is she?' I ask.

★

Ephyra lies in a large rock pool. Her peacock hair is splayed out round her head like a halo. She looks ancient. Her real years have leaped in and her face is like tissue paper.

'We brought her to the sea,' says Badger. 'There was nothing else we could do.'

'What happened?' I ask.

'She barrelled into you to save you.' I touch the lump

on the side of my head, feel where my ribs ache. 'Then she tried to stop the commander escaping,' says Badger, as we hold hands and stare at Ephyra. 'He shot her . . .'

'He shot her? That's OK,' I say. 'She'll heal. She's survived worse than that. Remember that time with the eel storm? She was ripped to pieces and . . .' My voice tails off. Badger isn't getting it. Why not?

'It's not just that,' says Badger. 'Before the commander escaped, he stole her saltwater charm.'

I freeze.

I begin to shake all over. I try to take a step backwards. Maura stops me.

'She was on land too long before we could get to her,' says Maura. 'You need to go to her now.'

I shake my head. It vibrates from side to side and I can't stop it.

Maura places her hands on my cheeks and holds me steady. One hand on skin. One hand on burn.

I realize then that it's not that people didn't want to hold me – I didn't let myself be held. There were always people who were ready to hold me.

Maura smiles through tears and crumpled eyes. 'Alpha, you have to do this now.'

★

I kneel beside Ephyra. Maura helps me, then takes Badger's hand and leads her away.

I can still see them; they're there, watching over me. I could call them if I needed to and I know they'd come running.

Now it's just me and my not-mam, my not-sister, my everything.

'Hey, you,' I say. Because what else do you say?

Her eyes open and I use my head to shade them from the sun. I touch her face. Even though she's in water I've never felt anything so dry. She feels like dust.

'Hey, my sweet,' she says back, and smiles. 'Sorry, I shouldn't call you that.' I can see the effort this takes and a little piece of my heart cracks off.

'I'm so sorry,' I say. I don't know what else to say. I want to tell her that the world stops if she stops, that she can call me her sweet a thousand times and that will never be too many, but the words bubble in my throat and they come out in a sob that I choke down and instead I smile through the tears.

'No sorries. I love you. You know that, don't you?' She tries to reach for my hand, but she's not strong enough, so I take hers, hold it under the water. 'Mermaids were not designed to love like this.'

I don't want to say it, not now, but I have to know. 'I thought I was just a favour.' Ephyra looks puzzled. 'I heard you tell Bobby you owed Cap'n one. That's why you looked after me.'

She sighs and squeezes my hand. It's faint, but I swear she does it. I can feel it grip my heart.

'Oh, my beautiful, headstrong you. Things can begin as a favour, but then they can transform. They don't have to stay one thing; nothing ever does. It doesn't matter about beginnings; it's where you end up that counts.'

I kiss her forehead. 'But you were going to leave me. For him.'

Ephyra tries to sit up. Her eyes flash. 'Never,' she says. 'My heart and yours are entwined.'

She smiles. 'I thought maybe we could be a little family. That's what he was saying about leaving. Me, him *and* you. You stole his heart too.' She pauses to catch her breath. 'All three of us searching for something. We found it in each other. *A new beginning.*'

She reaches out, uses all her strength to lift her arm and touches the orb on my wrist bone. Smiles. Drops her arm.

'Ephyra?'

'Yes, my sweet.'

'How come it's always black for a wrecking?'

'Now that is all down to Cap'n. Did you know that you can learn to tame the clouds?'

I can't tell if she's kidding or not. Keeping their shared mystery right until the end.

She closes her eyes. We don't have to say anything else. We've already said it and felt it a thousand times.

Ephyra begins to sing. The song for a wrecking. The song of forgetting. The song that leaves memory unformed. Her last duty is to protect me, just like it always has been since I was first in her arms and she kissed my face.

I gently press my finger to her lips.

'Don't,' I say. 'I have to remember this.'

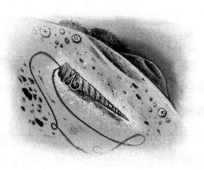

Chapter Forty

I am alone with Ephyra and then I'm not.

I kneel beside her as the sea surges. It bubbles and swirls, gaining speed, making a whirlpool. Out of it rise the mermaids of the Northern Clan. They are proud and triumphant, standing tall among the waves.

They begin to chant. Cobalt is at their head, Henrietta flanking her. They lead the others in song:

> Sister, we take you down to the depths.
> Sister, we take you back to the deep.
> Sister, we place you back with your maker.
> Sister, for you the tides always weep.

They chant it over and over, the words beating with the sea.

The sun moves across the sky, and still they chant. Still I kneel next to my not-mam, my everything, my Ephyra.

All I can hear from the chant is the word *sister*, echoing over and over. The mermaids are no longer chanting; now it's the waves repeating it over and over.

Over and over.

Henrietta leaves the water and steps on to the sand. She walks towards me and kneels down. Rainbow tears roll down her cheeks. I've never seen a mermaid cry.

Henrietta tries to smile at me, then she bends forward to scoop up Ephyra.

I scream and bat her away –

It's Cobalt that leaves the sea. It's the first time I've ever seen her on land. She reaches out to me. I shrink back. Cobalt takes me in her arms and squeezes me until I stop screaming. She looks at me.

'Ephyra is ours. She belongs to the sea. How do you think there are waves in the ocean? They are the heartbeats of our lost comrades, our sisters. We are the tides. We *are* the sea.'

Cobalt holds out a hand and takes a tear from my cheek. She bends towards Ephyra and I tense again, but she looks at me and I let her go towards her. She takes a strand of peacock hair from Ephyra and lays the tear on it. It clings like dew. She gestures for me to dip my head. I mouth, 'No.'

'Ephyra belongs to the sea, but I have never known a mermaid wish so much to belong on the land. That was because of you.'

Cobalt holds the tear on the strand of Ephyra's hair out to me again and this time I bow my head. She ties the strand round my neck. I watch as the tear turns opaque, into a perfect peacock-coloured pearl.

Cobalt bows. She turns her back on me and scoops Ephyra up. My not-mam is almost dust. Her scales crumble along the sand as Cobalt carries her to the sea, Henrietta beside them.

The mermaids take back their song from the waves. I feel hands in mine. Maura on one side, Badger on the other. Then I hear the singing echoed behind me too.

The Wrecklings fill the beach and they sing with the mermaids. Land and sea together, saying goodbye.

The mermaids turn to face us and the sea swirls

once more. Then they descend below the waves, taking Ephyra with them. White horses fling foam into the pure blue sky.

The song lingers on the waves long after they've gone. I stay on the beach until night falls. Badger never leaves my side.

Chapter Forty-one

Time is a blur. Cap'n and Kelvin are still away, trying to find Bobby and Verdigris.

I can't sleep. I hide at the top of the tower, curled up by the little door with the fist. Wait for time to pass. Badger brings me food that I refuse to eat.

On the third day, I hear clumping up the steps, heavy feet and boots. I curl up tighter, close my eye, pretend I'm asleep.

There's heavy breathing and a huge thump as Large sits beside me. He prods me.

'Oi,' he says.

'Go away,' I mumble.

He doesn't. Just sits.

Large is the most stubborn person I know, more stubborn even than me. I am not going to win. I figure if I sit up then he might leave.

We lean against each other in silence, our backs against the tower wall. I look up and all I can see is blue sky and clouds. They make me think about Ephyra, how she said Cap'n could tame them. I scrumple up my face and a tear leaks out. Large takes my hand. He doesn't say anything. Just carries on sitting there.

'She was killed because of me, because I was mean, because she left . . .'

My shoulders shake and I start to sob. I can't hold it back. He wraps his arm round me. I cry until I have no tears left. When I finally finish, Large says, 'No. She's dead because the commander killed her. You did not kill her. That's a fact.'

Large stands up and holds out his hand to me. He does the smile where his whole face lights up. I take his hand and follow him down the steps.

★

Four days later, when Cap'n returns, I'm sitting on my bench in the early-morning grey. His whole body shakes as he makes his way back across the garden to the safety of Old Ben.

I run to Cap'n and hold him tight. I don't ever want to let him go. He stinks. Bad. He kisses my forehead. Takes the kitten from his beard.

'She's too big for me now. Look – she's nearly all grown up.' Then he looks at me. The tiredness is etched into his face. 'Just like you.'

He hands me the kitten, now an almost-cat. She stretches and claws at my sleeve. He smiles.

Bobby and Verdigris are not with him. I thought he'd bring them back.

Cap'n walks up the path. Peter runs out and props him up on one side. When he reaches the door, Maura appears and holds up his other side. I watch them go in.

I take the almost-cat and go back to my bench. I put her on my knee and she kneads for a while until she's made me comfy, then curls up in a ball, letting out a little sigh. Her nose is bright pink. I tell her about the man with banana toffee, and the fiercest mermaid who ever lived.

★

At teatime, we're all laughing and joking, and this time Badger doesn't burn the toast. Jericho is doing an impression of Willis, but it's not nasty, it's spot-on hilarious, and Willis is laughing at it, shaking his head. All of a sudden, my throat catches and I feel bad for laughing.

I get up to leave, but Badger pulls me back down in my seat and puts her arm round my neck. She whispers in my ear. 'It's OK to be happy in among the sad, you know. She wouldn't mind.'

My eye fills. Large scooches across the floor and leans back against me, places his head on my knees. Flea hands me his football and a tear leaks out of my eye.

'Here we go again,' says Jericho. 'I thought you were hard?' Then he stops smiling and frantically looks around, worried he's taken it too far.

But that's what you need friends for. They know the bits of you that you try to keep secret. They take the mick, but do it with love above all else. Fought-for, hard-won, soft, tough love.

I burst out laughing. Jericho looks relieved, then laughs too.

Flea grabs his ball out of my lap and runs for the door. 'Last one to the pitch is a shrivelled sea lettuce!'

We all run after him, hollering not fairs about his head start.

★

I'm playing in defence and do a proper smart tackle on Willis.

'Mind my new leg!' he yells.

I say sorry and swipe at his other leg instead.

Maura yells for me.

I turn my head towards her, and Willis runs off with the ball, shouting, 'Ha!'

It can't be a bath, can it? That makes me think of Norma.

I trudge over to Maura, kicking the grass to slow down my pace further.

Everyone is whispering about Norma. What she did and didn't do. Why. Where she might be. If they've killed her. Some of them want her dead for what she did. I don't. I saw how she looked at Malcolm.

I haven't told anyone what she said to me. About how we shouldn't be hidden here. I need time to think that through.

'Hurry yersel'!' Maura yells. 'Or Cap'n will be asleep by the time you get up there.'

No bath? I zoom past her before she's even finished her sentence.

★

Cap'n is lying on his bed, the blankets pulled right up to his chin so he's just made of beard. It looks weird without a kitten in it.

I thought Blueberry, the not-kitten-any-more cat, was going to be mine, but cats are good at throwing curve balls and not doing what's expected of them. Kelvin now has a limp, no spleen and a cat. Not a bad trade-off.

Cap'n's eyes are closed and I don't want to wake him. I walk over to his desk and see Bobby's notebook lying there.

Bobby.

Where are you?

'Hello, Alpha,' says Cap'n, and I nearly do a swear out loud.

'Hello, Cap'n,' I say. I feel shy.

'Pull up a pew.'

I drag his desk chair to beside his bed and sit next to him. 'Did you find Bobby and Verdigris?' I pause. 'And Norma?'

'They're being held in Plymouth. We couldn't get close.' Cap'n's eyes can barely stay open. 'How you doing, kiddo?'

'OK,' I say, and shrug. 'Did you hear about –' I stop. Can't say her name. Then force myself. I want to hear it. 'Did you hear about Ephyra?'

'Yes,' he says. I expect him to try to make it better. He doesn't. 'That is always going to hurt. It will never leave you. The edges will soften, but it will catch you off-guard sometimes and leave you breathless. That's the price we pay for loving. For being loved.' He smiles. His face goes all crinkly, and he takes my hand. 'I promise you though, Alpha. It's worth the pain.'

He draws his hand away and puts his arm back under the blankets. Gets snuggled down once more. 'The hankie belonged to your mam,' he says. No preamble, just wham into it. 'She left it here, with you, in the box. There was a letter too.'

I open my mouth to speak, to yell, or I don't know what.

'Don't you go flying off the handle with me, or Ephyra. We were just doing what the envelope said, which was not to give it to you until you were grown. Which I think you are now.'

Questions, millions of them, dance through my head.

'What —' I say, then stop. Where do you even begin?

'The letter's in my desk, in the drawer you shouldn't know about.'

I want to be angry at Cap'n and Ephyra. How could they keep this from me?

I think of all the secrets we keep, the not-lies we tell every single day. I take a deep breath. It's time to be grown-up, to prove to him, and to Ephyra, that I'm old enough for the letter.

I stand. 'I'm going to let you sleep now,' I say.

He raises one eyebrow and says nothing.

I go to the desk and open the secret drawer. The hankie is there. Lying next to it is a letter. Bronze faded copperplate is on the envelope.

For my daughter,
once she's old enough to understand

I'm not sure if I am. If I'll ever be. But I take the hankie and the envelope.

As I'm closing the door behind me, I hear Cap'n say,

'I love you, Alpha. You were the first, the beginning. We've all just been making it up as we go along from there. I hope it was enough.'

I don't answer because I don't know what to say.

I close the door gently behind me.

Chapter Forty-two

The next day I'm summoned to No Entry by a shark tooth on my pillow.

The foam from the waves is whipped up and strewn all across the sand. Henrietta rises, swims through the breakers near the shore, then her tail shimmers and disappears and she walks towards me.

For a moment, a heartbeat, I thought it would be Ephyra.

I start to cry. Henrietta stands beside me and lets me. I didn't think I had any tears left, and yet they still keep on coming.

When I'm finished, I do a big sniff, just to let Henrietta know I'm done.

'Nice one,' she says, and grins. I do too.

We stand on the shoreline, looking out to the horizon. The seagulls caw and crash round Marsden Rock.

Henrietta doesn't look at me. 'We're leaving.'

'Because of Ephyra?'

She still won't look. 'Because of Ephyra, yes. And Verdigris. It's not safe here, for any of us, not now the commander knows where we are.'

'When will you be back?'

'Alpha, we're not coming back.'

I feel like someone has punched me. I'm going to lose everything.

'You can't,' I say, and Henrietta takes my hand.

She carries on staring out to sea. I do too because what else is there left to say?

I look towards No Entry. Then to my arm. My eye traces the sliver of a scar from where my wrist-bone nobble juts out to my elbow. That day feels like forever ago and no time at all. That's how my whole time with the mermaids feels, and maybe that's a little bit how they feel, living through waves rather than days and years.

I shake my head to stop the memories flooding in, and then realize I want them. They're all I have left.

They're treasure. The first time I entered In Deep alone, the surprise and anger and pride on Ephyra's face. Her grabbing me, swirling me round and round in the water until the bubbles fizzed into patterns in which I could see their history written. I was never meant to be there. Yet they allowed me in, trusted someone who wasn't their own.

'She loved you beyond tides. You do know that, don't you?' says Henrietta.

I watch the sun rise behind Marsden Rock, bathing everything in an orange glow. The hollows where the seagulls crouch look like they're being set ablaze. I touch my face.

'I know,' I say. And I do. I was loved beyond life by a mermaid. That part is as much of my story as my face, as much of my past. These things all squish together to make us *us*.

Henrietta turns to me, takes my hand. Her whole body is sparkling in the sun.

'Fair winds and following seas,' she says.

'Fair winds and following seas,' I say in reply.

She gives my hand a squeeze, then runs for the tideline and leaps. Her land legs shimmer and disappear, replaced by her powerful tail. She dives.

I turn to walk back up the beach, trying to work out not only what this means for me, but what it means for the Wrecklings.

I stumble over a piece of driftwood and put my hand out to break my fall. Something shiny falls from my fingers. I crouch down and pluck it carefully out of the sand.

My saltwater charm. I place it round my neck. The world wobbles, *whooshes*, and I feel the tickle itch as it burrows its way under my skin.

Chapter Forty-three

We're sitting in the base of the tower, playing Monopoly. Peter found a board and we've doctored it. The buildings round the edges are now all ours: Maura and Laura's cottage, Old Ben, the foghorn, the pillbox. The letter from my mam still sits in my pocket. Unopened. I touch it to make sure it's still there. I've tried to open it so many times, but I'm not ready yet.

Large leans forward and checks no one's listening apart from us. 'Henry and Wendy left this morning,' he says.

Willis looks round too, then throws the die. 'That's four Wrecklings gone, just this week.'

'What does that mean?' asks Flea, far too loudly, as he bounces up and down on his hunkers. We all shush him.

It's not that we're not meant to know, it's just that everyone is so on edge we instinctively don't want to add to it.

'Well?' asks Flea in a stage whisper.

No one answers because we don't know.

★

Once the mermaids left, there was confab after confab. We can't wreck without them. We can't be self-sufficient without wrecking. How do we stay here? Willis says our time is measured in weeks, not months or years.

We won't last until the cliffs get eaten by the sea.

Cap'n just smiles and says all will be well – we've hit rough patches before. But the smile doesn't reach his eyes. And he's lying. We've never faced something like this.

A week later, Hattie was the first to leave. Her bed was made; her clothes and guitar were gone.

It's not just the worry about what we'll do. The feel has changed: the magic, whatever it was, is no longer here. Not just because of Malcolm and Ephyra, and the mermaids leaving, but because of Norma too.

I've been thinking about that a lot, especially when I'm in my hammock at night and I can't sleep. What she said about this place not being right. That we shouldn't be hidden. And what Bobby asked too. *Are you happy here?*

★

'Four minutes to lessons and counting,' says Cap'n.

'Will you look after the board so Badger doesn't cheat?' Jericho asks Maura, who has the toddlers gathered round a table.

'Who me?' Badger puts on this offended look, but we all know that she sneaks down when she's pretending to go to the loo and raids the bank.

'Of course you!' says Jericho.

Maura laughs and says, 'Fine by me. That's a minute gone, and you've got to get to the top.'

We all go to move, then we hear voices in the hallway.

'Hello, anyone here?'

We freeze. Our eyes catch each other's. Maura grabs the toddlers, shields them with her arms. Cap'n stands stock-still, broom in hand.

'Hello?' Another voice this time. The footsteps draw nearer.

'We thought we could hear voices. Busting for a cuppa and a pee! Is this the cafe?'

Two people in matching bright red waterproofs appear in the hall. They wear bobble hats and waxy trousers. They've got gigantic stompy boots and poles dangling off each wrist. They're shiny and loud.

'Do you have a menu?'

Cap'n is frozen. We all are. We stare at the noisy, bright people.

Then Willis slowly stands. I can almost see the cogs whirring in his head. He puts on the biggest, most charming smile I have ever seen.

'Welcome!' he cries. 'You're early. No worries, you'll just have to wait a mo' while we get sorted. Have a seat.'

Willis guides them to the battered sofa and they sit down next to each other. One of the cats, a sleek grey one, uncurls from its spot by the side of the sofa, stretches, leaps up and curls back up in between them.

'How delightful,' says one of them as she strokes its head and the cat purrs in response. 'I read about these – a cat cafe!'

'That's a thing?' asks Willis. 'Of course it's a thing; of course we are! Flea.' Flea has his jaw to the floor. 'Flea!' yells Willis. 'Come and take their coats. Maura, kettle on.'

Flea goes dashing over to them, bows and holds out

his arms for the hikers' coats, dances on the spot. They giggle.

'How charming!' says one.

'How quaint,' says the other.

They struggle with their poles and layers and then pile them up into Flea's waiting arms. Once he's got the coats, he doesn't know what to do next. Willis shoves him towards the hall.

'I'm sure we've got some cornflake cake. Or how's about a nice bacon stottie?' Willis removes his little notebook from his pocket and takes out his pencil, licks the tip. The visitors giggle again.

I don't mean to make judgements, which we're not meant to do around here, but these people don't *look* wonky: they're too rugged and ruddy. Their clothes are expensive and new. They're not running from anything. But the Boundaries let them through.

Or have the Boundaries gone?

'They're not wonky, are they?' whispers Badger to me.

'Nope,' I say.

'They're not Wrecklings?'

'Nope.'

'What about the Boundaries?' she asks.

I don't have time to reply because Willis starts yelling orders, talking to the couple, getting us all chivvied along.

'After you've had a morsel and spent a penny, Alpha will give you a guided tour of Old Ben. He gets his name from the sign above the door, Old Benevolent. It was a society that kept mariners . . . Well, Alpha will tell you all about that, won't you, Alph?' says Willis.

I look behind me, just in case there's another Alph there. There isn't.

I turn back and the couple are not staring, or pointing or laughing, or scared. They're just smiling at me. Like this is dead normal.

They turn back to each other and discuss whether they fancy a bacon stottie.

Willis looks over at Cap'n, gives him a huge wink and sticks both thumbs up.

★

Now you know how you came to be here, to visit our beloved lighthouse that stands on the edge of Haven Point. And now you know too about the most ferocious and most loved mermaid that ever lived.

Epilogue

This time, although the dream is black and red and there's smoke and I'm choking burning, there is a face.

There's a face with a nose that curves like mine. I can't quite take it out of the shadow yet. But it's there.

I don't go back to sleep again. I wait. There's a full moon. I can see it lighting up the sky from my hammock. A sea-magic full moon. It's a gift from Ephyra.

I stare at the lump in the bed that is Badger. I want to whisper something. But I don't know what.

So I don't. I just creep out, trying to take the feel of the dorm with me. Remembering the breaths and the little snorts.

I grab my rucksack from behind the sou'westers and pull on my boots and coat. Take a little moment to remember Malcolm. I left some toffee among the daisies beside him yesterday.

I go outside, careful to close the door at the right speed to stop the creak, and breathe in deep. It smells of yesterday; nothing has woken up yet. I was one hundred per cent sure the sea would cry out and storm if I ever tried to leave. But it's still and calm.

I don't look at the soap box that gave me my name because I know it would send me running straight back inside. Or at the EMERGENCY USE ONLY bell, now there are no longer any mermaids to answer its call.

And suddenly, because I could see her face this morning, I know the time is right to read my letter.

My darling child,

It breaks my heart that I don't know your name, that I won't be the one to give you it. But, if I

can't be there to look after you and watch you grow,
then I don't deserve to be the one to bestow it upon
you.

I hope one day you're old enough to understand.
Richard and Ephyra will know when that time is
right. I entrust you to him, to them, to this place
where he has found safety and solitude. Maybe you
will wind your little fingers through his beard like
I once wound mine.

Know that I love you more than anything else
in this whole world. More than sea and sky.
Fair winds and following seas.

Yours always,
M. G. Edwards

I smile, trace my fingers along her words. I put the
letter in its envelope and place it back in my pocket.
Funny how what you've been searching for forever
becomes so small compared to what you thought it
would be.

I thought I needed to know why she left me, then I'd work out how to belong.

But I always belonged. I'm a Wreckling.

★

'Oi, going somewhere?' asks Badger.

My bum nearly falls out. 'You were in bed!'

'But I'm not now,' she says and grins.

'*You were in bed!*'

I told you Badger was magic. She plops off the wall, dragging her rucksack behind her, and lands softly beside me.

'Nope,' she says. 'I wasn't in bed, but my pillow was pretending to be me, just like yours.'

'How did you –'

'You are rubbish at hiding things from me, Alph, always have been.'

I humph. 'Going somewhere?' I ask.

'Yeah,' she says. 'With you.'

My throat does this catchy thing with sad heartache snot.

'You can't come, Badger. It'll be dangerous.'

She throws back her head and I quickly slam my hand over her mouth. She giggles under my palm. 'That is a rubbish laugh in the face of danger,' I tell her. 'You really don't –' I begin to say.

'I know,' she interrupts and links her arm through mine even though she doesn't need to. 'It's what best friends do.'

I look straight at her. She looks back at me.

'Am I staring in the right place for this heart-wrenching moment?' she asks.

I cuff her round the head.

'Oi!'

'*Shhhhh!*'

We put our rucksacks on our backs and walk towards the gate at the end of the garden.

I think about Verdigris, what the commander might be doing to her. About Bobby, held prisoner. I need to tell him I'm sorry. That he was right and wrong about everything. How I am happy here. How I *was* happy here, but things change. Nothing ever stays the same.

Nothing could be a more apt illustration of that than Haven Point. We're even listed on the internet now. Peter made us a website and we're connected to a thing called Broad Band.

Cap'n is happy. He says there was obviously always a reason for never getting rid of the cats. He's even cultivating a new kitten in his beard. That's the most important thing. He's happy because we're safe.

We can be safe even though we're no longer hidden.

Walkers come for butties, and Maura's bacon stotties are legendary. Rupert is in charge of the kitchen and always puts extra pickle in Kelvin's sandwiches because he still hasn't forgiven himself for squashing Kelvin, even though Kelvin is fine now and has forgiven him. I gave Rupert a big wodge of postcards because I still haven't forgiven myself for accusing him of being the spy. Maura and Peter teach BSL classes. We show people how they can make their buildings work for everyone. People still come and stay, but this time for holidays. Kelvin helps people to know their rights and claim them. Wheelchair users zoom up and down the beach in Jericho's rig.

There is so much laughter.

The Boundaries knew before we did that we needed to change and adapt to survive. They faded away. Let the world in. I still can't find it in me to forgive them for letting in the commander too though. That just wasn't on. Badger and I still can't figure that bit out, even if Norma must have had something to do with it. How could they let someone so evil in? Maybe it's that no matter how cruel the world can be, it's ours too and we need to claim a piece of it. You can't do that when you're hidden away.

I think of Norma. Poor Malcolm. She got it all wrong, but she kind of had it right. I wonder if she's with Verdigris and Bobby. Only one way to find out.

★

Last night, before I went to sleep, Cap'n came over to my hammock. He said something odd, something we say before an adventure, as a wish for the waves to guide us.

'Fair winds and following seas.'

I said it back to him as he walked away, and from both our mouths it sounded like a goodbye.

★

'How far is Plymouth?' asks Badger.

'How do you know about Plymouth?' I ask.

She taps the side of her nose. 'I know *everything*.'

Except she doesn't. Not quite. Not that I left the rest of my postcards in Jericho's locker so he can look after them until I get back, though I know he doesn't need to escape so much now that he has Willis. Whoever figured they'd be besties?! Not about the letter in my pocket, the hankie. That I'm no longer angry at Ephyra and Cap'n. Don't think I actually ever was. They found this bundle of a squally mess on their doorstep and they raised me as best they could. Look at me – they did a bloomin' brilliant job.

I bend down and pretend to retie the lace on my shoe so that Badger doesn't notice me take the letter out of my pocket, fold it in two and poke it into the hole in the wall where the mouse lives.

I'm a Wreckling. Because I know I belong, I'm brave enough to leave everything behind.

★

'Plymouth is far,' I say as we begin to walk together away from our red-striped lighthouse, the colour of poppies in brides' hair. Through the gate, me following Badger because I want to be the one who shuts it behind us.

'Yeah, I know,' Badger replies. She's quiet for about two steps, then she says, 'But how far?'

'The furthest we've ever been,' I tell her.

'Will Plymouth have the right sort of pirates?'

'Yes,' I say. 'Definitely.'

We walk in silence round the edge of the wall. Dawdling. Soaking in the spongy feel of the grass beneath our feet, the way the wind tries to eat my not-ear.

'Alpha.' Badger stops, looks heartbroken, like she's forgotten how to walk.

'What?'

'We never did name Cave Four.'

I take her hand. 'It's OK,' I say. 'Willis, Jericho and Large, they'll do that for us.'

'As long as Jericho doesn't write it, or no one will ever be able to read what it says.' Badger grabs the tear that has sneaked out of her eye and flicks it away.

I touch the pearl round my neck, held on a peacock strand. The orb on my wrist bone. The strand that has burrowed deep under my skin, an open-door invitation from my mermaid family.

'Ephyra's Place,' we both say at the same time, but not out loud.

We begin to walk away, but not before I remember to knock twice on the cool of the thick whitewashed wall.

Acknowledgements

I would like to apologize that this list is long. But also not apologize either, actually, because reading the acknowledgements in books is my favourite bit, so if you're a fellow acknowledgements lover I salute you and hope these are up to scratch.

Writing itself is very solitary but requires the support of wonderful people and organizations. A ridiculous amount of thanks go to:

Laura and James of Writers' Block North East, my journey back to writing began with you; Cove Park for offering me an Early Careers residency in 2019, supported by the Fenton Arts Trust; and ACE for a DYCP grant, which gave me time to write, supported by public funding from Arts Council England. New Writing North have been such a source of support and I owe you all endless posh biscuits; special thanks to Claire, Will, Ruth and the YP team. MIMA and especially Claire, you helped me work out how to be me. Our Penguin WriteNow cohort, you are all awesome.

All the incredible disabled women who offered guidance, support and humour, especially Vici, Karen, Kaite and JulieMc. Coll and Kevinski (C R Us!), I couldn't do this without you. Colin and Disability Arts Online, I can't thank you enough. The not-inspirational-in-the-slightest northern disabled posse, you rock. Steph, for reading bits for me and cheering me on. Richard, for Friday nights and poo bags. Dean, my constant supporter and entertainment guru. Bex, for the floor cushion and rants from your boot. Janey, Jen and Liza May and all the other AYME posse from so long ago.

The talented Durham Writers – K, M, L, M and A – did we ever pick a better name? The TWP, sistas unite! The northern spoken-word scene, for being so welcoming and having the best craic. My fellow Greater Tees Practitioners, so much began with you, thank you all and ARC. Dogs Trust Sadberge for Harper Lee, our literary rescue dog. David and Joanne at Kendrew House, for my excellent word home. The Darlo Cocktail Girlies, we need another trip away ASAP! Noisy Daughters Sarah and Fran, for pub rants, and Fran for being there for word vomit. My work wives, Jan and Sarah, for being there always, and to my OWF for terrorizing me into applying for things.

Did you know how much work and support goes into making a book come alive? It's A LOT! Rebecca, my incredible inclusivity reader, thank you from the bottom of my heart. Molly, you've had my back from the moment we met; you are the best agent in all the land. Wendy, your copy-editing skills are legendary, as is your kindness and ability to make me laugh. Emma, mentor and editor supreme, thank you for everything, and especially for loving Alpha and her gang as fiercely as I do. To all those in the Puffin family who have held my hand, and to those who will in the future, so many thanks. I have been so fortunate to work with not one but three incredible illustrators. Thank you for finding the heartsong of Haven Point and magically unravelling it in front of my eyes. Gillian, for the stunning cover – Old Ben actually glows! I can't stop looking at it, which is getting in the way of doing lots of other stuff . . .

Luke, for my childhood dream – not only of a map but of a cross-section; I keep spotting new things in Old Ben and need it as a duvet cover. Valentina, for bringing my characters and world to life, for the squeals of glee you keep making me do, and for the first time I saw the Wrecklings making bunting together. I will never forget that moment. And to Alice, for designing the most beautiful book in the universe. As soon as I saw the starfish as an asterisk I knew it was going to be magical. And it is.

Tom, my writing husband, you are the best in all the land – love, Auts. Carmen, for the heart-shaped flint and always being a step ahead and reporting back. Dot, for love and lions. Ballymaureen, for being the best un-family in all the land. Kirsten, for finding The Triangle, a full tummy and understanding about loops. Julie, my co-maker and co-wearer of big girl pants. Iain and gobscure – fellow lighthouse lovers and word legends. KB, this is yours, WB x. My Überwunderbud, my greatest cheerleader – what would I do without you? Kaye, the Cake to my Lizard, I love you so much – pop the kettle on.

My sprawling Northern Clan, thank you for a beach-based childhood and the marching ration tin. Nana,

Gran and M2 – I miss you. My Darlo family, both dogs and humans, you ruddy rock. Ryan, for our shared love of books I award you a Shining Smile Award. Alex, for asking the Sellotape or staples question so I didn't have to, having brilliant ideas, knowing replicas aren't always tiny and being such an important part of my world – don't ever stop writing. Sophie, I could not be more proud to get to be your sister. Mum and Dad, for all of the everything – words fail me, I just hope you know. Mads, my icklue suit, I promise not to put dolls on your screensaver ever again – that's how much I love you.

Marky Pants, this would be impossible and absolutely no fun without you, as far as they go.

About the Author

LISETTE AUTON is a northern disabled writer, activist, poet, novelist, spoken-word artist, actor, film and theatre-maker, and creative practitioner. She's an award-winning poet who has performed at Northern Stage, ARC, the Southbank Centre and the Sage, in pubs, in a crypt, at festivals, indoors, outdoors, on a bridge and in a launderette. *The Secret of Haven Point* is her debut novel.

Follow Lisette on Twitter and Instagram
@lisette_auton
#TheSecretOfHavenPoint

A Note from Illustrator
Valentina Toro

This book piqued my curiosity from the first page, and from then on, I couldn't stop. There is magic in this book. And for a moment it seemed to me that it could only be magic that made this particular book come to me as a commission.

While I read, I couldn't stop smiling. My whole heart smiled with every word, every character, every adventure. *It has to be magic*, I thought. *How could it not be?* This book came to me, and I had the huge responsibility to bring it to life. And now I, not only as an illustrator but as a writer, as a children's book enthusiast, as a disabled person myself, will treasure this book forever. This is the book I wish I had read when I was a child, and I am honoured and thankful to be able to illustrate it as an adult because now my inner child is jumping up and down, feeling loved and excited, and it is what I want every child who reads these pages to feel. I want them to feel powerful. I want them to think that the world can be changed, one book at a time.

About the Illustrators

VALENTINA TORO is a disabled illustrator and children's book writer from Colombia. She has written several children's books published in Latin America and has also worked as an illustrator for publishers around the world. What she likes most about making books is that, in them, she can imagine amazing worlds, like the one in this story.

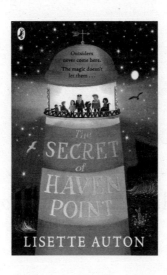

GILLIAN GAMBLE loves adventures and wandering, rich colours and flights of imagination, people-watching on public transport, cold North Sea air, bobble hats, big questions she can't answer and lying outside looking up and wondering what it's all about. She is a self-taught artist who learned while her babies slept, as well as a multi-award-winning social entrepreneur responsible for starting several community enterprises and a trustee of Unltd, a charity that supports social entrepreneurs across the UK.

Driven by a motto she picked up as a child that 'life is big – be all you can be', Gillian strives to bring a sense of creativity and thoughtfulness to everything she does and to see the wonder in everything and everyone.

LUKE ASHFORTH is an illustrator from Nottingham, UK. Luke has drawn for as long as he can remember, but when he studied animation at university and then went on to complete a masters degree in illustration, the love of illustration stuck for good. He works digitally, taking inspiration from stories and monsters from all over the world and making up his own along the way. With an aim to inject the whimsical and magical into his work, Luke loves interesting and fun characters with a good story to tell. He enjoys all things horror, fantasy and space, and you will most likely find him curled up with a book or trying to make people laugh.